Maya's Song

This is a work of fiction. All characters and events portrayed in this novel are either products of the author's imagination or are used fictitiously.

Maya's Song

Cover by Driven Digital Services
Map by Vicki B. Williamson
Editing and typesetting by Kingsman Editing Services

First Edition November 2019
ISBN: 978-0-9990605-1-3

vickibwilliamson.author@gmail.com

To the dreamers . . .

OTHER TITLES BY
VICKI B. WILLIAMSON

Finding Poppies

Key of the Prophecy — an Ellen Thompson Thriller

Maya's Song

The Pedagogue Chronicles
Book I

Vicki B. Williamson

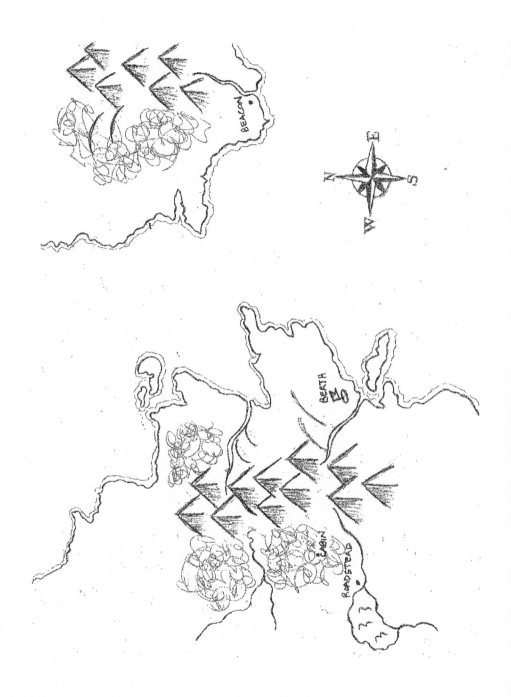

L IGHTNING STRUCK THE CLIFF, ILLUMINATING the two figures who stood at its edge.

"Once and for all, brother, with a grasp of our hands a challenge is cast." A harsh wind blew the woman's hair from her face to reveal a beauty so stark and cold, it cut. Stepping forward, she extended a hand from beneath the folds of her cloak. "When the Three and Three become One, the judgment will be made for good or evil."

Caleb stared down at her hand. He remembered a time when it had given succor and comfort. A time when his twin and he had truly each been halves of a whole. Where had that time gone?

"Come now, brother." At her words, he looked from her hand to her eyes. Eyes so like his own. "Or perhaps you are afraid you'll lose. Lose everything you've fought so hard for all these millennia."

Caleb's eyes narrowed with his sister's challenge. Even knowing she deliberately provoked him, he stepped forward. He would take this contest, and he would win.

With a quick motion, he grasped her hand. The slap of skin

against skin echoed over the raging ocean, louder than even the thunder.

"You are correct, Cassandra. It is time our conflict was at an end. When the *Three and Three become One*, we will know."

1

"OUCH!"

Maya turned to catch the culprit and wasn't surprised to see Teck standing behind her. The bane of her childhood couldn't seem to stop himself from picking on her. Her gaze fell, and she turned to continue through the shop. Why couldn't he just leave her alone?

"Whatcha doin'?"

With an inner sigh, Maya muttered, "Shopping," and headed toward the front counter. She wasn't surprised to hear his heavy footsteps on the wooden floor as he followed her.

Causing more irritation than pain, she flinched at another yank on her long crimson tresses. Halting, Maya spun around to confront him, only to be stopped by his pleased expression. He stood, bigger and taller than her, eyes sparkling with humor, hands on his hips, feet planted apart. He did look handsome, she grudgingly admitted.

"Your Names Day is tomorrow, huh? You'll be sixteen."

"Yes," Maya said softly, and a blush colored her cheeks.

Tomorrow, she'd be considered a woman to the small community she and her mother lived in, though they lived outside of town in a small cabin. She and her mother had never really belonged to this community. They found her lack of a father ample reason to ostracize her and her mother. Their prejudices didn't stop them from availing themselves to her mother's services as a healer, though, as she had an uncanny way with the healing arts. Plenty of them made the distance to the little cabin for her remedies. Maya preferred not to come into town, but today her mother wanted something special—something they couldn't hunt or forage for themselves.

Once again, turning from Teck, Maya moved quickly to the counter. Her mother sent some rare coins with her for the purchase of the precious sugar for her Names Day cake. She was also to stop at the fish market for their dinner tonight. As she waited for the proprietor to finish with another customer, Maya felt the heat of Teck at her back. Outside, her dog, Rory—a large mix—uttered a yip and planted his front feet on the door. He seemed to sense the confusion she felt when near Teck.

Purchase finished, the townswoman in front of her looked down her nose at Maya, sniffing in disapproval as if she'd caught scent of an unpleasant odor. Maya had an urge to smell herself even though she'd bathed just that morning. With effort, she ignored the woman and stepped around her. A smile split her lips as she faced the owner of the shop, where he stood behind the counter.

"G'morning, Maya. Happy Names Day to yah."

Mr. Bachmann, who had owned the shop for as long as

Maya could remember, was a nice man. He often allowed her mother to barter services for goods and trusted them if they needed to run a tab at his store. His trust was never in vain, as her mother always paid her bill.

"Good morning, Mr. Bachmann. Thank you." A warm smile touched her lips, and she relaxed.

"Sugar, ayah?" he asked when she told him what she needed. He measured out the amount from a large bin and wrapped it in paper to hand to her. "That mother of yorn making you a cake for your special day?"

"Yes, sir." Maya reverently placed the packet of sugar within her knapsack for the trip to the wharf, and then home.

When he told her the amount, she opened her hand to reveal one of the coins her mother had entrusted her with. The coin would more than pay for the sugar. The shop owner's eyebrows rose when he caught sight of it. "Now, Maya. Where'd you get that?"

"My mother's been saving for my Names Day."

Taking the coin from her palm, he turned it over before he placed it in a lockbox.

"Will you be runnin' a credit for the extra, or you needin' something else today?"

"No, sir. Just a credit."

With a nod and a quick glance at her, he turned toward the jars of sweets along the back wall. "Go ahead and pick yourself a treat, why don't you Maya." When she began to shake her head at him, he put up a hand to stop her. "My gift to you . . . for your special day."

Surprised and pleased, Maya selected a hard candy, and when he handed it to her, she placed it with the sugar. "Not gonna enjoy it now?" he asked.

"I thought I'd share it with my mother," she explained, another blush coloring her cheekbones.

With a stretch, the owner patted her hand and said, "You're a good girl, Maya. You have a nice day now and tell your mother 'ello."

"Thank you," she murmured. As she turned toward the door, she couldn't stop herself from risking a glance at Teck. Confusion filled her head when her pulse quickened. He'd stood still and quiet the whole time she made her purchase. As she passed through the door, she could hear Mr. Bachmann ask him what he needed, but she didn't wait to hear his response.

Outside, the sun fell on her face, causing her to squint against the brightness. In its welcome warmth, she had a moment of bliss before the bell above the shop door jingled and Teck stepped out. She tried to ignore him and, with a gesture at Rory, stepped down onto the dirt street and headed toward the lake.

"Maya, wait." She heard him plain enough but kept walking. She really needed to get away from Teck. He grabbed her arm and spun her around but broke the contact quickly as if she were hot to the touch.

With another sigh, she asked, "What, Teck?" Impatient, and not wishing to make a scene in the middle of the street, she looked left and right, making sure they weren't being watched. She wished he weren't so good-looking. A couple of years older than her, he was already a man in their community. He came from stock that stood tall and strong—even now, his broad shoulders blocked out the sunlight. Standing in his shadow made Maya feel even smaller and more vulnerable. As she waited for him to get on with whatever he thought he had to say, a breeze lovingly lifted his thick black hair and pulled it across his forehead. Her fingers itched to push back his hair, but she snapped her mind back to the present. As if offended by her thoughts, the same breeze snapped her skirt around her legs attempting to drive her away from him.

"Will you be coming into town for the harvest celebrations?" Had his face not been in shadow, and if she didn't know him better, she'd swear she saw a slight flush come to his skin. Almost as if he were at a loss for what to do, he reached a hand to pet Rory but stopped when the big dog issued a warning growl low in his throat. Maya placed a hand on her companion's head to calm him and gave Teck a look of dismissal.

"No, Teck. I have work to do and no time for the frivolousness of a celebration." Maya turned and walked down the street, pushing her relaxed stride to hurry. A few blocks away, she chanced a look back, a sigh bowing her shoulders when she saw he hadn't followed her. Teck confused her. She just needed to get the shopping done and get home. Looking down at her pet, she gave him a pat on the head. "Good boy, Rory," she cooed, causing the dog's tail to wag.

As Maya continued through town, she couldn't help but notice the looks that came her way. She was used to it, but no matter how hard she tried to rise above it, the townspeople's disapproval continued to wear at her. She'd give anything to take her mother somewhere where they could truly be part of a community. Accepted and loved. She'd asked her mother why she insisted on staying in the home they now occupied—why couldn't they move to another place? A place where the people didn't know them. They could be whomever they wanted, and no one would be the wiser—but her mother refused. She wouldn't speak of it and simply stated she would be staying here. Maya could find another home for herself. Now that her sixteenth birthday had arrived, her options were open. With a shake of her head, she gave a small chuckle at her foolishness. She would never leave her mother. They were all each of them had.

As Maya neared the wharf, she could hear the faint echoes of men's voices as they shouted back and forth at each other. Above her were the sounds of water birds. Their calls mimicked the working men. The fish markets weren't even within view when her nose told her she was almost there.

2

THE OVERPOWERING STENCH OF FISH entrails filled Maya's nose, and for a moment her stomach churned. After a few more breaths, the intensity of the scents became more bearable.

With a hand on the rail overlooking the water, she rose to the tips of her toes to locate a particular boat. The *Amerlin Clipper* was moored toward the end of the pier. She was one of the largest fishing vessels, able to travel closer to the middle of the lake and catch fish at greater depths. This made her the perfect choice for Maya to find a cuttooth bob—her favorite fish. They lived at the bottom of the lake and took expertise to hook.

With careful steps, watching for fishing lines and other debris along the dock, Maya made her way to the trade area near the *Amerlin Clipper*. Two sailors were busy selling their catch, and Maya was happy to see what she wanted among the items.

Taking an assertive step, she placed herself into the line with the other buyers and waited patiently for one of the sailors to notice her.

"Help you, love?"

She couldn't stop it when the corners of her mouth turned up slightly. His accent was foreign, but she liked the lilt of it. "Yes, please. I'd like one of the cuttooths. A big one, if you don't mind."

"Of course, of course." With a move quick from long practice, the sailor stuck his hand in the gill of the fish, flipped it onto a large stretch of paper, wrapped it quickly, and handed it to her. Maya gave him another of the coins her mother had provided her, and after a quick look at her, he nodded and pocketed the money.

With the fish and sugar purchased and secured, she was ready to return home. Maya was glad to be leaving town. The noise and abundance of humanity quickly became too much for her. She felt more at home in the forest surrounded by the wild plant and animal life. Along the dock, Maya called Rory several times, the temptation of rancid viscera almost too much for him to resist.

It wasn't until they moved into the shadow of the forest that Maya took a deep breath and felt her nerves dissipate. This was her world, her perfect place. Since she was a small child, she'd had an affinity for the plants of the wild. Her mother explained it, saying everyone was born with something special about them. Maya knew it was more than that, though, and chose to keep this ability secret from everyone except her mother.

When she sang to them, the plants would grow and bloom. They would reach for her when she called. She felt their energy within her.

As they moved along the trail, which led deeper into the forest and ultimately to her home, the earthy smells and sounds comforted her—the forest, fallen leaves, soil, faint scents of animals, the sounds of birdsong, small animals in the underbrush, and the distant gurgle of a stream. It was music, like a great symphony that filled her soul and gave her peace. She was a part of the nature around her, rooted in the rich soil.

Too soon, the path thinned and the cabin she shared with her mother came into view. It was small but quaint, and her mother insisted it be kept in good repair. A line of smoke meandered toward the sky from the chimney, telling her that her mother was beginning to prepare the last meal. Window boxes bursting with flowers caught her attention with their array of red, yellow, and purple blossoms. A healthy, well-tended garden peeked out from the rear edge of the cabin, reminding Maya she still needed to gather vegetables to go with the fish for tonight's meal. To the other side of the cabin was a small lean-to and corral that housed an old milk cow. For as long as Maya could remember, Old Meg had provided her with warm milk for her breakfast. Through the partially open door, she could hear her mother singing softly. She recognized it as a lullaby she'd sang as Maya grew. Her mother must be feeling nostalgic. Tomorrow was her Names Day after all.

When Maya passed through the doorway into the cabin, she was momentarily blinded by the darkness inside after the bright sun outside. Blinking, her vision adapted, and her mother's form stooped by the fireplace stirring something in a kettle.

Rory followed her in and busied himself sniffing every inch of the room—acting as if he'd been gone for a year instead of a few hours.

"Mother, I got the sugar and fish."

"Good, my love. Why don't you put the fish in the cool pantry for later? We'll make your cake this evening, after dinner and the chores are done."

"Yes, Mother." Maya moved into the one-room cabin without any conscious awareness of its amenities.

In one corner was a large feather mattress that she and her mother shared. It was covered by a homemade quilt, bright with colors and patterns. She valued it not only for the warmth it brought on cold nights, but for the memories of its creation. The quilt was a project they'd shared when Maya was a child. Its construction taught her the joy of taking her time to make something beautiful.

Maya set her pack down next to a small shelf attached to the wall, where treasures of a young girl, a beautiful blue stone, and a few cherished books sat. Later she would sit before the fire and read a few chapters to her mother. The book was always Maya's choice. Learning how to read on her mother's knee, it was years before Maya realized only a select few of the elders in town could read the printed word. She'd questioned her mother about how she had learned, but as usual, when queried about her past, her mother became evasive.

Placing the fish in the cool box and the sugar in a stone container next to the hearth, Maya reached for a basket she used for gardening and a bucket for milking.

"I'll get the chores done, Mother."

With an absentminded nod, Maya's mother waved her out. "Take the dog with you," she called, and Maya gave a whistle that had Rory jumping up from the bed he'd made on the floor.

As soon as she stepped into the sunshine and fresh air, Maya was once again in tune with the nature around her. Walking among the stalks and rows of her garden, she ran her fingers lightly along the vegetation. Vines wrapped gently around her fingers, and flowers turned their heads in her direction as if she were the sun living among them. A warmth filled Maya. Love wasn't an unfamiliar feeling, but what she felt here was somehow different. What she felt among the plants was deeper, to her core.

Gathering different vegetables, she was disappointed to see her favorite, a chostle pepper, wasn't ripe enough to pick. She so loved the sharp, crisp taste with fish. Humming low in her throat, she gently placed her fingers around one and smiled to see it swell and ripen within her grasp. Plucking the dark purple vegetable, she held it to her face and inhaled, looking forward to their meal. She placed it in her basket and continued her chores, weeding, hoeing, and watering the plants, her mind on tomorrow. What would it bring? What did being an adult mean? Would there be any changes? She couldn't imagine what those changes might be. Happy within her world with her mother, she still longed for adulthood.

After finishing with the garden and taking the basket of vegetables to her mother, she headed to the corral and Old Meg. When the cow saw Maya, she let out a deep lowing.

"I know, Meg, old girl. I'm coming."

The corral gate opened easily, allowing Maya and Rory to slip through. The dog touched his nose to that of the cow in greeting and then wandered around the paddock, checking out the scents. Maya moved to the lean-to and retrieved a small stool and then returned to the cow. With a gentle hand, she patted Meg and planted the stool next to her with the bucket under her full udders. Meg stood docile, munching her cud, seemingly lost in her own thoughts.

Placing her forehead against the cow's warm, slightly prickly belly, Maya allowed the motion and mindlessness of milking to lull her, and her mind began to wander. She found her thoughts, not for the first time, turning to Teck. The image of him in town, the large smile spreading across his face, had her pulse quickening in an unexpected but pleasant way. Shaking the thought, she stopped milking and placed a balancing hand on Meg's side. Meg glanced back at her and then resumed her stance. Maya shook her head, reminding herself how frustrating Teck could be.

"I hate him." With an inward assessment, she realized this statement wasn't really the truth. Somewhere, somehow, her feelings for Teck had changed, grown. Her eyebrows pulled together as she realized this notion did not make her happy. Is that what turning sixteen would bring? Would her feelings no longer be hers to control? As anger started to replace confusion, Rory jumped up and barked, advancing to the edge of the gate. With a quick look past the bulk of the bovine, Maya saw the subject of her doubt step from the forest.

What the . . . why would he be here?

Eyes fierce, Maya almost upset the bucket of milk as she stood and moved around the cow. With a soft, "Rory," the dog quieted and sat patiently by her side, tongue out, looking from her to the man. "What are you doing here? You're not welcome here." Her stance stiff, hands in fists, Maya tried to ignore the increase in her breathing and the flush that heated her cheeks. She'd never had these feelings before. And for Teck? Her body's betrayal was unacceptable.

As he moved toward her out of the shadows, she noticed he had his hands behind his back, and in the bright light of the late afternoon sun, his blush was obvious. "I made something for you. For your Names Day."

She didn't respond. Her curiosity was roused; it wasn't often she received a present. A step or two more and he was just on the other side of the corral post. He hesitated now as if afraid. She wondered how that could be. She didn't know him well even though they grew up in the same area, but everything she knew pointed to him being an indulged and arrogant, but well-liked, young man. She was sure he'd never wanted for anything.

She remembered all the times he'd picked and pulled at her while they were growing up and had a moment of clarity. He'd seemed so pleased to have her attention. It annoyed her, but now she wondered if he just wanted her attention the way children go about getting it. Maybe that was his aim all along. This thought sent a rush of blood to her cheeks, and she looked at Teck more closely.

Heaving a deep sigh, Teck pulled a bow and quiver from behind his back. The quiver was full of arrows with newly created fletching, bright with color. The bow was a thing of beauty, etched with swirls and carved with realistic leaves.

Maya's breath left her lungs in a whoosh, her body relaxing. "You made this?" she asked, taking a small step toward the offering. Her hands were itching to touch it, to run her fingers over the fine wood and carvings on it. He gave a small nod, watching her intently. "You made it for me?" Unable to resist any longer, she ran a finger softly over the surface. With a shift, Teck slid the bow and quiver through the fence, thrusting it at her.

"Here, take it," he said roughly.

At his tone, Maya looked up from the bow into Teck's eyes. When their gazes locked, he dropped his and intently studied the ground. A small smile curved her lips as she watched him, enjoying his discomfort. She felt in control, something she lost every time he towered over her, and now that power moved through her. As she reached to take the bow and quiver, she lightly trailed a finger over the clench of his hand. His gaze flashed back to hers and he released the bow so fast, if not for her quick reflexes, it would have ended up in the dirt on the corral floor.

With a quick step back, Teck watched her. She swung the quiver full of arrows across her body along her back and, with expertise gained from long practice, stepped on the lower limb of the bow to pull the string and rest it in the string nock. After a nimble step back, she quickly brought the bow up to shoulder height and drew the string. Knuckles on her cheek, the other arm outstretched. Time stopped, then she slowly released the tension in the string. Maya turned to Teck to give him her thanks for such a fine gift when her mother's voice stopped her.

"Teck?"

They turned to see her mother coming toward them.

"Ma'am." Teck dropped his head in greeting and moved a pace from the corral.

With a quick look from him to Maya, her mother said, "You're just in time for last meal. Please stay and help us begin our celebration of Maya's Names Day."

"Mother—" Maya began uncomfortably, but Teck talked over her.

"I'd love to." Maya's mother took Teck's arm and walked toward the cabin.

"Mother," Maya muttered under her breath. She shook her head in disbelief when her attention was again captured by the bow in her hands. She reached back and pulled an arrow from the quiver to examine it. The fletching was soft with flecks of red, perhaps from the belly feathers of a sparkling swallow. The shaft was straight and strong, and the arrow had been finished with a metal tip. Long hours went into its construction. *Why,* she wondered. *What does he want?* When Maya's stomach grumbled, she decided to put aside her questions for now. She grabbed the bucket of milk before following her mother and Teck into the cabin.

The first thing Maya noticed when she entered the cabin was the wonderful smell of simmering vegetables and freshly cooked fish. No one cooked like her mother. The fish, after it had been cleaned and stuffed, had its skin sewn together with twine to hold herbs inside. Maya knew there were freshly made biscuits in the warming pan to the side of the fireplace. If it wasn't for Teck's presence, this would be a perfect meal.

"Maya, put your gift away and set the table for last meal." Moving from Maya to Teck, her mother looked up at him. "Would you like to sit, Teck? I bet you'd like a mug of cool water." When he nodded in agreement and took a seat at the small table, Maya's mother continued in her chosen job as hostess. "Please, Teck. Tell us about the present you brought Maya. I had no idea you were so talented."

Maya moved into the room, sparing a glance at her old bow propped by the door. She walked to the other side of the cabin and reverently laid the new bow and quiver down safely in the corner. With a roll of her eyes for her mother's attempts at conversation, she got three of the mismatched plates and cups and three eating utensils.

As her mother talked, she moved the pan with the fish and set it in a place of honor in the center of the table. Maya placed the biscuits in a basket, then this too went to the table, along with a small crock of homespun butter.

Setting the table was an exercise of control for Maya. She felt Teck's eyes follow her every move as she shifted around him. Why had her mother invited him to their meal? Shouldn't he be heading home? Walking through the forest after dark could be dangerous.

"Maya, come sit and visit with our guest."

As Maya took her seat, she paused midway, hovering over her chair, her gaze fixated on the dog. Allowing herself to drop into the seat, she stared at Rory, who was sitting by Teck's chair. Teck absentmindedly pet the dog's head, and it was obvious Rory was loving it. His eyes were closed, and his tail made a small swooshing sound as it moved on the floor. *Traitor,* she thought and threw a dirty look at the man and dog. Rory looked sideways at her in that ashamed, distinctive dog way but didn't move away from Teck or his large caressing hand.

Maya's mother sat at the table and passed the dishes around. "So . . . the bow and quiver? You made it specifically for Maya?"

Even in the dimly lit room, Maya could see his skin flush red. "Yes, ma'am. For her Names Day."

"Please, Teck. You're eating at our table. You can call me by my given name."

The embarrassment was obvious on his face as he looked from Maya to her mother. Taking pity on him, the older woman said, "Sylvan. My name is Sylvan."

"Sylvan." With a small nod of understanding, he continued. "Yes . . . Sylvan . . . I made it for her Names Day."

They continued to talk, but Maya gave her attention to the meal. *Finish it and get rid of him,* was all she could think. The cabin was her haven, next only to the deep forest, and she didn't want him here. The feelings he aroused in her were confusing.

Soon, though not soon enough, the meal was finished. Teck jumped up to help Sylvan clear the table, but she stopped him.

"Why don't you and Maya step outside. Maybe take a stroll, and she can show you her garden."

"Mother . . ." Maya couldn't believe her mother was throwing her at him like this. What was she? A burden on her or something?

"Go now and quit your complaining."

As Maya and Teck left the cabin, Rory gave an excited yelp and ran after a rabbit in the evening light. The sun was dipping quickly now, and soon it would be totally black except for the light of a full moon rising from the mountain. With her eye on the dog, Maya muttered, "Well . . . thank you for the gift. It really is beautiful."

* * * * *

TECK WATCHED HER, BUT SHE wouldn't lift her face to look at him. With a firm grasp on his courage, he reached out to run his hand down her arm to her hand. Her skin was warm and soft. As before, it was almost as if a bolt of lightning were moving through him when he touched her.

When she didn't shy away from him, he kept her hand in his and turned them toward the path to town. Teck liked the sensation of walking with Maya at his side. He had always liked her, though he'd never been good at showing his feelings and would pick on her just to have her attention. Now, however, he was a man, and tomorrow, Maya became a woman. The days of picking and irritating her were at an end. They walked in silence, hand in hand along the bank of a lake to the edge of the meadow where Maya lived. Reaching the tree line, Teck turned toward her, and this time, she met his gaze.

"You're welcome, Maya," he whispered. Reluctantly, he released her hand but, with a smile of satisfaction, turned toward town. Tomorrow was going to be a big day. Rory ran along with him for a bit, but at Maya's whistle, the dog headed back.

3

CALEB STARED AT THE WORLD below. It was one of many. Just another contest to fill the long days of his and Cassandra's lives.

He realized, as he watched the pretty blue and green orb, that he was tired.

For the longest time, almost past his memory, he'd allowed his sister to win their contests. He wanted her happy. Wanted her to love him as she used to when they were children.

With a sigh, he moved away from this view. Perhaps for the first time, he was seeing, she was a different person. The sister he remembered, that beloved sibling, was long gone. Now, she lived only for the power. Each time she consumed a world, turning it black and cold, she became more powerful. The life forces and the magics filled her until she craved it all the more.

Maybe it was time he stopped this farce. Stopped sacrificing world after world to his sister's need.

Pacing, his thoughts spun.

When he passed the pedestal with the ancient tome resting

on it, he paused. All worlds had prophecies. Predictions for the outcomes of change. It was this world's prophecy that he and Cassandra battled over.

She scoffed.

He believed.

With a step he neared the book. Old and worn, it had seen many a millennium come and go. Caleb gave a wave of his hand and the book's pages flipped, the sound of them feather-light in the room. When they stopped, he looked down to once again read the words.

In a time of strife, in a world of fear,
age will come for three of the blood.
When the core is joined,
Three and Three become One,
and darkness will be consumed by light.

A small smile tugged at the edges of his mouth and he pulled a hand from within the folds of his cloak, opening it to reveal three stones. Each was a different color—blue, green and ivory—and each was etched with a different symbol. He knew them to be powerful, ancient magic. This magic could be used to influence his win. Just this once, he could break the rules, help where needed. The stones could be the beginning of this help.

Rolling the stones with his thumb, he planned. This world, he knew, was different. Magic still moved through the blood of certain family lines.

He and Cassandra both knew of whom the prophecy spoke.

If he could lay the work, push them the right way, he could see this world's prophecy true.

It would take finesse.

In the perfect moment, they would need the Three to join— to become One. Only then could the prophecy be fulfilled, and Cassandra stopped.

4

THE AIR IN THE CABIN was warm and comforting and smelled faintly of the cake that had been baked earlier in the evening. The fire was banked, and glowing embers provided a filtered light that fell gently upon the two sleeping women. The homey image was ruined when Maya issued a moan, which broke the silence of the room. The dog pricked his ears. With a whine, he moved to the edge of the mattress to watch her. She jerked and gave a startled cry before lurching upright on the bed. Alarmed, the dog jumped back.

Maya looked blindly around the room. She didn't realize where she was at first. Her chest heaved, and a layer of sweat stuck her nightgown to her back. The dog caught her eye and she placed a shaking hand on his head. The connection gave them both comfort, and the canine leaned into her leg, offering what relief he could. Maya glanced from the dog back to the remnants of the fire, and then behind her to check on her mother. Sylvan slept soundly, unaffected by the nightmare that woke her daughter. Lying down a bit stiffly, Maya continued to caress Rory's head and with measured, deep breaths, calmed her nerves.

The dream was fading from her memory, leaving just an impression. An atmosphere of expectation. It had her edgy upon waking. There was a man in her dream—that much she remembered. The man and then the light. A blinding light, but one that didn't burn. When she woke, it all seemed so important, and now as it evaporated, so did the urgency.

She sat upright again, placing her bare feet on the floor. The cold planks robbed what little heat resided in her feet. Stomping gently, she stood and walked quickly across the floor. With a poker, she stirred the embers and placed a log on them, watching the fire eagerly find the new fuel. Hypnotized, the dream drifted further and further away.

"Ah, Rory." At his name, the canine stepped to her and bumped her elbow with his head. "You're a good boy." She gave him a small pat. Thoughts of the dream filling her head, she turned from him to wander across the room. She thought if she could just remember what was said, then she could act. What act was necessary, she didn't know, but her mind and body were poised—sitting on the precipice of a need, of a forward motion. The harder she tried to capture the dream, the further it drifted from her thoughts. As her eyes swept the room looking for hidden answers, her sight was caught by the gift from Teck. Nearing it, she ran her fingers over the intricate woodworking that he had so painstakingly created. Teck continued to confuse her. She was old enough to know what he wanted, but she couldn't fully understand why he wanted her.

She didn't even think he liked her until today. And this line of thought wasn't helping her to get back to sleep. Unable to grasp the intensity of the emotion she felt, Maya yawned and headed back to bed. Under the covers, with the fire flickering in the room and the dog breathing heavily on the floor below her, Maya once again drifted off to sleep.

* * * * *

THE MAN'S EYES OPENED WITH the first stirrings of magic. The feeling of it, even the scent of it, woke something buried within him. Taking a deep breath, he held the essence in his lungs, savoring it. So long had he waited for her to be revealed. He didn't know why the shroud was removed, and not caring, he expelled his breath.

"Orson," he bellowed. The echo of his call had yet to dispel when the chamber door was thrust open and a small, ugly man rushed in, nearly tripping over his own feet.

"Yes, my master," he muttered, prostrate at the edge of the bed.

The night was chilly, the dwindling fire no longer heating the room. The man in the bed didn't notice as he pushed the covers back and swung his legs to sit upright on the mattress. Memories from his childhood spun through his mind. Images of Sylvan as a young girl, the old remembered desire—both for her and her power.

"She's been unveiled."

The small man hustled backward to avoid being trod upon

when his master strode through the room, pacing back and forth. Jumping to his feet, Orson grabbed a night jacket and held it open for his master, offering it even though the man ignored him. When his master still ignored the offered jacket, he slipped by and stirred the embers of the fire, tossing in logs to warm the room.

"Get my clothes," the master barked, causing Orson to hustle into the wardrobe and begin pulling items out. Continuing to pace, the master rubbed his hands together, his face breaking into a large, toothy smile. "Finally. After almost two decades, Sylvan will be mine."

5

MAYA'S NAMES DAY BLOOMED BRIGHT, sunny, and warm, and she couldn't wait to get into the woods. Part of the food she and her mother ate came from traps Maya laid each night and checked each morning. The act of moving through the forest, being a part of it and one with the plants, centered her mind and spirit. Today was no different. She'd woken with a light ache in her head and the feeling of having not slept well. She knew she'd been up once due to a dream but now couldn't recall what it was about.

"Yes, Mother!" she yelled back hastily to Sylvan's warning to be careful, and then she and the dog disappeared out the door. Shaking off the feeling of a night ill-spent, she stopped partway across the clearing to tilt her head back and feel the warm sun on her face. Today she was dressed in shades of brown. The homespun cloth of her pants, a coarse long-sleeve shirt, and vest were crafted with her mother's loving, capable hands. She had a burlap bag to help transport game home, and on her hip was a hunting knife. Today, she'd opted to leave her bow at home since it wouldn't be necessary for trap checking. Her fingers itched with the need to try out the new bow, but just as strong was her desire not to be unduly influenced by Teck and his present. With a stubborn lift of her chin, she'd turned her back on it and walked out of the cabin.

Rory yipped happily as he ran ahead of her as if calling, "Hurry up! Hurry up!" She looked at him and, with a small laugh, followed into the shadow of the forest. Small animals scurried out of their way, and irritated birds called overhead, but Maya just laughed at them all. It was the perfect day. Her perfect day.

AFTER CHECKING HER TRAPS AND coming up with three fat, young hares for their next few meals, Maya swung by her favorite spot near Edelberry Creek. A dense covering of clover and wildflowers blanketed the bank. It was like this every spring, and Maya loved to take advantage of the natural bedding. It was a magical spot for a young girl to dream away the hours, braiding flowers into her flaming locks or making collars from tree sprigs for Rory. Today was no exception. Dropping down close to the water's edge, Maya laid the burlap sack in the shade of an old oak tree where the rabbits would keep in the cool. Near her, Rory rolled in the fragrant blossoms, grunting and sneezing as the pollen irritated his nose. The sun was bright, and the air smelled heavily of flowers crushed under Rory's weight.

Time passed without measure as the muffled sounds of bees and far-off birdcalls accompanied the soft gurgle of the stream. Finished with her garland of blossoms, Maya realized how quiet Rory had become. She smiled gently to see him sleeping in the warm sunshine. His legs would twitch occasionally, and she imagined him chasing rabbits in his slumber. Humming a tune of her own design, Maya placed the crown of flowers upon her head. She lay back as the blanket of vegetation welcomed her with open arms, and closing her lids, she blocked out the late morning rays.

When she heard a voice, she cracked open her eyes and shifted her head in the direction of the sound, but it didn't cause her any fear or worry, just curiosity. There was never anyone this far out in the woods, and listening closer, her brow furrowed.

The voice grew closer and louder, and Maya could tell by its tone it was that of a man. Staying flat and staring absently into the blue sky, Maya concentrated. The man crooned a melody as he neared. Though she couldn't understand the words, the sound of his voice and the song resonated with her, and a flush heated her skin. Her brow wrinkled to pull to mind the memory they stirred. When the man's presence was imminent, the melody stopped and in the sudden quiet, Maya slowly sat up to look in the direction of the stranger. His figure was still within the shadow of the trees. Maya expected him to startle at seeing her, but the man spoke as if he'd known Maya had been there all along.

"Hello."

"Hello," Maya replied easily.

"Happy Names Day to you, Maya."

Maya rolled to her knees to fully face him. "Do I know you?"

"I need your help, Maya."

6

THE DOG WOKE AS THE girl slept and he wandered about, as dogs do, to smell the scents left by other animals, and contribute his essence to the area. Through his seemingly aimless meandering, he kept his ears and eyes on the young woman. She was the leader of his pack, and wherever she went, he went.

She mumbled and twisted in her sleep, so Rory trotted back to sniff at her and whine. When a vine ran between his legs, Rory gave a yelp and jumped much higher than a dog his size should be able to. With a step between the vine and the girl, he gave a warning growl, but the vine continued its straight track for the girl. The dog moved forward with a louder growl, which halted in a yip when he saw the vine was not alone. Other vegetation—ivy, flowers, and weeds—moved toward the girl's sleeping body. Even the trees in the area seemed to bow toward her. The dog had seen many small happenings between the girl and the flora of the forest, but this abundance was something new. When he realized the girl now slept soundly and peacefully, covered with a blanket of greenery, he gave a *hmph* and lay beside her, placing his chin on his forelegs. His eyes stayed wide open, and at every noise or movement of foliage, his eyebrows shifted. Normal sounds resumed as birds called, and a small rodent ran through the glen as the dog held vigil, but the girl slept on.

7

I N THE COMPLETE QUIET, MAYA rose slowly to her feet. "What help could I give you?" she asked the man. "I'm just a girl."

"Oh, my dear." The man shook his head and peered at Maya through narrow eyes. "For good or bad, soon you will know that just isn't true."

His words sent a shiver up Maya's spine and a spike of fear to pierce her heart. A fog of foreboding covered her, making it hard to draw a breath—and the very air around her thickened.

The change in the day came quickly as clouds covered the sun. Birds fell silent. Maya studied the sky and then shifted her gaze back to the man. Rising, she stepped closer, but the nearer she got, the farther away the man appeared. He was fading, slowly, washing from the day. Second by second, his image became fainter and fainter, wisping into the air. On a breeze, his final words landed in Maya's ears. "Your mother needs our help. You must hurry. We must stop The Three from never becoming."

A SOUND LIKE AN EXPLOSION reverberated in the distance, waking Maya. The vines and brambles pulled swiftly back. Rory leaped to his feet to spin about as the vegetation disappeared. When Maya opened her eyes and sat up, they were almost all gone, and the ones that remained caressed her hands. Maya gazed at the horizon where the sound had occurred—the direction of home. The sky was full of birds. Faintly, she could hear their frantic calls.

"Mama." Maya jumped to her feet and took off at a sprint. Rory fell in beside her. He quickly outdistanced her and disappeared into the forest.

Pulling up at the edge of the tree line bordering her clearing, Maya peered at the cabin. A scowl creased her brow as her way became barred by tree limbs. She gazed through them to the smoldering cabin. The branches continued to interlock in front of her, and while it didn't alarm her, she didn't understand it. Her hand on the bark, she hummed a tune low in her throat. The branches, like fingers, pulled back to allow her to pass.

Smoke rose from the cabin, but not the warm, happy sign of dinner being cooked. This smoke was seeping from the roof and as she watched, the flicker of flames erupted behind the windows. Her eyes darted around the deserted clearing. Maya's heart quickened when she couldn't locate any sign of her mother. Breaking into a sprint, she headed toward the cabin. Her skin chilled. At the cabin door, Maya raised her arm to protect her face from the heat of the flames. She stepped over the threshold and scanned the interior of the burning cabin. There was still no evidence of her mother.

Like a magnet, her gaze flew to the far corner of the cabin where her new bow and quiver still lay. She looked around at the fire. She still had time. She couldn't leave it.

Overcome by a coughing fit, Maya bent at the waist. She needed to hurry. As she straightened, she noticed her rucksack by the doorway. With a quick grab and toss, she hurled it outside and away from the burning cabin. Turning back to the inferno, she looked at the room and headed in.

With each step farther into the cabin, the heat intensified. It was as if the flames were waiting for her to make this one fatal decision, this overstepping of her bounds as a mere mortal. "Come play with us," they teased, licking at her skin.

Maya crouched at the waist to aid her breathing as she continued across the floor, but still, she coughed with each breath. The cabin wasn't large, but she couldn't seem to make any progress getting to the other side—it was taking a long time to make her way through the inferno. Sight limited by the tears streaming from her eyes, Maya allowed her instincts to lead her the few feet to the back wall.

Finally, she bumped against the solid wood. Her hand shook as she reached down to touch the carved bow. Switching it to her other hand, she grasped the quiver and strung it about her body and then turned to head back the way she'd come. When she looked toward the door, she couldn't stop a startled gasp, which caused another coughing fit as her eyes beheld the blaze. It was hard to tell where the door was.

Flames licked up the walls and across the ceiling. Like living beings, they moved and shifted, calling to her in the roar of their voices. Their colors vibrant and intoxicating. Just as she thought she saw faces in the flames, another coughing fit drove her to her knees. She looked up, searching for the faces—the beautiful, deadly faces.

She tried to find air, but her lungs felt tight. Her throat burned, breaths coming in shallow pants. Bow clasped desperately in her hand, Maya gave a last look to the door and heard a ceiling beam crack. A shower of sparks landed around her as her body collapsed on the floor.

A WET NOSE AND A high-pitched whine. The cloying smoke. An intense blanket of heat. Still the coughing with every breath.

Lifting her head, Maya turned in the direction of the dog. Rory pushed his head under her arm and body.

"Rory? What're you doing here, boy?" Maya barely recognized the sound of her own voice. It was low and raspy, and pain flared in her chest and throat. She didn't know how the dog had found her within the burning building, but his insistence swept aside her questions. She pushed to her knees, and with one arm around him, they began to move. The flames consumed everything they touched, belching out acrid, black clouds of smoke and soot. Nearing the beacon of the doorway, she halted. The bed was ablaze, burning the last remnants of a once beautiful quilt. As a sob escaped her already weakened frame, her body attempted to crash in on itself. The dog moved forward, again pulling the girl with him, and soon they were clearing the cabin. Fresh air washed over them as they continued to crawl away from the pyre that had once been her home.

Maya collapsed onto the cool grass and curled into a ball. Hacking smoke from her lungs, she lost her grip on consciousness.

The crack of a collapsing building and roar of the consuming fire penetrated Maya's stupor. With a bone-deep weariness, she pushed to her side and peered over her shoulder. It was twilight now, and the firelight burned bright. Maya watched the cabin's burning remains for just a moment more. Rory lay to her side. Nearer to the cabin, half the distance she'd crawled, lay her rucksack, and her hand still grasped the bow. Maya wobbled on loose legs and made her way back to the sack on the grass, Rory keeping pace with her. She bent to pick it up and had to catch herself before tumbling headfirst to the ground. With one hand on the sack and the other forearm pressed into her thigh, she heaved a great sigh and pushed herself upright. With a last look at the cabin, she turned and walked to the tree line. She needed a moment. A second to rest, to get her head together and decide what to do.

The flames reflected in her eyes. Maya appeared to be an otherworldly being—a creature come down to this planet to wreak havoc on its citizens. She could have been a beast straight from hell, her eyes ablaze like her flaming hair. As her world burned to nothing, she became a woman without a home. A woman on the cusp of change.

Tearing her eyes from the destruction, Maya scanned the glen and saw the evidence of many riders at and around the homestead. Trampled grass and rut marks from what looked to be a heavy wagon cut the area.

She needed to get moving, but although her mind was anxious, pushing her to get up and find her mother, her body was at its end. Without her permission, her body was shutting down.

The motion of the flames drew her once again. She stared so long that her eyes became dry and her lids drooped. Finally, they closed altogether, and the girl slept again, the dog next to her and the crackling of flames in the background.

* * * * *

IN A FAR DISTANT CASTLE, Cassandra stared into the flames of her hearth. The light caressed and lit her graceful features. So beautiful, yet her soul had long ago turned black and charred like the logs in the fireplace. Looking within the flames, she watched as the first steps were put in motion. The girl escaped from the cabin with the dog's aid.

This one would be a problem. For Cassandra to win the contest, for this world to be hers, she would need this child to fail, and for Cassandra's champion to win.

The girl must be kept weak. Her allies halted before they reached her.

Cassandra stepped away from the hearth, her thoughts spinning. So simple, she thought. The orb, the pedagogue. If she could but influence the girl—make her fear the orb—then the pedagogue, and with it the Three, would never be.

8

THE DOG LIFTED HIS HEAD and watched the man run into the clearing. When Teck caught sight of what had become of the cabin, his footsteps faltered, and he stumbled, almost falling to his knees.

"Maya!" His scream bounced off trees and startled an owl into flight. The dog's ears twitched forward and then back as the shrill sound reached him.

The man slowed his gait as he approached the cabin, now smoldering with hot embers of a life that was. The charred ruins still contained enough heat to cause the man to stand back, unable to enter and search for any remains. He stood, defeated, his head and shoulders hanging, yet he was unable to move away.

When a breeze buffeted him from behind, Teck's head wrenched up and around as if catching a scent. Teck and Rory stared at each other for a moment and then, at a run, Teck made straight for the canine. As he neared, he noticed the bundle behind the dog. When he realized who lay there, he stopped, unable to move closer for fear her image would fade. She shifted in her sleep, giving a small cough and turning more fully on her side. Teck dropped to his knees, all power gone from his limbs.

He stayed that way, watching her, until the sun began to rise on the horizon.

* * * * *

WITH ANOTHER SMALL COUGH AND rubbing of her eyes, Maya looked around, confused. She reached out an unsure hand to run it down Rory's body, grounding herself in the familiar. With a shift, she sat up to look straight at Teck. She stared at him a moment, captivated by his expression, and the moment froze. His eyes seemed to glow with an inner madness, and the intensity both pulled and pushed at her. She fought with the urge to flee from him and the desire to run to him. In the next moment, he blinked and the look, along with her confusion, was gone.

Shifting her gaze over his shoulder, across the clearing, she caught sight of the remnants of the cabin. Small tendrils of smoke still rose from the charred remains, and an occasional creak or pop would sound from the burnt wood. The clearing was permeated with the scent of smoke. The scorched fireplace stood as testimony that this had once been a home. A place where meals were cooked, laughter sounded, stories were read, and love abounded. All around the chimney were the blackened fragments of dreams.

Maya stood as if in a nightmare and approached the cabin.

Rory stayed next to her, his body leaning in slightly to touch her leg. When she passed Teck, he too rose and followed her silently. For a moment, she simply stood and said nothing.

Then, with a quick step, Maya moved around the rubble and ash. The only other living thing on the homestead was the old cow, Meg, but she hadn't seen her.

The smell hit Maya's senses before her eyes could register what they saw in the early morning light. The stench of an eviscerated carcass had her turning her head to staunch a gag. What type of man would feel the need to slaughter an old, harmless cow?

Speaking over her shoulder to Teck, she said, "I need to find my mother."

"She wasn't in the cabin?"

With a small shake of her head, the panic of the previous day returned to her. "No. When I got back, the cabin was on fire, but she wasn't in it." Maya scanned the immediate area. "There were riders."

"Did you see them? Did they see you?" Now, Teck looked around the clearing. "Do you think they're gone?"

"They took her." Maya walked closer to the cabin. "They came, and they took her."

"Why?" Teck turned from the corral. "Why would they want your mother?"

Shaking her head again, confusion filling her brain, Maya turned from the cabin to look at Teck. "We've always been safe here. I don't know who or why." When Rory neared to sit by her leg, Maya looked down and gave him a small smile. She patted his head and then squatted to wrap her arms around him in a hug. "Good, Rory. Good dog. You saved my life yesterday, didn't you, boy?"

"Maya, what's going on? Why was your mother taken?"

"I need to leave. I need to find my mother."

Shaking his head at her, he took a step forward. "I don't understand."

Maya didn't know how to explain it to him. She didn't even know if she should try. "I know you're confused, and soon it won't matter since I'll be gone."

"No. If you're leaving the valley, I'm going with you." His eyes widened, seemingly as surprised by his declaration as she was.

"You don't mean that. You have a life here, a family. You don't want to go into the wilderness with me." Maya turned to walk across the field, Teck close behind her. "I need to find my mother, and I'm willing to face everything that goes with that, but I think you need to go home." Maya moved swiftly to the tree line and her small pile of belongings. She kneeled and gathered the bow, quiver, and her rucksack. Standing, she gave Teck one last glance and said, "Good-bye, Teck." With a pat on her thigh for the dog, she headed into the brush. She had an extra set of clothes and some supplies by the stream. Finally, they would come into use.

With a sure step, Maya pushed her way through the undergrowth until she reached a faint game trail. The trail led to the water and her spare belongings. She didn't know exactly where she would be going, but the riders' tracks headed in the direction of the mountain pass and out of the valley. Over the mountains was the city of Berth, and it was to that city she would head. Even if she didn't find them there, she hoped she would find someone who knew something.

AFTER A QUICK DIP IN the cold creek, Maya felt refreshed and able to think. She dressed in her spare hunting garb and laid her newly washed clothing on a rock by the water's edge. Then she inventoried what belongings she had. There wasn't much. Along with the extra clothing were a flask for water, some trapping equipment, and a jacket. Before she left the valley, she'd pick up her traps—they could come in handy for collecting food along the way.

Maya paced in a circle and argued with herself. She was anxious to get going, her thoughts returning to what her mother must be going through, but she knew she would fare better if she was prepared. Being ready for anything was something she'd learned at an early age, so rushing off into the wilderness without thinking went against her nature.

At the edge of the creek, under an oak tree, she found the bag still containing the three rabbits she'd gathered the day before. Thanking all the gods that they hadn't been stolen by a predator, she decided to take another night to smoke the meat and allow herself a good start on her journey. While she was doing that, she could gather young branches for the construction of additional arrows. Maya reached into her new quiver and pulled out one of the arrows Teck made. The ones she made wouldn't be as fine a quality, but they would do.

She'd been making serviceable arrows for years, and she and her mother hadn't gone hungry yet.

When the rabbits were skinned and cleaned, she cut the meat into strips and hung them from an improvised rack over a newly built fire. The smoke and heat would do its job overnight, and by morning she and Rory would be ready to leave the valley in search of her mother. Spreading her jacket by the fire, Maya sat and worked on an arrow. She had plenty now, but she wanted to keep her mind occupied.

The heat and eye strain in the waning evening light did its job, and she soon became sleepy. Sliding down to lie flat, she drifted off.

The dream began almost immediately.

THIS TIME IT WAS A woman. Maya felt a sense of unease but couldn't understand why. And she talked, hissing in Maya's ear. Whispers of a place and a person. Whispers of an orb. Fear ran through her body.

"Stay away from the orb. It is full of dangers," the woman said. "Go back to the man and make a life. Your mother's not worth your life." And with the fear came a dazzling, glowing light.

Just as a scream pressed itself against her throat, a cooling wave swam over her. Soft as a lullaby, a man's voice came to her. "Be calm, child," he said. "Listen and find your mother."

WHEN MAYA WOKE, SHE RETAINED much of the dream, though only vague recollections of the woman. So beautiful, so deadly.

The man's voice and his directions stood out as if his directions were imprinted on her mind. Not only was she to go to the city of Berth, but she was to seek out a priest. How she would locate this priest, she didn't know, but the man was very clear this priest was to play a major role in her future. He even had a name—Patrick. She hoped he was real and she didn't get killed on the way to Berth. The forest outside the valley held many dangers. If she made it through them, she still had the mountains to cross. And what was the light in her dream? She should be afraid of it. Instead, she felt drawn to it. But then would she, like a moth to a flame, be burned? She could only hope to find the priest, and to find answers.

After packing her meager belongings into her rucksack, Maya swung it onto her back along with the quiver of arrows. With her bow in hand, she headed toward the rising sun. She would navigate with the sun, keeping its path in front of her in the morning and behind her by night.

But first, the forest. She'd never traveled far from the cabin. Other than the town of Roadstead, they never needed to turn to other people for anything, and even then, it wasn't often. She knew her mother had come from outside the valley, but other than that, she never discussed her past.

As Maya moved away from the valley floor and to the edge of her known world, the forest seemed to darken. The forest always being a place of safety and security, she questioned her senses. Stopping often, she scanned the area to discern whether this shadowing was true or a figment of her imagination—an outer manifestation of her mood. The forest seemed normal enough, but even the birdcalls were odd and heavy, seeming to drop straight from the air. Once or twice, she swore she heard footsteps alongside her, but watching Rory relieved her anxiety; he didn't seem worried.

The first day ended without incident. Moving off the path, she searched for a suitable place to make camp. She'd made good time today and was feeling optimistic. If she could continue at this rate, she figured they'd reach the mountain pass in under a week's time. About a half mile later, she heard the faint gurgle of water and pushed through some brambles to discover a small stream. The bank rose on the far side and would provide protection from both the elements and any animals that might pass by. Maya dropped her belongings and began moving outward in circles, gathering enough wood to keep a fire going into the night. Returning to her spot, she cleared an area, and after collecting serviceable stones from the stream, she placed them in a circle with wood in the middle. Utilizing the flint fire-maker she'd had with her spare clothing, she soon had a small blaze going.

She knew she should save the rabbit jerky she'd made last night, but the day had drained her both physically and emotionally. Collecting water from where the current quickened, and a healthy pile of the wood, Maya wrapped her jacket around her shoulders and lay on the bank. Rory finished his nightly wanderings and, smelling a bit ripe, lay near her to fall instantly asleep. Maya envied the dog's clear mind. Though tired, she couldn't put her thoughts away and relax. She wondered where her mother had ended up, who had taken her, and why. Did it have something to do with her past? Or was it just a random raid? A melancholy feeling fell over Maya. A tear trickled down her cheek and onto her lips. She was lonely, scared, and worried for herself and her mother.

She'd never been alone before, but she couldn't allow herself to begin considering all the possibilities of what may or may not happen. With a determined set of her jaw, she swiped at the tear, drying her face. All she could allow herself to think about was moving forward. After what felt like hours of staring into the fire and still not coming up with any answers, Maya fell into a troubled sleep—and the dreams followed her.

MAYA RAN. IT WAS DARK and dank. Her throat and lungs burned as she pulled in another harsh breath. She splashed through a bog of stagnant water, falling to her hands and knees, saturating her clothing with the stench of the mire. Looking over her shoulder, she watched for whatever was after her to show itself, her breathing ragged. With a push, she was back on her feet and moving, but all around her everything stayed the same. As if she were running in place. Hollow sounds echoed, her breathing so loud it drowned out everything but the fast and frantic beat of her heart.

Fire burst from the ground in front of her, and with a cry, she pivoted to change directions. Her feet slipped on the wet ground and she almost went down. She fought to run faster, but it didn't matter. She had no idea where she was heading. She ran blindly, moving on pure adrenaline. Another burst erupted to the side and she shifted to move farther away. Dimly, it came to her that she was being herded, moved where someone or something wanted her to go.

Pushing through the semidarkness, she concentrated on staying calm, to control her breathing and not allow fear to direct her. If she could only think. Another burst of fire, closer this time, derailed her thoughts and sent her scurrying along another path. Behind her, disembodied voices echoed faintly, and then louder. They were getting closer. The cackle of laughter had her increasing her speed only to dig in her heels and pivot as another tower of flames erupted. *Faster. Faster.* It was all she could think, the rationality of her thoughts gone in the panic.

WITH A SCREAM CAUGHT IN her throat, Maya sat straight up, woken from her troubled sleep. The sun peeked over the horizon. Her fire had burned down to embers. Across the fire from her and the dog was a pile she couldn't identify in the dim light. She grabbed her hunting knife with a slightly trembling hand, her eyes never leaving the mass. One second more, and the bundle moved, revealing Teck's profile. Stretching, he turned fully onto his back and looked at her.

"Good day, Maya," he said as if it were normal for him to be in her campsite.

"What are you doing here?" Her voice came out breathless even to her own ears.

"I'm coming with you. I told you that you weren't leaving the valley without me. The road is dangerous." Sitting up, he rubbed his eyes and ran a hand over his stubble. Its raspy sound made the hair on her arms stand up.

"I don't need your help. I can protect myself and find my mother on my own."

Teck nodded. "Your mother was always kind to me. With or without your permission, I'm going to find her. Seems only smart that we travel together." Having said that, he stood and began to gather his belongings. She watched him for a while, and when he bent to grasp a belt with a short sword and scabbard, she chuckled.

"What's that?" she asked, pointing at the weapon with her chin. When he looked at her, she snickered again. "Why do you have a sword? It's not as if you know how to use it."

His brow furrowed. "Of course I know how to use it. Do you really think my father would raise a son who didn't know how to use a sword?"

"Oh, I'm sure you're a great swordsman," Maya said with all the sarcasm she could muster. With another laugh under her breath, she shook her head, stood, and gathered her belongings. Deciding not to argue with him further about their traveling arrangements, Maya drowned the remnants of their campfire and they started out of the forest toward the mountains.

* * * * *

TRAILING BEHIND THE PAIR, SNIFFING where he would, Rory stopped. Giving a small yip, he eyed a cat squatting on a branch high in a tree. It was a large cat, about forty pounds, and had streaks of brown and green in its fur.

The cat watched Teck and Maya with big, yellow eyes until they turned a corner, and then he looked down his nose toward the dog. Rory gave another small yip before he placed his forelegs on the tree and wagged his tail. The cat stood leisurely and stretched from the top of his ears to the end of his tail. Taking a step along the length of the branch, the cat again looked at the dog. Seeing he was still being observed, he leaned forward, and with a smile, said, *"Boo."*

Rory, having never been in a situation where a cat spoke to him, jumped down and with a yelp, ran to catch up with Maya. The cat watched him go with a pleased look on his feline face. After a moment, he jumped from his perch where he'd watched Maya sleep and strolled after the trio.

9

CASSANDRA PACED THE CONFINES OF her room atop her castle. Outside, the wind howled and the beginning of a storm whipped rain droplets against the windows.

Finally, after so many eons, the pieces were in play. Two of the Three moved toward their destinations. Now just to decide how to influence them. She and her brother were forbidden to use their powers, to become directly involved, but free will was so boring and mortals so much fun to play with.

Cassandra paused before a large ceramic bowl. Like the fire, she was able to use liquid to see. This bowl was filled with a unique water, which moved in a thick, blackish swirl. With a few ancient words and a motion of her hands, the water cleared to allow the woman to view not only this world, but many others. When the desired image filled her view, her hand once again moved, and the view stopped.

Cassandra's gaze sharpened, and she leaned forward. With a lick of her lips, she decided which players to move.

10

TWO DAYS LATER, TECK, MAYA, and the dog cleared the densest part of the forest and the mountains were at last in sight. The crags rose above them in the distance, the miles yet to travel deceptive in the clear air. With the trees gone, the ground turned rocky and the sun baked down on them, though the breeze coming out of the mountains was cool and brought to mind shady spots with cool water to drink. They'd filled their canteens in the last stream they'd found, and it didn't appear there would be any fresh water until they reached the other side of the mountain. When they found snow, they could melt it to drink. Until then, water would be limited. It was hardest on the dog, but he could roam far and wide in search of water.

MAYA AND TECK DRANK SPARINGLY from the water left in their canteens. If they could just get to the pass and the snow, everything would be all right. The days and nights were long, and after three days, they felt the lack of water in their systems.

Maya had never been in an area so devoid of plant life, and this absence drained her senses. She not only felt the scarcity of water and food, but her spirit was shrinking, starving for the life forces that fed it. She'd quit complaining about a headache a day ago when whining didn't get her anywhere, and it even seemed to make her feel worse.

They continued to trudge toward the mountains, but by now both were becoming dizzy and disoriented. More than once, each of them had stumbled and almost fallen. But to stop would mean death. The only salvation was in moving forward. Or going back, which she would not do.

The weather had continued to cool as they progressed, and every day they watched the sky for rain or snow. The clouds hung heavy and swollen above them, but what was promised was never delivered.

They climbed the next rise, hoping to see snow on the other side. Maya stood at the top, dumbstruck. Her mind swirled with thoughts she was unable to hold on to. Below her, the bowl of land opened to reveal nearly a hundred men sitting around firepits, sharpening tools, preparing food, and mock fighting in hand-to-hand combat. The sound of the camp had been masked by the ridge she and Teck had climbed, and now she couldn't believe the horde of men were real—that they hadn't heard them or smelled the cook fires. Staring at them, her mind was numb, and she couldn't process the danger they were in.

They were seen immediately, so there was no time to go back the way they'd come or even drop to the dirt. A flood of dirty men came at them, the level of noise they made intensifying as they neared.

Maya spun to run, but Teck grabbed her arm. "No, don't run. They'll be on you before you can get far, and there's nowhere to go."

When she tried to free her arm, he gave her a small shake.

"They're animals. Running will drive them into a frenzy." Fear lit her eyes, and he added, "Maybe we can talk our way out of this if we keep our heads."

Maya stared at him, hoping he was smart but thinking he was crazy instead. Then the mass reached them. Men jostled them from side to side as more poured up the rise and into them. Rory crouched, head and front quarters down, a mighty growl issuing from his chest. Prepared to defend, his hackles rose, but before he could act, one of the men clubbed him across the head. Maya cried out and lunged for him, throwing her body over Rory. Already swinging again, the club connected with her shoulder. A spike of pain expelled all the air from her lungs, and before she could draw in a full breath, the men surrounded them and easily pulled her to her feet. As the raiders grabbed and pulled them into the camp, the dog was left for dead, lying with blood running from his ear and mouth onto the rocks.

The bandits pushed and pulled at them. Hands were everywhere on Maya. Men tugged at her hair and clothing. They touched and sniffed at her as she was forced past them, shoved to the center of the camp. The smell of the men caught Maya's breath in her throat and caused her to gag. She and Teck were separated, and although she slapped at the hands that rubbed and pinched her, it did her no good. The men laughed at her efforts and kept her moving with thrusts, kicks, and punches. At the center of the pit, she was pushed to her knees as the men fell back.

This is it, she thought. A hot spike of panic burned in the pit of her belly, and she was shaking by the time it reached the tips of her hands and feet. Her head ached, and she blinked repeatedly to try to clear her eyesight, but it had narrowed to a mere pinpoint. She'd never fainted before but thought she might as she sucked in great gulps of air.

An unnatural silence fell over the gathering, the breeze hot and heavy. When Maya heard footsteps coming through the loose rocks, she looked from between strands of her hair. A man was approaching. He wasn't like the other men, though, or like any man she'd ever seen. He was huge. He had long, snarled hair hanging from his head down his back and onto his chest, and a long, unkempt beard with debris gathered in it. Even in her panic, Maya wondered what kind of man this was. When he stopped a few feet in front of her, the men threw her bow, quiver, and knife at his feet and then fell back. She hadn't even felt the weapons being stripped from her. They treated this man with reverence and more than a little fear, and she thought, maybe, to them he was a god. Standing in front of her, the man stared for a time and then looked to the side. Turning her head to follow his gaze, Maya saw Teck in a similar position, on his knees, head bent, with his weapons laid out in front of him.

A large smile crossed the big man's visage. He threw back his head as a loud guffaw exploded from his frame. His teeth were brown and broken, and with the sound, his eyes went wild. In a language she didn't understand, he yelled something to the men and they answered with an excited, deafening roar. One of the men grabbed her by the upper arm and pulled her to her feet. Her injured shoulder screamed in protest and Maya sucked in a breath. Before the man pushed her forward again, he rubbed a hand down the small of her back and breathed in her ear, "You'll be a fine entertainment, dearie."

She spun her head around, hoping she'd misunderstood him—that there was still help to be found—but the look in his eyes, and those of the other men she passed, confirmed she was in trouble. She looked left and right, searching for Teck or some way out, but he was nowhere to be seen. The hands continued with their exploration and punishment as she was shoved forward toward an outcropping of large stones. In the middle of the rocks, she saw a small cage, and after the man fiddled with the key and lock, Maya was thrust into it and the door slammed shut behind her. Men stood looking in, leering at her, rubbing dirty hands over their lips and whispering among themselves. She pushed herself back against the far side of the rock wall, staying well out of reach of their dirty, grasping hands. Her breaths came in great gasps, and her heart beat so fast and hard it rocked her frame. She'd never find her mother now. She was going to die in this encampment, and she feared death wasn't going to be the worst of it.

As NIGHT NEARED, THE MEN settled down around the campfires. They tore into barely cooked meat and slurped liquid from tankards. They shot looks in her direction that kept her nerves at a fever pitch. Great shivers racked her frame as she sat in the cage, her arms wrapped around her shoulders, slowly rocking. A man walked near the cage and, pausing, tossed a bladder to her. Maya stared at it for a moment, as if it might bite, then she gingerly reached out to grasp it. She opened it, smelling it suspiciously before she took a sip. Water. It smelled and tasted like water.

She sipped the fluid, trying to keep her mind off what lay ahead of her, her thoughts spinning as she searched for a way out. Standing, she moved to the front of the cage, ever vigilant of the men, ready to jump back if one approached. She studied the lock and bars, running her fingers over their rough surface, but she didn't see any way she could open it without a key. As time passed and nothing happened, her breath and heart returned to a steady rhythm. She only heard the low voices of men and the wind whistling above them.

She was peering out at the camp when her vision caught what appeared to be the edges of a fog rolling in. Fog? She hadn't been in the mountains before but didn't think it was normal to get fog. Even in their valley, fog only appeared by the edge of the lake when the humidity was right. Now, in this dry mountain air, she watched suspiciously as the mist moved in.

Grasping the bars, she observed it. It didn't advance like a normal fog. This vapor moved at will, between and around the men and fires. The haze moved right up to the cage and snuck through the bars like fingers. She stepped back from it, unsure. When she came up against the back bars of the cage and could retreat no farther, she reached out and allowed it to play across her hands. With a hesitant breath, she tested the scent as it floated by. Yes, it smelled like fog—crisp, fresh, and cold.

The men didn't seem concerned, continuing with their night. After a time, they began nodding off to sleep, one after another. Some lying down and some dropping where they were.

By the time all the men were unconscious, the fog had grown so thick, Maya could only see a few feet past the bars of her cage. The illumination of the cook fires gave the mist an unearthly quality. Everything was quiet and eerily so. Even the sound of water dripping off the nearby cliffs reverberated back into this space. She walked to the front of the cage, and her footfalls echoed back at her hollowly. With her hands gripping the cold metal, she tilted her head and listened. Turning her attention again to the lock, she studied it. No matter what was happening, this would be the perfect time to get free and run. Giving the bars a small shake, Maya looked around hurriedly when the sound seemed to bounce in the fog. In the distance, a low bang echoed as if a helmet or pot had fallen against some stones, then all was again quiet.

A shiver ran up her spine. Crossing her arms, she put her hands in her armpits to warm them. She didn't know how long she stood looking out into the camp, but after a time, she realized she could see into the distance. Her view was indistinct, but bulks of sleeping men could be discerned from the deeper pockets of mist. As she watched and waited, from between the men, something moved—it was coming toward her.

At first, her mind grasped the notion it might be Rory. The figure walked on all fours and was cast in gray, blending in easily with the evening. No noise came from it, no footfalls or sounds of any kind. When it got nearer, she saw it wasn't Rory, and was surprised to see it was a cat. A big cat. Walking straight to the cell, the cat sat and looked at her with large, luminous yellow eyes. Tearing her gaze from it, Maya looked over it to the camp, not sure if the feline was alone, what was happening, or where the cat had come from.

A soft purr issued from it and then it said, "My lady, why do you not free yourself?"

Maya froze, her breath caught in her throat. She blinked hard, and then her gaze fell back to the cat. For a moment, it caught her in a staring contest, but then she broke the contact. Blinking rapidly, she looked around, scanning over her shoulders and even turning in a complete circle to locate the speaker. When she saw there was no one else around, she turned back to the cat.

"Did you just speak to me?" Just saying the words made her feel foolish, and she looked around again, this time to make certain no one was witness to this interaction. Dehydration and stress were taking its toll.

Completely ignoring her, the cat stretched out a hind leg and began to clean himself. Maya sighed in relief. "Okay, Maya. You're not losing your mind. Get out of here and everything will be all right."

The cat gazed at her with widened eyes. "And how do you plan on getting out of there? You seem to be void of any useful ability."

Maya's legs folded, and she sat on the cold earth. It was official—she was insane.

Walking to the bars, the cat looked up, studying them and Maya. After a moment, he rubbed his body against the outside of the bars. Turning in a complete circle, he again sat to face her, his tail wrapping elegantly around his front feet.

"I suppose you expect me to get you out of here?"

In a whisper, Maya said, "What are you?"

The cat looked her over. "I, my lady, am a dirkcat. My kind has served the realm for eons. I suppose your mother didn't tell you anything about dirkcats?"

"No. No, I've never heard of a dirkcat and certainly have never heard of a cat that could talk."

"Of course not. That mother of yours always was headstrong."

Maya's heart jumped. "My mother?" She rose to her knees and leaned into the bars. Her words coming out fast, she said, "How do you know my mother? Do you know where I can find her?"

"Well of course I know your mother. Your mother and I have been together for many a year." Turning his back on her, the cat wandered away from the cell.

"Wait," Maya called in a whisper and stood to grip the bars. "Where are you going? Don't leave me." Standing on her toes and stretching her neck, she watched the retreating cat. Her voice cracked with emotion at the thought of losing this new acquaintance and possibly her freedom. The idea of finding herself alone again without an escape filled her with terror.

The cat turned and stared back at her. "All right, my lady. Let's go then. We have a long way to travel." As he said these words, the lock popped and the cage door opened, swinging out. Maya released the door, standing in the entryway. The cat turned again and started away.

Shaking off her stupor, she whispered, "Wait. Wait for me." With a ginger tread, she stepped from the cage, looking left and then right. When nothing came at her and no one attempted to keep her in the cage, she trailed the cat through the camp, hurrying to keep up with his departing figure. He led her around the bodies of men and between campfires. As they neared the edge of the encampment, Maya stopped.

"Wait," she whispered. "Hey cat, wait. We need to get Teck, our weapons, and I need to find what happened to Rory."

Stopping, he stared at her with those large, yellow eyes. "Those things are unimportant. You and I need to be moving." And he turned from her to continue away.

"No. No, I'll not leave without Teck and Rory."

Once again, the cat stopped and studied her. "All right. But I'm telling you this delay is a mistake." With a change of direction, he moved past her.

Toward the middle of the camp, they approached a large tent made of animal hides. In a pile to the side of the tent opening were their belongings and weapons—Maya's bag, bow, quiver and knife, and Teck's sword and long knife. Gathering them in her arms, Maya looked at the cat.

"Where is Teck?"

With an arch of his neck, the cat indicated the tent. Maya looked at the tent and then back at him with wide eyes. He ignored her and sat to rub his forelegs over first one ear and then the other, diligently cleaning himself as if there was nothing more important to be doing. Seeing no other way around it, she quietly set down the weapons, her knife in hand as she moved toward the tent flap.

"Stupid cat," she muttered and stepped through the flap of the tent.

Inside, the room was softly illuminated by the light of lanterns. The large, dirty man was asleep, snoring loudly, sprawled on a pallet by the far wall. Looking from him to scan the interior, Maya's eye caught a silhouette in the corner. When she neared on silent feet, she first saw a pile of black hair and then identified Teck. He was laid out on the ground on his stomach. A rough cord encircled his neck to run to his feet, which were pulled up behind him. Intertwined with that was the rope holding his arms tightly behind him. He was gagged, but Maya saw the flash of his eyes in the light. As she neared him, she made out dried blood on his temple and swelling and bruising around one eye. Blood seeped around the gag in his mouth. Inching forward and keeping one eye on the giant in the corner, Maya crept to Teck. She quickly cut the cords holding him.

"Maya," he uttered when she removed his gag.

"Shhh . . ." With a gesture toward their exit, he nodded.

Standing, Teck swayed on his feet and almost went down. Maya placed his arm around her shoulders and put her arm around his waist, helping him upright. Two of his fingers were bent in an unnatural position. Her heart thrummed and fell into her gut, but she tried to remain composed.

With soft steps, Maya moved Teck toward the exit. A few paces from the tent entrance, she stooped, picking up two canteens. They were heavy and sloshed when they moved. Slinging them across her body, she got a better grip on Teck and moved on. They entered the dissipating fog of the night, and the cat stepped forward and caught Teck's attention.

"What's that?" he mumbled, his lips swollen.

"It's a cat," Maya responded. Teck looked blankly at her. As she moved from under his arm, he planted his feet to stop himself from falling. Stooping, Maya again picked up their weapons and packs. She pushed them onto different parts of her body and then put an arm around Teck again, starting forward with a lot of effort. Teck offered no resistance and allowed her to pull him along toward the side of the camp. When they cleared the men and fires, Maya helped him to sit and placed their things next to him.

"What are you doing?" he said as she backed away, catching her breath.

"I need to find Rory." She turned and started back into the camp. Teck tried to rise. Maya turned and held out a palm. "Stay here. I'll be right back."

"Maya . . ." he whispered into the fog, but she was gone.

MAYA MOVED SILENTLY AND STEADILY through the sleeping camp back to the place where they'd first been taken. It was the last spot she'd seen Rory, so it was here that she'd begin her search. She tried to steel herself to see his lifeless body. She only remembered him being clubbed.

When she arrived at the crest they'd scaled coming the other way, she paused and took a deep breath to fortify her courage. Silently, she cursed the small stones when they rolled and skittered downward with her movement, afraid any moment the camp may decide to waken. Her luck held to the top, and with the ambient light from the fires, she started down the other side, looking for a large gray dog. She saw nothing. The only indication of his having been there was the displacement of stones from their confrontation and a splash of dried blood on a few of the stones. Kneeling, she touched the stain and softly said the dog's name. Where could he be?

The camp was large. She had no way of knowing which direction he went, if it was under his own steam, or if one of the men moved him. Was he even alive?

Maya stood and climbed back up the bank of rocks. She would move through the camp to Teck, but by a different route, and see if she could spot the dog. She knew the odds of locating him weren't in her favor, but she needed to try something.

Sidestepping around the men, Maya kept her eyes open for any sign of Rory or of the camp coming awake. Occasionally, one of the men would stir, turning or uttering a snore. She would freeze, thinking her luck had run out, but then they would quiet and she would move on. Keeping her senses alert, she thought it odd that there weren't any other dogs in the camp. It would be natural for a few scavengers to fall in with the men and travel with the easy pickings of food. A troubling thought that maybe they ate the dogs had her looking more frantically for her friend. When she made it to the other side of the camp with no insight into where he might be, she knew she needed to turn back and get herself and Teck to safety. Blinking rapidly to stop the flow of quick tears, she turned back toward where she'd left Teck.

Coming within sight of him and seeing him alone, she scanned the area for the cat. He was nowhere to be seen.

"Where did the cat go?" she whispered.

His eyes panning over the area, Teck said, "I don't know. He was here a moment ago."

Sighing deeply, Maya grabbed their things and assisted Teck. He hissed with pain before gaining his feet, but the same pain was ample motivation to put the camp behind them.

"Let's get out of here," Maya mumbled, mostly to herself. "He'll catch up, I'm sure."

"You didn't find Rory?"

"No. There was no sign of him."

"I'm sorry, Maya." He tried to catch her eye, but she moved past him. Without acknowledging his sympathy, she moved off into the night, trusting him to follow her.

11

THE SHRILL SCREAM DISTURBED A small colony of bats in the upper reaches of the room. They shifted and resettled but seemed to stay alert to the scent of danger.

Head thrown back in frustration, Cassandra began to laugh. The tone and pitch of it neared hysteria as the servants fell back to the shadowed edges of the room lest they draw her attention. Moving back from her scrying bowl, she softly cursed.

"Brother," she muttered. *"Brother."* How could she have forgotten his sharp and crafty mind? She would need to think harder, play rougher, and always remember he was her twin. He would strive to win just as she would. Her long, tapered fingers tapped on her thigh as her mind worked. She was certain it was he who sent the cat to the girl.

So now, after all his losses, he would dip his hands into the field and play dirty.

The wind came through open portals of the keep and whipped the length of her gown to surge under her skirts and bring a welcome chill to her skin. She barely noticed, her mind occupied with other things. Anticipation filled her, and a smile creased her face. It was about time he began to plan in earnest. This would make the contest so much more interesting.

She must push the girl. She was pivotal to everything. The dreams were the perfect vehicle to motivate and turn the girl— she was so receptive, but others used the dreams too. She couldn't be scared off... not yet. What fun would that be? Caleb must be allowed to think he may win.

She moved to the dais and sat at a large throne-like chair. With a tug to straighten her gown, she folded her hands in her lap and stared into the nearby flames.

Shaking herself out of her reverie, she directed her thoughts once again to the problem. The girl. The mother. The coming of the Three. The town of Berth held many dangers for one so innocent as Maya. She would try to get to the temple in search of the priest. He was one of Caleb's. He would aid her on the quest of the Three and put her feet on the path. If she made it that far, Cassandra could manipulate her. She could yet turn this her way.

Since her brother saw fit to aid the girl, Cassandra would manipulate the other side.

* * * * *

CALEB PACED THE CRAGGY ROCK cliff, his mind on his sister and the coming of the Three.

So much depended on this girl. For so long he had waited, and to have it all fall to the whims of fate and a young girl—

there was only so much he could manipulate. He'd planted the seeds in the sacred stones. It would be up to the Three to locate and use them.

He'd given a gentle push by sending the cat to her, but there was only so much aid he could send. So much of it would be left to chance.

And his sister. She wouldn't adhere to the rules of the game. Though he was mostly blind where she was concerned, he knew it was not within her nature to play fair. And her pieces were so many—evil in the hearts of most men and women.

The cat was an ally to the girl. There would come others he could rely on to help her in her quest. He would have to be diligent to scent out his sister's minions.

12

MAYA AND TECK TRAVELED FOR miles before they felt it was safe to stop. They knew the men from the camp would likely be coming after them, but physically, both were at the end of their endurance. With all he'd been through, Teck pushed himself further than Maya would have imagined he could. When he went down for the second time, she began to look for a place to rest.

They were far beyond the tree line but not yet into snow. Investigating a break in a pile of large boulders, she decided it would have to do as a resting place for the night. Darkness was falling and would soon be upon them. It would be cold, but even if they had fuel to make a fire, it wouldn't be safe to do so. This small crevasse would provide them with limited security from the elements and mask their presence if they were followed. Maya figured it would take them a couple more days of hard walking to clear the mountain pass and take comfort in nearing the town of Berth.

Pushing her way between the boulders, Maya moved some

of the small rocks and laid their belongings out, using various articles to plug holes and limit the wind, which was picking up.

"Come on, Teck. Get in here. It'll have to do."

Teck eyed her and with a shrug, bent over to work his way in. His body loomed over her at one point and he paused momentarily, looking down at her. She shifted to the side, making as much room for him as possible.

"Let me look at those fingers of yours."

He sat awkwardly facing her and extended his hand, catching his breath as she took it within the warmth of her palm.

"I'm sorry, I don't mean to hurt you," she whispered.

Unable to control his reaction to her, he allowed her to think it was pain that changed his breathing. While she looked over his injured digits, running her fingers lightly down the unnatural angles, he stared at the part in her hair. He could smell her. A musky, earthy essence that he wanted to dive into. He took one deep breath after another, filling his lungs with her.

When she looked up at him, he lost himself in her eyes and almost didn't hear her say, "I'm sorry," before she jerked his index finger straight.

Pain erupted up his arm and he pulled back from her with a yowl. "By the gods!" he cursed and held the injured hand with his other.

"We're almost done," she said, reaching for him. "Let me finish and wrap them before they begin to swell."

He didn't want to give her his hand again. The pain quickly became a steady manageable throb, and he really didn't want to feel that again. When he looked at her with the intention of having her wait, she raised one eyebrow and, suddenly, he felt like a child. Setting his jaw, he extended his hand to her, prepared for the worst. Maya was quick to straighten his other finger. Wasting no time, she wrapped the hand in an extra shirt she'd torn into strips. He'd be limited if it came to a fight, but at least it wasn't his sword hand.

When he lay down, Maya turned her back to him and covered them with her jackets, creating a cocoon to hold in their body heat. She scooted backward until she almost touched him and then tried to relax and get some rest.

Teck could feel her heat and knew he wouldn't be getting any sleep this night. He longed to reach out and just touch her but wasn't sure how she'd react. He listened to her breathing change as she dropped into an exhausted sleep, and he allowed himself the luxury of rubbing a strand of her hair between his finger and thumb.

WOKEN IN THE MIDDLE OF the night by Maya rolling over and snuggling into the warmth of his body, Teck held perfectly still, not even breathing. When her hands snaked under his shirt and she sighed contentedly, he thought he was dreaming. His lids blinked heavily.

Surprised he'd fallen asleep earlier, he now had no illusions about getting any additional rest. His body's ready response to Maya, though ensuring his own warmth, was not something he could sleep through. The way she snuggled with her head under his chin allowed him to wrap his arms around her and breathe in the scent of her hair. She smelled of the land and wild — growing things. Taking a large inhale of her essence, he got comfortable and enjoyed her closeness.

Too soon for Teck, Maya began to stir. When she pushed herself back from him and tilted her head to meet his gaze, he was spellbound. She was so beautiful. Soft and warm, just coming out of sleep. He didn't even think as he lowered his head toward hers, capturing her lips with his. The touch of her caused a tingling through his body, and when she gave a gasp of surprise, he pushed his advantage to deepen the kiss. Her taste was everything he could have imagined. She moved closer and pressed a leg between his to wrap her arms tightly around his middle. Teck placed a hand on her back, moving her shirt up, and caressed her spine, right above the rounding of her bottom. With a small moan into his mouth, Maya moved even closer.

A moment later, Teck pulled gently back from her. As if in a trance, she opened her pale green eyes. Gently, running a fingertip over her temple, he pushed her hair behind her ear. What he saw in her gaze — the passion, innocence, and confusion, registered and he took a deep, calming breath, separating himself from his desires. What he wanted from Maya wasn't a momentary romp, a quick tumble within the warmth of their coats. He'd always wanted Maya, but it was a lifetime he yearned for. He would do nothing to break her trust. He would protect her with his sword and body from all the threats of this world, even himself.

He allowed her the time needed to come out of the dream of desire, and when her mind began to work, he saw the sharpening of her eyes and the blush of her skin.

"Oh, um Teck . . ." She stumbled over her words as she pulled from his embrace and moved as far as possible from him. With her back to the stone wall of their shelter, she wouldn't meet his eyes. She began to gather her belongings and pointedly stared outside as if watching for something.

"Maya," he began and had to stop himself from reaching to her.

"No, Teck. You don't need to say anything. It's me . . . I'm sorry I took advantage of you. I just . . . ah . . . I don't know what I was thinking."

A small smile curved Teck's lips and he fought to conceal it. He didn't want her to be offended and, truly, her inexperience was endearing. "Maya, I've been wanting to do that for a long time. You didn't take advantage of me."

Maya's gaze swung to him, her eyes large on her flushed face. "Really?"

With a nod, he kept his gaze on her. "Really." Reaching to gather a few of his belongings, Teck said, "Maybe we should be heading out. We still have days until we clear this mountain range."

"Yes. I think that's a good idea."

No matter what he'd said, Maya still seemed embarrassed. It would be better to place a bit more space between them and concentrate on their travels.

Maya crawled from the shelter of the rocks and stood to stretch. Sleeping on the cold, rocky ground wasn't either of their idea of a comfortable bed. When he stepped out, Maya moved forward to give him room to exit.

The sun was cresting the hills and it looked to be a beautiful day. A good day for walking. After stepping away for some privacy, Maya came back to the area just as Teck was coming from the other direction. She had her pack and quiver on her back, and a firm grip on the bow. He was just finishing adjusting his belongings—strapping on his sword in its scabbard, straightening the knife on his hip, and closing his jacket. Taking his canteen, he opened the cap and offered it to her. With a soft thank you, she sipped and handed it back. Teck drank, screwed the cap on, and swung the canteen over his shoulder.

Watching his movements closely, Maya asked, "How is your hand?"

Looking down at the wrapped appendages, Teck wiggled his fingers slowly within the bandage, withholding a cringe at the dull pain. "Good. You're a good healer, Maya."

She blushed at his compliment and looked off in the distance.

"You ready?" He asked, glancing up the hill.

Maya nodded, walked past Teck, and started up the rise. He fell into step behind her.

THEY HADN'T GONE FAR WHEN clouds rolled in to cover the warm sunshine. The chill in the air came quickly, but with the exertion of their climb, they didn't complain. The cooler air felt good on their sweat-covered skin. Conversation came infrequently as they put their energy into placing one foot in front of the other.

About midday, the snow started. Walking became increasingly treacherous as they slid repeatedly on the mud and slick stones. Twice, Teck steadied Maya when she would have fallen. The cold worsened the higher they went, and although they didn't discuss it, both knew finding shelter was going to prove difficult.

The day waned, and the sun continued to dip, but on the horizon a moon began to rise. Maya stopped and looked back the way they'd come. She could see no evidence that they were being followed, but she didn't think they should stop for the night. Turning back to look up the mountain, Teck watched her.

"I think we should continue to move," she said as she neared him.

"Yes, okay. There's no shelter to be found anyway. If we stop, we're apt to freeze to death. At least walking is helping to keep us warm."

Nodding, Maya passed him. Speaking over her shoulder, she added, "If we can just make the summit, heading down should go faster. Even if it's days until Berth, we'll be able to find shelter and make a fire. Get something to eat."

Teck didn't add anything else and simply followed her up the mountain.

HOURS PASSED AND STILL THEY climbed. Maya's boots were wet from the snow and her feet were numb. Her breath puffed out with every exhale. If not for the continued exertion, they would surely be freezing.

She was conscious of Teck behind her, but all conversation

had halted hours ago. They both concentrated on staying alert and moving one tired foot in front of the other.

Maya stopped, looking down at her feet, and Teck almost ran into her. "I feel as if we're heading down. Do you feel it?"

"Yes. It happened a bit ago. We must have crested the mountain in the darkness. Let's keep moving and see how far we can reach tonight."

A surge of excitement and expectation filled Maya, and a small smile curved her lips. Finally, they were getting somewhere.

13

THE CREVASSE BETWEEN THE ROCKS smelled of the girl. Rory spent a long time sniffing the area, front to back. Mixed with the girl's scent was that of the man. Sometimes, his scent confused the dog. He had a distant feeling of the scent being unwelcome—it made him feel like growling and maybe biting. But the newer feeling was warm. One of the man becoming a member of Rory's pack. Through all these images and feelings, the dog deferred to the girl. She was the leader. Where she led, he followed.

Now he must find her.

Rory and the cat had been tracking the girl and man for days. Under normal circumstances, he knew he could have overtaken her quickly, but these circumstances weren't normal. He hadn't been himself since the camp, where his confused memories were of loud sounds, harsh smells, the girl's terror, and his own fear. Then nothing until the cat.

When he woke and saw the cat standing over him, he wanted to growl, to snap, but he couldn't make a sound.

Without effort, as if he were being lifted by an unseen force, he took to his feet and walked, following the feline. The cat smelled bad and the dog didn't want to go with it, but he had no choice. His feet followed the cat.

When they stopped near a bubbling pool of water, the dog lapped eagerly to quench his burning thirst. His throat was so dry. His exhaustion made him dizzy. At one point, the cat laid a dead rabbit at his feet. He licked the blood from the carcass, igniting his hunger. Tearing into the animal, he consumed it in big gulps. After finishing and licking the remnants from his paws, he looked eagerly to the cat who ignored him completely. It leisurely cleaned its own fur and then turned in a circle, lying down. It covered its nose with its tail and fell asleep.

When he woke, the day progressed much like the previous. He needed to find her. Within him, no other instinct existed.

That night, the cat once again supplied food and somehow found water. Each day, Rory felt better, his head clearer and his body stronger. Finally, the cat and he could travel at a speed that got them closer to the girl. Moving quickly the next day, he and his companion crested the mountain and he knew they were very close to their quarry, her smell fresh to his senses.

Rory picked up his pace, practically tripping down the hillside, anxious to again see his girl. When a strange smell hit his nose, he stopped midstride, whining low in his throat. He lifted his head, nose in the air to taste the wind. His head dropped below his shoulders. With a gleam in his eyes, he surged forward.

14

TIRED AND NEEDING TO REST, Maya continued to push forward. She and Teck had been on their feet for days. When they'd reached the tree line a few hours ago, a change had occurred deep in her. The trees, grasses, and bushes radiated a power, a life force that filled her. When they came across a small stream, she thought they'd found paradise. They would follow the stream, and if they could find shelter that would conceal them, tonight they would have a fire. Keeping her eyes open and alert, even through the fog of her exhaustion, she watched for game. A bird perhaps.

Maya nocked an arrow. She moved stealthily through the underbrush, her eyes keen, her senses open to the area around her. The sun cast speckled streams of light through the canopy of the trees, and a gentle breeze blew the welcome scent of green, growing things. Maya was in her element. Just let a bird or rabbit show itself.

Moments later, one did just that—a bird taking flight. Maya drew the bow, aimed, and let an arrow fly. The bird issued a small squawk and fell to the ground. Taking a bird in flight with an arrow wasn't easy, but Maya had been hunting for as long as she could remember. And as good as she was, she was better with the bow Teck made her—its balance perfect and its pull smooth.

With a hurried step, Maya went to the bird and kneeled. Pulling the arrow from its body, she placed the bird in her game bag that hung from her waist and wiped the arrow on her pants leg. Teck stopped behind her, and as she rose, she faced him, meeting his smile with one of her own.

Maya missed the next bird, but she wasn't discouraged. That was the nature of hunting. Hitting a bird in flight every time was almost impossible. When the third bird flew, Maya aimed and fired. The arrow hit the bird in the head and knocked it from the sky. She killed it before it could regain consciousness and put it with the other in her game bag. Looking around, she spotted the arrow a short distance away. As she kneeled to grasp it, the brush behind her rustled. She twisted just as Teck yelled out a warning. Five men leaped out as if they'd been waiting for them. They came from the camp, their odors ripe and strong. Teck stepped to confront them, and three of the men faced off with him. He pulled his sword from the scabbard with his good hand.

Turning from his companions with a smile at Maya, one of the remaining men advanced on her. He rushed her and grabbed her arm, wrenching her to her feet. Using the impetus of this motion, Maya swung one arm from behind. In her hand was the lone arrow she'd retrieved. Her aim true, she jammed the arrow into the man's neck, driving it in until it came out the other side. Blood spurted from the wound, covering her to the elbow and staining her shirt. His eyes widened with shock and disbelief. She released the arrow as his body fell, lest she be pulled down with him.

Pivoting, she pulled the hunting knife from her waist and moved toward the fifth man. Behind him, Teck clashed with the others. With each sweep of his blade, he made short work of them. One was already dead on the ground and the other two had looks of surprise and rage. Red oozed from their bodies from a multitude of cuts. She paused momentarily, watching over the shoulder of the last man, her gaze tracking Teck's movements—smooth and confident as he cut the men down. He was right when he'd told her he was good with a sword. No, better than good. The man advancing in front of her drew her attention, and crouching with the knife in her fist, they locked eyes as she waited for him to make a move.

Just as he took a step toward her, she heard a noise from behind. A fierce growl made her jump, and a large gray mass flew by her to tackle the man. Rory straddled the bandit, silencing a scream, the man's throat in his jaws before Maya could even register he was there.

"Rory," she breathed, her shoulders slumping with amazement and released tension. All at once, emotions she hadn't realized were buried surged to her chest, and she almost cried in joy and relief.

She watched the altercation for a moment but had to look away. She wondered if this wasn't her pet. The dog was brutal.

He ripped out the man's throat with a mighty shake of his body. At the sound of the rending flesh—a wet, tearing sound—Maya bent at the waist, a dry heave catching in her throat and making her eyes water.

Tipping his head back, Rory arched his neck and a howl issued forth. Maya's eyes darted up. Hair rose on her arms and a shiver streaked down her spine. She'd never seen this side of him. He'd become a powerful, vengeful predator.

The howl ended, and Rory sniffed disdainfully at the body at his feet. He glanced toward Teck, who, with a well-aimed thrust of his sword, finished the last man. Then the dog looked over his shoulder at Maya, turned, and padded toward her. For just a second, Maya had a surge of fear. The large gray dog, his muzzle and forelegs covered in blood and goo, didn't bear any resemblance to her companion. When he came near her, he sat and looked up at her, tongue hanging out.

Maya gave a sigh of relief and dropped to her knees in front of him. She threw her arms around his neck and buried her face in his fur. She'd thought him dead.

"Oh, Rory. Good boy, Rory, good boy."

* * * * *

WHEN RORY HAD CAUGHT THE fresh smell of his mistress and the man, along with the harsher scents of the strangers, he'd broken into a run. After the last couple days, it felt good to stretch his legs and feel the muscles respond. The smell of the men's blood came to him on the breeze and in an instant, an instinct washed over him like nothing he'd felt before. The urge to protect, to kill if need be, was all he knew. When he broke from the brush, seeing the girl standing defenseless—without tooth or claw—against the bigger assailant, the dog reacted without thought. To bite and tear were his only desires. The man's throat felt good in his maw, the warm blood right on his tongue. Finished, his enemy dead under his feet, his howl of victory burned true in his throat. Partway through, sanity returned. When he approached her, he could smell the fear on her, so he sat and waited for her to come to him. And she did. She even said the words. *Good boy.* He didn't know what they meant, but he knew the way they made him feel. The approval, love, and acceptance from the girl, the leader of his pack, was as necessary to him as the air he breathed.

He heard the man, their companion, approach, and when the girl pulled from him, he felt and heard the change in her. Her breath quickened, and before she rose, her fist clenched tight in the heavy fur of his nape. Leaning her weight into him, she stood and flung herself at the man.

* * * * *

WHEN MAYA LOOKED FROM WHERE she gripped Rory to where Teck stood watching, she felt an overwhelming thankfulness wash over her. They were alive and their enemies dead. She didn't give it a moment's thought as she stood and launched herself into Teck's arms. When he caught her and wrapped her in his warmth, she hung on.

Death had been so close to them. Now it stilled in the bodies of their assailants. The smell irritated her nose and the color stained her skin and clothes, but they were alive.

Releasing her, Teck stepped back. "Come on, Maya. Let's move. There may be more of them."

She couldn't speak—her throat was dry—so she nodded quickly. Looking around the area, a shiver of revulsion passed through her. She stepped wide around the man she'd killed with the arrow, unable to fathom how she did it. Now the sight made her uneasy to know how little she thought before killing a person. The dog trotted by her side, and when she reached down and placed a hand on his head, she calmed a bit more.

THEY WALKED FOR HOURS WITH Teck now leading the way. As the scent of their adversary's blood floated to her from her clothing and skin, Maya's stomach yearned to purge itself. The farther down the mountainside they went, the warmer the day became, and the blood soon dried on their bodies. It no longer created such a strong scent but became stiff where it had soaked them. Rory's coat, where it had once been wet, was firm and spiky and showed a deep maroon against his pale gray fur. The texture of it was worse than the scent had been. Every so often, she'd forget and scratch her nose or move her hair, and the stain and feeling of her hands threw her back into the fight. Her memory kept playing over the body of the man she'd killed. It was different than hunting. She'd never really had a reason to consider it before. Killing a man. How he'd lain there, blood streaming from the wound on his neck. She feared she'd never get the image out of her head. The shock in his eyes before he fell. Even the sound of his body as it made contact with the ground. She tried to get the thoughts out of her head and think of their future. Fleeing the area, they'd left the stream behind and she prayed for water of some sort soon so she could clean the carnage from her body.

Not long after, Rory gave a small yip and broke into a trot. He quickly disappeared from their sight, and when he didn't return, Teck looked at Maya with raised eyebrows. She just shook her head at him. Who knew what was in the dog's mind.

They continued for another half mile before the sound of gurgling water came to her. "Teck." She stopped and grabbed his arm. "Do you hear that? I think there's water ahead." He smiled at her, and they picked up their pace. It wasn't long before they smelled the water.

Pushing through the underbrush, the trees parted, and ahead of them was the most beautiful stream. It gurgled where it ran over rocks, and downstream, it broadened into a pool surrounded by lush vegetation. The sun shone warmly down on them, glinting off the water. The smell of the dampness and growing things filled her lungs and forced out the scent of blood and death.

"It's a paradise," Maya whispered reverently.

She didn't know if Teck heard her. He dropped his pack and moved toward the pool. Reaching behind his head, he caught a handful of his shirt and pulled it over his head and off. Maya watched him, captivated by the ripple of muscles in his back and shoulders. He tossed the shirt down and unbuckled his sword, allowing it to fall to the ground, unheeded. As he neared the water, he balanced on one foot to grasp a boot and pull it off. With that done, he reversed his stance and pulled off the other boot. These, too, he dropped to the ground as he kept moving forward. Unlacing his pants, he pushed them down past lean hips and stepped on the end of each leg, forcing them off over his bare feet.

Maya knew she should turn her back, but she'd never seen anything so beautiful. The sunlight played over Teck's body as if it were sculpting him out of rock. She stared as he moved into the pool of water and only let out a breath when he was covered to his shoulders. Maya took a step and then two toward the pool. Teck dunked his head under the surface and sputtered out a mouthful of water when he came back up, pushing wet hair from his eyes. She kneeled at the water's edge and scrubbed her hands with sand and water, removing the dried blood. When she looked from her hands to Teck, he was watching her.

"Come in, Maya." He spoke loudly enough to be heard over the flow of water. "Don't be shy now."

Was he speaking of their kiss in the rocks? It was true, she hadn't been shy. Now she wasn't sure. "One of us should keep watch. Who knows if more of those men are tracking us."

"The dog can keep watch," he said with a jerk of his chin at the shore. She looked over her shoulder and saw Rory lying on the bank, coat wet, panting in the sunlight. "He'll warn us if someone comes." He was right. Rory would alert them in plenty of time.

She stayed where she was. An ease moved through her as

her discomfort fell away. She could do anything she wanted. She and this man faced death more than once, and her journey had just begun. Who knew what tomorrow, or even today, might bring? She could be dead at any moment. Why shouldn't she grasp this opportunity? They were alive, at least for now. They were alive, and she wanted to live.

Maya stood slowly, and excitement hit her. Excitement so heady, she felt dizzy. Her heart felt heavy pounding in her throat, and her breath became shallow. Teck's eyes almost glowed with his need for her. In her mind, she replayed the sight of him as he walked toward the pool. She wanted to touch and taste that skin, and the new desire thrilled her.

She pulled off one boot and then the other. She set them down carefully on a rock at the edge of the pond. Her vest came off next, and as she grasped the bottom of her shirt, she again glanced at Teck. He hadn't moved. When she laid her shirt beside her boots and vest, she released a breath she didn't realize she'd held.

The sun and the gentle breeze brushed her skin. Closing her eyes for a moment, she simply enjoyed the sensations that came to her from inside and outside her body. She realized, then, that she couldn't wait for Teck's hands to create their own sensations. When she unlaced her trousers and pushed them down her legs, she looked at him and her lips curved in a smile. The power she'd felt at the corral behind the cabin returned in full force. Her body held the mastery women have felt through the ages.

Naked, she stood, straight and proud. This moment, this

decision, would change everything after it. With acceptance, she stepped into the cool water of the pond and the open arms of the man who waited.

* * * * *

TECK WATCHED, HIS BODY TENSE as Maya disrobed. When she bent to remove her pants, he became so lightheaded he feared he might fall face first into the water. He was afraid to blink, lest he miss something. She was a thing of beauty. Like a wild sprite surrounded by the forest. He moved slowly for fear that he would scare her away.

When she stepped into the water, he moved forward to meet her. Her red hair was like fire in the sun. Her pale skin bright in the afternoon light, it called to him to touch and taste. He couldn't—wouldn't—resist. What would he do if she pulled back now? Could he let her go? He didn't think so.

When Maya stepped into his arms, he quit worrying about his own control and simply enjoyed the feeling of her. Her body felt soft, her touch gentle. She wound her arms around his neck, and when her breasts pressed against his chest, he'd have sworn the doorway of the beyond opened for him alone. She'd said the forest and pond were paradise, but paradise was being in her arms. He'd never felt anything to compare.

He swept her long hair back from her face and over her shoulder. His hand followed her hair to run over her shoulder and down her side. At the small of her back, he paused to draw her closer. She gasped as his full length met her softness. He lifted her, and without guidance, she wrapped her legs around his hips. Bringing his hand back to her hair, he grasped her at the nape and pulled her head back, linking his mouth with hers. Their tongues played a mock battle as he walked with her toward the bank. Lowering her to the long grass, he lay atop her and with ease, slid into her. The joining made her gasp. With a soft breath, she said his name. When he turned and found her lips again, she arched into him.

They moved together in a ballet older than the ages, older than this world or the next. Teck curled his body around hers, laying his face in her neck to breathe her scent. Moving swiftly now, their breaths erupted in pants and groans. When she crested, Maya's back arched, head thrown back, and eyes wide. Into the light of the afternoon, she stared, blind from eyes that glowed a bright blue.

IN THE POND, TECK AND Maya splashed and washed the sweat of travel and passion from each other.

"We should be getting out," Maya said. "We still have a fire to make, birds to clean and cook, and besides, I'm wrinkling like an Arrok berry." Teck laughed. He swooped her up in his arms and carried her to her clothing and pack. Stepping to his belongings, he pulled a pair of pants from his pack and pulled them on, then stomped his feet down into his boots.

"You get covered and I'll gather some wood." As he walked by her, he leaned down and ran his hand over her head and down her hair. When she looked up at him, he gave her a quick kiss. "Take care of my girl. I'll be right back."

Maya realized she was watching where he'd left with a stupid smile on her face. "Come on *girl*. Get up and get something done," she berated herself. She pulled a shirt from her pack and slipped it over her head before dressing completely. Covered, she washed their bloody clothing in the stream. Laying them over some bushes for the night, hoping they would dry, she put the packs against some larger boulders. It would be a good place to make a fire and spend the night. She cleaned the two birds she'd shot earlier and, searching for a moment, found a tree with small, strong branches to make skewers. Sitting, peeling the bark from the green branches, she glanced up as Teck came back. His arms were full of timber. With a small smile in her direction, he kneeled by her and began to make a pit for the fire.

WITH A SMALL FIRE GOING and the birds cooking, Maya and Teck relaxed, lying back onto their packs, feet stretched toward the warmth of the flames. Earlier, he'd taken her hand in his. Now, while they discussed the coming days, he ran his fingers over hers and along her palm. His touch was relaxing her, and she didn't know if she'd stay awake to eat.

"Your mother. Do you remember anything that might help us?"

"Nothing. I don't even know if her kidnapping was a random act by raiders who took the opportunity or if it's something more. My mother would never tell me anything about her past." Maya sat up and stretched her shoulders. "I know I must find her, but part of me is worried I'm leading us to the wrong place. Another part of me is certain this path is correct." She looked at her hands, realizing she was wringing them. Flexing her fingers, she rolled her shoulders back, trying to relax. "I just don't know."

"What makes the part of you certain?"

Glancing over her shoulder at Teck laid out with his feet next to the fire, Maya debated with herself on how much—if anything—she should tell him. Would he think she was mad if she confided about the dreams? About the man in them? Or the woman?

She looked away for several moments. Teck didn't speak, but she felt him watching her. Finally, he ran his hand up her back and got her attention.

"Come on, Maya. You can tell me. It can only help for both of us to have all the information."

He was right, of course. Still worried about his reaction to her story, Maya lay with her head on his shoulder. She felt safer talking to him this way. He couldn't see her face, and she didn't have to see the possible derision in his.

"I began having dreams a few nights ago. First, dreams of a man, but recently, they've taken on a darker feeling, as if I'm in danger, and there's a woman. I recall running, but I don't know what from." A shiver passed through her frame and Teck pulled her in tighter, wrapping an arm around her shoulders. "I realized the dream of the man came to me days before my mother disappeared and then again on that day. His words are never clear. I can't remember it like this conversation." Pushing up on one arm, she searched his face. "He wants me to find my mother, and it's he who has instructed me to go to Berth. I'm to meet a man there—"

"A man?" Teck interrupted, a scowl coloring his face.

"Yes. The image in my mind is foggy, but I think he's a priest."

Rubbing his hand up and down her arm, he asked, "What makes you think that?"

Maya thought for a moment. How did she articulate her feelings about this man? "Well, in my mind, I can't see him clearly, but the feelings he projects are of a profound holiness. His image is stained with an odd blue shade—like a summer sky." Snuggling back into Teck's body, Maya thought back. "He's nothing like the holy man in Roadstead. Master Umber always made me feel . . . uncomfortable. I thought it was because Mother didn't like him much."

Shaking off the memories of the small village and the people residing in it, Maya wrapped an arm around Teck and moved even closer. Her voice was low as she spoke, half-asleep. "All I know is to go to Berth and find the priest."

15

WAKING FROM THE DREAM, MAYA'S eyes snapped open, her thoughts fully alert. Sitting quietly, mere inches in front of her face, was the cat. Neither moved nor said a word. Maya blinked slowly and watched the feline, not certain it was really there, or if she was really awake. She might still be in her dream. When a breeze blew through the camp and the cat's fur ruffled under its touch, Maya decided she must be awake.

"Hello, cat," she murmured.

The cat didn't say anything. Glancing over her shoulder at Teck, Maya slowly sat up and again faced the cat.

"Where have you been? Why did you disappear?"

When Teck shifted behind her, the cat turned and walked away.

"Who are you talking to?" He placed a hand on her hip, and she welcomed the warmth of his skin.

"The cat is back," she answered him without turning.

Pushing himself up on one elbow, Teck looked around the

area for the animal. "Where did it even come from in the first place?"

With a small shrug, Maya admitted, "I'm not sure, but I'm glad it did. I don't think we would have escaped the mountain camp without it."

The sun was just beginning to make an appearance over the distant mountains, and since they were both awake, Maya stood and began to ready her things.

With a yawn and a stretch, she asked, "Do you think we'll make Berth today?"

Nodding, he said, "I've never been there before, but I'm thinking today or tomorrow, probably."

Acknowledging her understanding with a small motion of her head, Maya scanned the area for Rory. With a small chuckle, she pointed the dog out to Teck as he stood and moved up behind her. Following the line of her finger, he saw Rory sitting with the cat who rubbed across his front legs and chest. Rory's tongue hung out, and he seemed to be smiling at the attention.

"Cat's almost as big as Rory," Teck observed. Turning from the sight and shoving items into his pack, he muttered, "At least they seem to know each other."

With a wrinkle of her brow, Maya watched the animals for a moment more. They did seem familiar with each other. Turning from them, she hefted her rucksack and waited for Teck to do the same before they started out.

THE DAY GOT WARMER AS Maya, Teck, Rory, and the cat made their way down the mountainside. The trees became a forest with the addition of broad leaves and viney growth. Maya's hands brushed the rough bark of trees and the soft featherlike leaves of viney plants. She felt more and more like herself as the day progressed. Water became more frequent, and the debilitating thirst no longer racked their bodies.

As they walked, Maya and Teck gathered berries, roots, nuts, and other edible growth, which they snacked on throughout the morning hours. Catching a rabbit, Maya placed it in her game sack with wild vegetables she'd collected. She began dreaming of the stew she'd prepare when they stopped for the night. With the injection of water and food, their young bodies rebounded quickly. Strength filled them, and their muscles responded to the forced march. She realized the cat hunted during the day when Rory appeared with blood on his paws and muzzle. In their own way, each of them was recovering from the ordeal in the man camp, and the trek over the mountains.

As the sun tipped toward its resting spot, they made their way across another stream when Teck stopped. "It doesn't appear we'll make town tonight. Let's find a suitable campsite."

With a nod of agreement, Maya made her way downstream. They soon chanced upon an outcropping of rock and a thicket. She raised her eyebrows at him and when he nodded, they started forward. After clearing the spot of sharp rocks, Maya set down her pack and game bag and moved off to gather wood for a fire. Teck mimicked her actions but headed in the opposite direction.

* * * * *

CASSANDRA WATCHED THE LITTLE GROUP from her viewing bowl. The liquid pulsed and swirled as if alive. The air in her castle cold, the atmosphere foreboding.

Now would be a good time to see if this girl was as powerful as the Telling foretold. Would she be able to withstand all the world and Cassandra had to throw at her? When Cassandra won this contest with her brother, she needed to know if this girl would be worth all the trouble. The power in this world was pure, its essence drawing her with every touch. When this world was hers to have, the girl's power would be hers too.

She closed her eyes and reached out, calling one of her servants, Mikel—a promising man of low ethics. He'd been with her almost from the beginning of his life. The malice and depravity oozed out of him. And even luckier, when he learned of the girl, he'd have a reason to hate her.

* * * * *

CHANTING LOW IN HIS THROAT, Mikel cut his hand. Squeezing it into a fist, he allowed fat drops of blood to fall into the fire. They sizzled upon coming into contact with the flames. The smell of charred fluid filled his nostrils, and he began to sway in tempo with his chanting.

His mistress had called upon him, and he was always happy to serve her. It was she who gave him his power, she who saw potential in him, she who showed him who he could be when all others failed him. She made his life worth living.

He had loved Sylvan. As a boy, they had grown up together. He thought they would make a life. But she had betrayed him. Told of the girl, Mikel had become furious. He would dispose of this problem—this evidence of his beloved's betrayal. With the power of his mistress, the girl would soon be dead. And with her death, his mistress would fulfill his bidding.

Chanting louder, he called upon his dark mistress for this gift, and in the flames, he saw the realization of his desire.

* * * * *

ARMS FULL OF WOOD, MAYA approached the campsite when her attention was drawn to the sound of frantic barking. She dropped her load and broke into a run. As she moved into the area around their chosen site, Teck arrived from the forest near her, his arms also full of wood. She scanned the area and rushed toward Rory's barking, only to have Teck intercept her and grip her arm.

"Wait."

"But, Rory—he'll be hurt."

Looking across the clearing, they watched as Rory fended off a small, furry animal. Long and sinewy, its body ran like water over the ground. Its size was like that of a normal cat. Perhaps it wasn't dangerous, just curious. Then, upon closer inspection, they saw the abnormally long claws and teeth. When Maya stepped closer, intent on separating her pet from this unknown creature, the animal's attention turned from the dog to the girl. Large eyes locked on her as it lifted its head to smell the air.

A low growl issued from the animal, and with unnatural speed and ferocity, it headed toward her, its body rippling and seeming almost to float across the ground. For a moment, Maya stood still in shock, and then the realization it was coming straight for her had her backing up. When it increased its speed, she felt a moment of panic before she turned to run.

"Maya!" Teck yelled, but the claws on the rocks and a high-pitched whine drove her forward in horror.

Maya reached the tree line, and just as the monstrosity threw itself at her, she leaped to grab a branch, pulling herself up and over the outcropping with a swing of momentum. The animal reversed directions, tearing up the ground with its claws and giving an almost human scream of rage and frustration. Its elongated snout darted left and right, rows of teeth snapping as it rushed to hurl itself against the base of the tree trunk.

Crouched on a branch, Maya looked down at it, startled to see its eyes gleam with a higher intelligence and hateful malice. It jumped upward toward her, tearing and spitting, and she felt lucky when she saw its claws were not conducive to climbing. Unable to reach her, it dug furiously into the ground at the base of the timber. Claws flung dirt and grasses all around. Maya looked up as Teck and Rory approached. They moved slowly, each of them keeping a keen eye on the beast. Rory began barking again, lunging at the creature who ignored him in its fixation on the tree and Maya. The sound of the animal—its grunts and growls—blended with the sounds of Rory's barking. Maya was sure the racket would bring the band of men back down upon them.

Watching the creature, she tried to identify what kind of animal it was. She'd never seen anything like it in the forest, and she'd been exploring the woods for almost as long as she'd been walking. It appeared to be a blend of many animals into one. Cat, bear, badger—all ferocious animals when bent on a cause, and now the cause was her.

The animal continued its assault on the base of the tree, but Maya's heartbeat began to calm and her breaths evened out. She thought herself safe as long as she remained where she was. She caught Teck's eye, hoping he might have a plan. Just as she was about to yell out to him, though, her perch moved. It was just a slight shift, but it caused her to grip the tree tighter and bury her face in her shoulder. The animal became even more frenzied. Heartbeat flaring, Maya looked to the clearing where Teck drew his sword and headed toward them at a fast clip. Nearing the creature, he stabbed violently with his blade, burying it in the animal's hindquarters, drawing blood. The creature screamed in pain.

Turning from the tree, it rushed Teck. His eyes widened, and his face paled with the animal's change of focus and the speed of its attack. He staggered back, the swishing of his weapon as it cut through the air only adding to the din, but in his panic, he missed the animal.

"Teck!" When he tripped and fell, Maya jumped from the tree. Landing solidly on both feet, she wrenched her hunting knife from its sheath and called for its attention. It halted its forward movement toward Teck, lifted its head, and released a strange call. Turning, it slithered back toward Maya.

Maya swallowed tightly as the creature's eyes locked on her, and her hand with the knife trembled. Dimly, she heard Rory barking, but she didn't dare take her gaze from the animal.

Now, instead of speed, it stalked forward, step after slow step, its claws digging into the ground. Taking a deep breath, unconsciously registering the scent of the newly torn earth, Maya stood her ground, her legs shaking so badly they almost buckled under her weight.

Behind the animal, from the corner of her eye, she saw Teck regain his feet, but she couldn't take her gaze from the creature.

The nearer it got, the more her mind began to fog over from the crazed look in its eyes. In the back of her mind, she screamed to move, to get away, but her mind was hypnotized by the animal. Teck moved toward her at a run, but she knew he'd never get to her in time.

The scent of the soil penetrated her consciousness. The odor, along with the smell of the stream and foliage along the edge, filled her lungs and expanded through her being. Like a spark to a waiting match, her fear of the animal ignited a seed within her. Her mind fuzzy, her magic reached out to protect.

Just as the animal was mere feet from her—its hind haunches bunched for the final jump—an eruption of green sprang from the soil around the animal. All manner of plant life grew in a split second to create a dense wall between the animal and the girl and to bind the creature in vines and roots.

Squeezing and twisting, the mass held the animal within its grip while it crushed tighter and tighter. A different sound came from the beast now. No longer furious and triumphant, pain colored this sound—pain and fear. Maya dropped to her knees, pressing her hands to her ears to block the agony of the creature's cries. With one final twist, the vines yanked and the animal silenced as it was torn apart, blood and gore flying in all directions.

Teck moved around the new jungle of plant life and the nightmare it contained. He stepped quickly to Maya to grasp her by the elbow and help her to her feet. Keeping a wary eye on the scene of destruction, he stepped back, taking Maya with him. When they were a few safe feet from the slaughter, he pulled her into his arms.

"What happened?" she whispered. She shook her head to clear it, the fog still invading her senses.

"I don't know," he said. Loosening his arms from around her, he directed her back. "Let's move away. We don't know what that was or what happened with the plants."

"The plants are mine," she said, but instead of moving with him from the animal carcass, Maya stepped slowly toward it.

"What do you mean, yours?"

Maya didn't answer him but walked toward the killing.

"Maya."

The plants, once so alive and violent, now lay flat on the ground, their leaves wilted and shriveled. Approaching the mess, Maya squatted down to study the confusion of green splashed with red. All was silent for a long time and then, without warning, a branch shot out into the air toward her. Startled, she fell backward to land on her bottom, but the branch had already fallen back to the ground, lifeless. Breathing hard, Maya inched back and then stood.

"You okay?" Teck's voice came from just behind her.

Without looking at him, Maya nodded. She would need to explain her magic to him. Part of her didn't know if he would believe her, or he may think she really was losing her mind. First the dreams, and now the plants. The bigger part of her mind was focused on the plants. Always, in the past, they had been her friends—gentle beings. But this was something entirely different. This violence.

She'd been so afraid of the animal; she was past thinking. And then it had just happened, the plants and the tearing and all the blood.

* * * * *

MIKEL GROWLED AND KNOCKED OVER the grate containing the fire he'd been watching. Coals, ash, and flaming embers spilled out onto the floor, but the man paid it no mind as he turned from the center of the room to walk to the door.

How could my beast have been defeated? He had seen the girl's demise in the flames. He'd been promised the fulfillment of this desire. Never before had the images his mistress sent him not come true. A small shiver of apprehension fingered up his spine, but he buried the feeling and thought again of the images in the fire.

He'd had her, he knew it . . . then everything had changed. Where had that power come from? The plants—so formidable. He paused in his pacing and his thoughts turned.

If only I could harness all that power. My mistress would be pleased.

Taking a deep breath, the man calmed his thoughts but allowed them to spin and shift. Soon the corners of his lips turned up in a smile.

* * * * *

MAYA HAD THE FIRE GOING and her stew simmering. It smelled wonderful. Teck, having buried what was left of the animal, came to rest beside her. Rory had lain down next to her a while before and was now sound asleep a short distance from the fire. Maya hadn't seen the cat. If he didn't show up soon, she'd need to decide if she should seek him out.

Her concerns were laid to rest later when the cat wandered through the camp and lay down next to the sleeping dog. He seemed unaware of the earlier excitement.

What had *happened earlier?* The creature had seemed to know her—to want her, even. And then the plants. She'd never seen them react in such a way. She continued to bang her head around all she'd seen and felt but still was no closer to the answer.

"So." When she looked at Teck, he was staring at her. "You wanna tell me about the plants?"

Maya shifted until she was facing him. Laying it out, she

told him of the power she had over plants. How it had aided her life and how she'd always thought of the plants as her friends. She even told him about the small gifts she'd received over the years from the trees.

Teck nodded occasionally but didn't interrupt her telling. He didn't look skeptical when she would have thought he should.

Leaning forward, she took his hand in hers. "But I've never seen them do anything like that before. I don't even know what that was."

"It's obvious they were protecting you."

"Protecting me?" She sat back, a scowl on her face. "Do you really think so?"

"Yes, they killed the animal that was going to kill you."

Maya nodded, looking off toward the trees. She never would have thought the plants capable of such an act. It put the gentle flora in a different light, and she wasn't sure what she thought about it.

16

MAYA STARED DOWN AT THE city of Berth—her mind awash with questions, her body flooded with emotions. Never had she even imagined man could build something so complex, so large. The small town near her home was the largest settlement she'd ever experienced. This was something totally unique to her.

The city filled the scope of their sight. Walled, it stretched north and south. From where she stood, Maya couldn't see the entirety of the surrounding wall. It was expansive as the forest, it seemed.

"Have you ever seen anything like this?" she whispered to Teck, somehow thinking if she spoke louder, something would happen. Perhaps bringing the many denizens of Berth down upon them.

"No. This is like nothing I've ever imagined."

Rory whined beside Maya, and with a reassuring hand on his head, she glanced back at Teck. "How will we ever find the priest?"

Teck stared at Maya for a full minute and then took her hand. He stepped back from the side of the hill leading into the valley. "Come here. Let's sit and talk."

Back in the trees, with the view of the city no longer monopolizing their thoughts, Teck said, "Tell me more of your dreams."

"I've told you everything," she began with a shake of her head, but with a lifted hand he stopped her.

"No, Maya. Concentrate."

"The dreams are foggy. Gone almost as quickly as I wake."

"There must be more you can give us—"

"No, there's nothing."

"What are you afraid of?" he asked gently.

Maya stopped talking so quickly, her jaw hung open. Afraid? What did he mean? She wasn't scared. Her jaw snapped closed and her breath exploded as the fullness of the emotion hit her. Fear. It was fear in the pit of her stomach. The dreams, the man, and then the woman. Though neither was scary by themselves, it was scary when each of them invaded her brain— her thoughts. And recently, the other dreams, the dark ones— what were those? She pushed them from her mind.

Jumping to her feet, she stalked off into the tree line to stand with her back to Teck. Deep breaths helped calm her. *Think*, she told herself. Pivoting on a heel, she stared at Teck, who hadn't moved.

"Okay." She slowly walked back to him, her hands on her hips. "Okay. Let's say I am afraid. What of it? The dreams are still misty. Hard to understand."

He patted the ground next to him with one hand and reached to her with the other. "Come and sit with me. Let's relax and talk about your dreams. The information on the priest came to you through your dreams. Maybe there's something helpful you're not remembering."

She heaved a sigh, took his hand, and plopped down next to him. Her brow furrowed, and she looked like a child with her bottom lip protruding.

"Tell me about the first dream you remember."

Teck took her through her memory of the dreams from the night before her Names Day to the dream the night by the pond.

"What did you see the man doing?"

"He was in the forest with me."

"That was the first one you really remember. Was there any other time?"

"He came to me at the end of one. The woman had been in that one. She scares me, though I don't remember much about her. Beautiful. Deadly. He came and chased her away."

"Are you afraid with him?"

"No. With him I'm calm. Peaceful."

"Okay. What more can you tell me about each of them?"

* * * * *

TECK WAS SILENT. HE ALLOWED her time to think. The wind blew over them through the tops of the trees, howling but not reaching the couple sitting below.

As he watched Maya, something moved within him. An air

of intuition perhaps—she was so much more than he'd first imagined.

"The woman, she had a loss. A loss of something or someone who altered her life. Tearing it apart, changing her. I think it had something to do with the man. Like they're connected in some way." Seeming to concentrate hard and center her mind, Maya gripped his hand and pushed to get more information from her confused thoughts. "All right. The priest. I know if I see him, I'll recognize him, but how will we find him given the size of the city?"

"When I'm confused and looking for something, it helps if I close my eyes and try to put myself back to the last time I remember seeing it. Doing that might help out with this, too."

When she looked skeptical he said, "Close your eyes for me, Maya." She looked up and raised her eyebrows but then closed her eyes, blocking out the smile he flashed. "Think of the image of the priest. Can you see anything around him? Is he in a room? A building? Are there any sounds or other people?"

With a deep breath and closed eyes, Maya's body relaxed. This time, when she spoke, her voice was soft, hollow, as if coming down a long tunnel. Teck leaned forward to catch every syllable. A shiver passed down his spine. Something other than memory was at work here.

"He's walking down a corridor. It's quiet, but in the distance, I hear voices—chanting. They're deep, like men's voices. His steps are scuffing the floor but he's hurrying. Frantic. He's searching behind with every few steps. He expects to be stopped. Oh my, his heart is pounding. Someone's coming.

He needs to do something, find something, before they stop him."

Teck leaned forward, pausing before taking her hand in his. He still wasn't sure what was happening. "Can you tell what or who he's looking for?"

With her eyes still shut, Maya slowly shook her head. "No. But I can tell it's important to him."

"Look around, Maya. Is there anything to identify where he is?"

"A tower. He's moving through an outer walkway now. In the distance, I see a tower. Tall and thin with a . . . a bell? Yes! A bell at the top." Maya opened her eyes, excitement splitting her lips in a large smile. Teck leaned back to observe her. Her eyes were a bright shining blue, but now they faded to their natural shade of green. She leaned toward Teck on her knees. "From the inner courtyard, I can see a tall bell tower."

"Good job, Maya. Good job." Grabbing her shirt, he pulled her to him and planted a kiss on her lips. When they parted, a smile passed between them. Did she know there was more going on here than her memory? What was happening within her to make her eyes shine? Teck began to question who Maya really was, though he was surprised and pleased to realize he held no sense of fear. No fear of her or of what was happening within her.

She'd given them a starting point. The bell tower. A point of reference.

It was still early in the day, so they grabbed their belongings and headed down the hill. Maya whistled to Rory to keep him close.

TRAFFIC PICKED UP CLOSER TO the gates. Merchants moving in search of commerce. They would set up their temporary shops, and at the end of the day, these same merchants would pack up and head back out of the city, the cycle of travel part of their lives.

Maya and Teck walked among horse-drawn wagons, man-drawn carts, and simple merchants with their wares on their backs. A fine sheen of dust coated their skin and clothing, and breathing in the thick air required more effort.

Maya's head tilted back as they neared the gates. The wall ran from it on either side beyond the scope of her vision. It towered above the citizens, and as they passed through the arch of the gateway, she elbowed Teck. She drew his attention upward with her chin. Guards patrolled the top of the wall, passing within inches of each other. Weapons threw shafts of light as the sun reflected on burnished surfaces. Their faces, hidden behind armored masks and helmets, turned toward the masses below, ever vigilant.

Teck leaned into her to whisper, "A lot of armaments for a peaceful merchant town."

Maya nodded. It would bode them well to keep their eyes open.

AS THEY MOVED AWAY FROM the hub, they entered a tunnel of vendors' shops. Barkers yelled at prospective customers to catch their attention and lead them to their wares. Dogs barked, and Maya kept a constant eye on Rory. Raised as a country dog, the city sounds and smells had him looking about in confusion and excitement. Maya realized the cat had disappeared again as they neared the city walls. She wasn't worried and figured he'd show at some point. She'd given up attempting to understand what made him tick and where his loyalties lay.

Eyes wide, Maya couldn't believe the variety of items offered. Fruits—apples, berries, and some she couldn't identify; hanks of meat; squawking chickens; fish; breads—loaves of golden and even dark rye; bolts of brightly dyed textiles and finished clothing; and ornaments—jewelry, hair adornments, and scarves for women. And weaponry—knives, bows and arrows, and swords. All beautiful with in-depth artistry. They passed stalls with men in brightly colored garments selling herbs and crystals for healing and magic.

They passed an alley, and the dark recesses drew Maya's gaze. Toward the back, against a side wall, a figure stood. He almost went unseen, the sun unable or unwilling to penetrate the dark, narrow aisle. Maya's head swiveled to keep the figure in sight, but in seconds, they'd moved past him.

A flutter moved over her frame and she looked forward again. Her thoughts turned inward. What was it about the figure? A cold shiver passed through her, and she tilted her head back, allowing the sunshine to warm her. When she grasped Teck's hand in hers, he turned a quizzical look her way. Giving her head a small shake, her lips turned up gently. She laid her head on his arm and relaxed as his heat and strength moved through her. Teck continued to lead them into the city.

* * * * *

SMILING AS HE PACED THE room, the man who worshiped the dark mistress thought of what he'd been told. How wonderful that the girl had unwittingly come to him. She was now exactly where he wanted her to be. When he gave a small chuckle of delight, the servants setting out his supper hesitated and glanced at each other. Realizing their mistakes, they hurried to finish their tasks before he noticed them. It would never be healthy to be the one he noticed.

Turning toward the table, the room now devoid of servants, Mikel sat and began to eat his dinner. The lamb was cooked just as he liked it, charred on the outside and bloody on the interior, but so preoccupied was he with his plans for the girl, he didn't even notice the chef's fine work.

17

LIGHT FADED AS THE SUN dipped behind buildings. A cool evening breeze picked up as the trio moved through the city streets. Maya closed her eyes and allowed the air to cool her overheated skin. She pushed her long tresses back and lifted them from her neck, emitting an audible breath as a current of air shifted around her.

"How much farther do you think it is?" she asked Teck.

"This city is so large, we might be miles from the bell tower in your vision." His lips pursed, and he looked away. Tired and hungry, frustration plagued him at their continued lack of success. Twice, they'd spotted a tower in the distance and twice, as they moved closer, Maya had dashed his hopes by telling him it wasn't the *right* tower. At this rate, it could be days, if not weeks, before they found what they looked for.

"I'm sorry, Teck."

He glanced down at her as they walked, taking in the dark circles under her eyes and the scuffing of her feet. Why was he complaining? He was bigger and stronger—if he was tired and hungry, she was surely exhausted and famished. He'd find them food and shelter and they'd start out fresh in the morning. He moved closer and wrapped his arm around her shoulders.

"Don't apologize. You've done nothing wrong. I'm sorry for being short-tempered." When she looked up at him with her large, soft eyes, his heart thumped painfully in his chest. "Food. Let's find food and somewhere to sleep. It's been a long day and we're both spent. Tomorrow will be better."

Maya gave a nod and followed.

18

THE NOISE OF AN INN drew them around a corner. Lights, sounds, and smells assailed them, even above what they'd come to regard as normal for the city. Every window of the building blazed with light. On the second and third floors, silhouettes moved behind gauzy draperies. Inside and out, people swarmed—travelers and townies alike. Dirty, tired, jovial, and inebriated, all by separate measures.

Maya stopped in her tracks, looking from the tavern to Teck. "You're kidding, right? We can't stay here."

"We've walked for miles," he responded. "I think it'll be our best bet."

"What if Rory's not allowed?" She glanced at the dog who sat by her side, eyes and ears trained on the activity down the street.

"Let's check it out before we move on. All they can say is no, and they might say yes." With a pleading look on his face, he took her hand in his and lightly pulled her onward. "Come on. We're both done in."

They passed by people who didn't notice or care about them, each too involved in their own lives. Ever alert, they passed into the main hall. More tavern than inn, a large bar presided over the far wall, but this tavern had rooms for rent. Rooms mostly occupied by women plying their trade. The raucous laughter of males and females alike reverberated in the large room, along with bawdy comments, which, more than once, caused Maya to blush.

The air in the room smelled of old brew, dirty bodies, and the smoke of pipes; a pot hanging over the fire belched an aroma of cabbage stew. Maya found herself breathing so shallowly, she soon felt lightheaded.

With her back to Teck as he spoke with the proprietor, Maya surveyed the room. She'd never seen anything like it. She kept one hand on Rory and one on the hilt of her hunting knife. People swarmed by them, bumping and jostling, causing an occasional low growl to issue from the canine's throat.

Finished and with key in hand, Teck turned to take Maya's upper arm in the other.

"C'mon. We're at the end of the hall. Let's hope it'll be quiet enough to get some sleep."

"I don't think anything could keep me awake at this point," she muttered and followed him to the staircase.

Up a flight of stairs and down the hall, they dragged themselves, keeping a tired but steady vigilance out for the men and women coming from the other rooms. With a click and push, Teck opened the door and surveyed the room before allowing Maya to enter. Empty. Empty of people and empty of just about any kind of amenity. Against the far wall was a bed with an old, dirty blanket thrown over it. When he walked to it and pressed the surface with a large hand, he felt the rushes that filled it. Not the most comfortable and probably infested with bugs, but it would have to do. A small, wobbly table sat next to it, and on its surface a lamp, half-full of oil, rested.

When he'd closed the door behind them, the noise muted and Maya expelled a heavy breath. Dropping her bags, she smiled as Rory lay next to them, his head nestled atop one. With a sigh, he closed his eyes and was instantly asleep. She kneeled by him and patted his head, causing his eyelids to twitch.

"Good boy, Rory."

"I have an idea." With forced energy and enthusiasm, Teck moved toward her. He helped her to stand and said, "Let's leave our stuff locked here with Rory and get something to eat. There's a kitchen downstairs. We'll sleep better with our stomachs full."

"Okay." She smiled at him. "But if I fall asleep at the table, you'll have to get me back to the room."

"Deal. We'll leave the door locked and Rory here."

Maya refused to leave without her knife but agreed the bow and arrows would be unnecessary in the tavern. Ready, they stepped out of their room, locked the door, and Teck pocketed the key.

Loud voices still filled the main room, and the impact of it rocked Maya's senses. She was certain there were more people in and out of this business than in the whole town of Roadstead—or at least it felt like it.

Taking pity on their faculties, Teck led them along the wall to a table in the back. If he'd ever needed confirmation of Maya's beauty, it came in glances—both covert and bold—that men threw her way. Not only were her looks striking with her small feminine frame, crimson tresses, and large, luminous eyes, but she projected an innocence—one some desired to protect and others to subvert.

Every look directed her way he met with a challenge. Some men turned away, unwilling to question his possession of her, but the bolder stared back, some even smiling.

Maybe, he thought, *this wasn't such a good idea.* When Maya sat at a table, Teck decided they were committed to the spot. He scooted in beside her, his back to the wall. They'd eat quickly and return to the relative safety of a locked door.

When the waitress came to their table, Teck was sure she spent most of her hours entertaining men upstairs. She had a brashness with her breasts mostly exposed, showing heavy and sweaty when she bent over their table. She made it obvious with her blatant stares she would be happy to spend time with him, no matter he was with Maya. When she brought the bowls of stew and two tankards of ale back to their table, she dared to go so far as to rub her hip along his shoulder and lay her hand on his cheek. Jerking back, he threw her a forbidding look and then a guilty one toward Maya—who, luckily, was occupied watching an altercation across the room. With a shrug, the waitress left them to their meal. A meal they wasted no time falling upon.

The stew, though mediocre, warmed and filled their bellies.

Maya began to yawn as Teck pushed his bowl aside and finished his ale.

"I may just lie down here, the noise and commotion be damned," Maya uttered.

Standing, Teck gave a small chuckle, pulled her gently from her seat, and with an arm thrown around her shoulders, they plodded their way toward the stairs.

Their thoughts only on the bed that awaited them, and their eyes focused on the stairs, neither of them saw the waitress until she stepped in front of them. Giving Maya a push, she moved into the empty space. She twined her arms around Teck's frame, pressing her large breasts tight to his chest. With a gasp, Maya started toward her only to stop when the woman whispered in Teck's ear, her eyes on Maya—her voice pitched loud enough to carry. "Hey there, darling. I'll see you in a bit as we planned." Leaning into him, she quickly traced his lips with the tip of her tongue. Teck grabbed her shoulders and peeled her body from his.

"Get away from me, woman," he snapped. "I don't know you." But he could see the damage was done. Maya, young, impressionable, and new to love, saw only the woman and heard her words. She stared at the woman, her color riding even higher in her cheeks. Tears pouring from her eyes, she turned to Teck.

"How could you? After we . . . what we did . . . I thought—" Breath catching, she pushed through them and ran for the door leading to the street.

"Maya!" Teck yelled, trying to push past the woman who

once again placed herself in his way. "Maya, wait!"

But she was gone. She slipped around and through the crowd to disappear out the door and into the night.

With a shove, Teck disengaged himself from the woman, thrusting her behind him as he headed after Maya. Larger and not as spry, the few seconds' head start aided her. When he pushed open the door, she was gone. Lost into the darkness.

19

MAYA RAN INTO THE NIGHT. Fleet with the pain of betrayal, blind with tears, she ran on instinct, not sure of her path. Finally, not knowing where she was or how she'd gotten there, she collapsed, sobbing against a wall of a building.

In her mind, all she saw was the voluptuous woman, her attributes pressed against Teck. Of course he'd want her. She was knowledgeable—not a naïve girl. How could Maya hope to compete with that? It was her own fault, she berated herself. He'd never spoken of love. She was a silly girl to have given her heart so fast. Mentally bashing herself, she remembered that only a week ago she didn't even *like* Teck. She would have gladly seen him pursue another woman.

Sniffing, she stood straight, wiping her tears away with trembling fingers. A deep breath in and out—and another, and she felt more centered.

"Okay, Maya," she said aloud, "enough of playing the fool." Standing, she placed a hand to the wall to steady herself and calmed her mind to think. She couldn't believe she'd left with no thought for Rory or her own safety.

Stepping from the mouth of the alley, she looked left and right, but she had no idea where she was. She remembered the sign outside the pub had a fish on it. A fish jumping from the water. Come morning, she was sure someone could give her directions back to it. Finding a safe, secure place to spend the remaining nighttime hours was her new priority.

In the distance, men's voices—raucous and loud—echoed down the street. Slipping into the shadows of the alley, she crouched silently as the group of revelers passed her location. Maybe she should just stay here.

"Did you see where she went?"

Freezing, Maya realized another group had neared her location without her realizing it. These men were silent and sober.

"She came this way."

"Well, find her you idiot. Director Quinttock isn't going to be pleased if we lost her. He doesn't accept failure."

A third man joined the discussion. His voice was low and deep. "She couldn't have gone far. She was in no condition for endurance when she flew out of the tavern." Maya straightened at his words. Tavern? What *she* were they looking for?

"Well, we have to find her before the man does. Ol' Gert got well paid to create this opportunity and we won't waste it. Spread out and don't come back until you have her." The low threat wasn't missed by Maya as the men moved off in separate directions. Maya stayed quiet and small, willing herself to blend into the background.

Was she paranoid to think the men were talking about her? What could she have that they might want? And the woman — the woman at the tavern — were her actions deliberate to drive Maya away? To put her on her own so the men could get to her? And she'd made it easy for them. Stupid! She kicked herself. So stupid. Teck must be frantic worrying about her.

Listening hard, Maya concentrated on the sounds of the night. It was quiet, at least for a city. The quietest she'd heard. A dog's bark echoed in the distance, and the wind whistled through the buildings, but that was all. Moving with stealth toward the mouth of the alley, she paused, straining her ears for any sounds of the men. Nothing. All was quiet.

Slinking down the lane, keeping to the wall, Maya moved. There was no way to know if the direction she chose would take her closer to Teck. All she could do was try.

A few blocks later, her luck ran out.

She rounded a corner and came face to face with a man, almost running into him. His expression showed surprise first and then recognition. As a large smile spread across his face, it was confirmation he must be one of the men who searched for her.

Maya kicked out, catching him directly between the legs and dropping him to his knees. She turned and bolted back the way she'd come. His bellow of pain and outrage followed her down the street. Farther on, another man stepped from the shadows. Maya skidded to a halt and swerved down an alley. She heard his footfalls pounding, spurring her on.

She flew out of the alley as another man cut her off. Whooping, he gave an exclamation of glee—the predator after prey. The other men, converging on her, took up the call. Their voices and pursuit threw her into a panic. A doe fleeing from a pack of wolves.

Running, her heart pounding and breath rasping, her body forgot its exhaustion in the wake of fear. She was fast, but they were many. They rounded her up, closing off avenues and shutting her down. Soon there was nowhere to flee. They corralled her with their bodies, her back pressed to a wall, arms outstretched, hands grasping the stone. She sucked air in and blew it out but still felt out of breath. She swiveled her head, searching for an avenue of escape. The men's demeanor, their faces. They leered at her as if at any minute they might set upon her, rending her flesh from her bones. Her panic scented the air, and they bathed in its fragrance. She was outnumbered, out muscled, with no route for escape. The hilt of her hunting knife bumped her forearm and reminded her of its presence. Would it be of any help? Her against many with just the aid of a small knife? Not willing to lose without ever trying, Maya ripped the knife from its sheath, brandishing it at the men, first left and then right. They easily evaded her thrusts, laughing and slapping at her, instigating her to fight harder.

Maya's breath hitched in her chest and her throat burned. Panic was coming fast now.

"Halt!"

Another voice broke the tension and the pack visibly recoiled, pulled back from the precipice of assault and murder.

"Back. Step back," the voice shouted, and the tension dropped further.

Through the ring around her, a new man pushed. Confident in his control, he bit and snarled at the animals he commanded. They'd tasted the promise of her surrender and blood but didn't have it in them to question his dominance.

"Maya," he said, stepping to her, his avid gaze taking in her panic. "At long last we meet." With an ease that ashamed her, he pushed her knife to the side, twisting it from her numb grip. With a cringe, she turned her head from him when he laid a palm on her cheek. She froze, waiting for the violence that still colored the air.

"My master is anxious to speak with you." Stepping back, he looked her over—from the top of her head to her booted feet. "And how happy he'll be to see what a beauty you are, much like your mother."

His words caught her attention and she turned wide eyes to him. What did he mean? Did he know her mother or where she was? Studying him, Maya saw an unimposing man, one she'd never laid eyes on before. Short in stature, his frame small and head covered by a thinning coat of gray hair. Not what she'd thought from the command in his voice.

"Come with me, pet." He held out a hand, and when all she did was eye it like a snake, he prompted, "With me or them. The decision is yours, but those are your only two options."

Looking up from his extended hand to his eyes, Maya pulled her gaze away to survey the circle of men beyond. They were under control with the man's presence, but behind each of their eyes she saw the gleam of violence. The promise of brutality.

With no other options, Maya straightened from the wall and placed her hand in the man's.

"Good girl." He smiled at her and she instantly regretted the decision she'd been forced to make. This man was no salvation, just another form of victimization.

When he took a step back, she took one forward. With an audible click, an iron cuff snapped around her wrist. A tug and a shift and he'd spun her, grabbed her other wrist, and cuffed it to the other behind her back. Spinning her back around to face him, he grasped her chin—silencing a gasp that escaped her.

"Finally." He smiled again, his eyelids drooping low. "My master will be so pleased." He turned to walk away from her back through the ring of men.

"Take her to the temple," he said, and then he was gone.

20

WHEN TECK RAN OUT OF the tavern after Maya, he looked around in surprise at how fast she'd vanished. A large group of people milled around the entrance with others coming and going. Teck looked over the heads and quickly crouched to look between them, but Maya was gone.

With a curse, he turned back to the tavern. *What the hell was that all about?* When he stepped into the inn, he surveyed the room, his aim to find the barmaid and question her about what had just happened. He didn't see her right away, but then she pushed out of the back room, her arms laden with mugs of ale. She had just set the tankards down when Teck grabbed her upper arm and hauled her to the back of the room.

"Hey!" she yelled and slapped at his hand, but he had her in his grip.

When he reached the back wall, he spun her and pushed her up against it, leaning the bulk of his weight into her. "What was that?"

"What, darlin'?" she purred, running her hands up his chest and over his shoulders.

With a quick step back, he once again tore her from where she'd wrapped herself around him. Cursing, he pulled her hands down and pushed her back into the wall.

"That fiasco at the stair. I gave you no indication I'm the least bit interested in you."

"Aw . . . did your little girl get upset?" She smiled a wicked smile and cocked her head.

"Gods!" he cursed and released her, turning away and running a fist through his hair. Looking into the room, his mind thinking fast, he almost missed the waitress's next words.

"He was right. Worked perfectly."

Teck spun back around to lock eyes with the woman. "Who was right? What worked perfectly?" Once again, he grabbed her shoulders and with force, slammed her back into the wall. His worry for Maya tearing at his mind, his fingers dug into the skin on her upper arms.

"Ouch, darlin'. That hurts," she whined and tried to break his hold.

"*Who?* What did you mean?"

"Okay." She stopped struggling and looked him in the eye. "The man. He came in and told me what to do. Said the girl was sure to leave you, and he was right. She bolted just like he said."

"What man was this? Is he still here?" Teck's brows wrinkled as questions ran through his mind. He scanned over his shoulder, looking for someone, though he didn't know who.

Shaking her head, her messy braid swinging with the motion, she stared at him, her eyes big. "No. Some little guy.

I've never seen him before."

"What did he look like?" They were looking for her mother. Why would some man be setting a plan in motion to take Maya?

"He was short. Barely as tall as me and skinny. He was old, his hair gray—what there was of it, anyway."

"He didn't say anything else?"

"No. Can you let go of me now?" Finding her bravado again, the woman shrugged off his loosened hold, and pushing at his chest, attempted to move past him. Teck looked down at her, a scowl on his face, but then took a step back and allowed her to hurry past. She threw a final worried glance over her shoulder as she went through the door to the back.

"Damn it," he muttered. Not bad enough Maya was out in the city—alone and upset after dark—now there was some strange man after her.

Walking slowly back through the tavern, Teck let his mind work on the problem. He didn't even know if she'd gone up or down the street in front of the building. How was he to find her? He was a good tracker of animals, but that was in the woods, where signs were left by their passing. He stopped as an idea occurred to him, and a smile parted his lips.

Moving quickly, he pushed past drinkers to the stairs. Taking them two at a time, he hurried to the room at the end of the hall. When he opened the door, the light from the hallway spilled across the floor and crept up the bed. In the middle of the light, the large gray dog lifted his head from his mistress's pack.

Teck's grin widened.

21

MAYA DIDN'T KNOW HOW LONG she'd walked with the men surrounding her. Since the little man left, they hadn't spoken to her or touched her. She was thankful for that, but if thanks were to be given, she couldn't come up with much else. Her arms were numbing from being stretched behind her back. Her adrenaline long gone, the exhaustion weighed heavily on her. The last couple days—really the last couple weeks—were long and trying, the worry, travel, and stress catching up with her fast. More than once in the past mile, she'd tripped over her own feet, catching herself at the last minute. This was no easy accomplishment with her arms cuffed, but she was afraid to fall. Afraid the men would plod over her as they walked on like mindless beasts, and if they didn't, she was afraid of what else they might do.

THE SUN WAS JUST BREAKING over the horizon when she saw a building rising in front of them. The closer they got, the larger it became until it filled her vision. Its color the same as the buildings surrounding it—the same stone was used in every building in this city—the ornate work around the door and windows made it stand out. Stunning images of angels and demons, flora and fauna, different stages of the sun and the moons of this world. This must be the temple the little man spoke of. Temple of what, though. What or who was worshiped here?

The group of them, she and the men, stopped in front of the building, massive doors barring their way. With a loud bang and groan, it slowly swung open. Its ponderous movement and moan reminded Maya of an animal in pain. The morning sun peered around the main steeple of the temple, and as if on cue, a bell began to toll. Maya looked toward the sound to see the tower from her vision just a few blocks away. Recognition hit hard, and with wide eyes, she looked between the tower and the temple, realizing the courtyard she'd seen the priest in resided within the walls of the temple before her. The priest she sought may very well be within its walls right now. Somehow, unplanned, she ended up right where she wanted to be—even if she didn't want to be with her present company.

With the door fully open, its dark maw gaped at her. Nothing moved within its confines for several minutes. Not wanting to draw attention to herself, she shifted her feet. Her vision dulled, her eyelids drooped, and she feared her body was getting ready to shut down.

From deep within the building came scuffling, pounding, and the shifting of many footsteps. Someone, or a whole group of someones, moved toward the opening. Blinking rapidly and straightening her body, Maya prepared to meet whomever this new threat might be.

Men in white robes spilled out of the door. Maya didn't know what to think. These men weren't dressed as the priest in her vision, however, they would seem to be priests of this temple. When the robed bodies filled the top of the stairs, Maya didn't have to wait long before another man stepped forward. It was the man from the alley. The man who, with just his voice—and perhaps his reputation—controlled the pack of men around her.

The small man stepped toward her. Maya stepped back. He smiled and grasped her arm, pulling her forward. Too exhausted to put up a fight at first, she followed him up the stairs and through the throng of priests. Digging in her heels, she tried to wrench her arm from his grasp, but his grip was like iron. He dragged her up the stairs and through the doorway.

The interior of the building held a chill that was absent outside. Pulled along behind him, her skin pebbled with the cold. The smell of cut stone, incense, and the intangible essence of the cold assailed her nose as she huffed breaths and pulled back from the man. A look of amusement colored his face at her attempts to thwart him.

"Where are you taking me?" Maya asked him over and again, but he ignored her, dug his fingers into the soft skin of her arm, and continued to drag her further into the building.

When they reached the end of a long hall, a pair of uniformed men stood by a large, wooden door. They didn't even look her way, and she realized that, perhaps, a woman being dragged here was something they'd seen more than once. When she and the little man halted, one of the soldiers pushed open the door. Beyond it was dark, and a dank smell issued forth. The soldier moved with them to light a torch and proceeded down a short hallway to a set of stone stairs. Water leaked down the walls to pool along the stairs, reflecting in the torchlight and making the steps hazardous.

Down several flights, the dripping echoed in a confined area that made her long for wide, open spaces. For the greenery of a forest and the smell of fresh running water. Neither man said a word, though the deeper they went, the louder their breathing became. Exertion and lack of fresh air took its toll on them all.

Finally, the stairs ended, and a blackness stretched before them. Without hesitation, the men advanced into the complete darkness, their only guide the sparse light from the torch. The flooring, dirt and damp, smelled of the land, but not the healthy freshness of newly turned soil. This smelled of rot, ancient growing molds, and the reek of things long dead. It was cool, but Maya broke out in a sweat that ran down her face and between her shoulder blades.

The trio reached a metal door with a large locking mechanism. Across from it and down the hallway on both sides were additional doors. She wondered if there were other prisoners. Maya listened intently, but no sound other than the running of water reached her ears. The little man uncuffed her hands, and just as she began to pull her stiff arms to the front, the soldier pulled a large ring from his belt. Using one of the keys that hung from it, he unlocked and pulled open the door. For a brief second, Maya caught a glimpse of the interior of the room before she was shoved in and the door pushed closed, leaving her in total blackness.

She spun to throw herself against the door. "Wait!" Her frantic call fell flat as if the air in the room were so thin it could not hold the words. A small window in the door slid open.

Through the window, the little man looked at her with a sick smile. "Sleep well," he muttered and slammed the window shut, blocking out even a promise of light.

Oh, how she wished she'd never left Teck.

"Wait!" she shouted. But she was alone, her only companion the dripping water.

Turning to place her back against the door, Maya stared out into a darkness so thick she was sure, if she reached out, it would fill her hands.

Standing perfectly still, she listened. No sounds came to her straining ears. No breathing, no gnashing teeth, and no clicking claws.

Her imagination tried to fight free, but she forced it to remain sane. She was alone, and there was plenty to fear without dreaming up nightmarish beasts.

She slowly inched along the surface of the door to the wall. It was stone, rough and damp under her palms. When she reached the corner, where another wall met this one, she pressed her body into the space. Her breath came rapidly, and in her ears, the pounding of her heart created a rhythm. Unsure what to do, Maya crouched, making herself as small as possible. There was an illusion of protection at the juncture where the two walls and floor met. Now, all she could do was wait.

22

TECK HID, LOOKING AT THE temple from the darkness of an alleyway. Beside him, Rory waited. They'd tracked Maya through the city quickly but not quickly enough, missing her before she was taken into the building. He'd need to get inside and get her out before something happened to her. Having no idea who took her and toward what end, it was better to assume the worst. He would take down the city if need be, but first he needed a plan.

Men in robes and men with weapons milled around the front of the temple. People passed on the street, throwing glances at the imposing building. The men never looked too long or held someone's gaze. Even conversation quieted the nearer they got to the building but would pick up again as they left it behind.

A company of soldiers exited the large doors and made their way into the city. They moved past Teck's hiding place in loose order. He again searched the thinning groups at the dais of the temple door. He moved forward until within distance.

When a large soldier passed by, his attention on where he was going, Teck grabbed him with an arm around his throat and hauled him into another alley. His mind focused and his eyes staring straight ahead, he tightened his grip, arms locked, one hand behind the man's head. He held on until the flailing man quieted. No longer straining, his body malleable, Teck grasped his head in a tight hold and, with a sharp twist, snapped his neck.

He stripped the body, moving quickly, his eyes continuously scanning the area. When naked, he buried the man under a pile of refuse along a wall. Slipping into the uniform, he tied his garments together and hid them behind a container, which looked as if it hadn't moved in a millennium. He almost tripped over the dog who'd moved next to him. Staring down at Rory, his mind went blank. What to do with him? He couldn't take him back to the tavern. Even if he did, he'd need to change into his own clothing again and then back into the uniform. There was no time. His instincts screamed that he needed to get to Maya and get to her quickly.

He placed his hand on the dog's head, staring him in the eye.

"You're a good boy, Rory," he whispered, causing the dog's tail to whip from side to side, clearing a spot on the floor. "I'm gonna find Maya. I need you to stay safe until I return." As the man and dog stared at each other, Teck swore the dog understood him, a light of knowing almost human in the creature's eyes. "Okay," he muttered, removing his hand. "Which way did they go?" Striding to the end of the alley, he looked both ways before he moved into the street. He walked with a quick and confident step.

Not a mile later, Teck saw the backs of the unit of soldiers he'd seen earlier. His success depended on looking like he belonged. He was sure the uniform helmet would help with that, and he hoped they planned to head back to the temple, or this would all be for nothing.

Sidling up to the last man, Teck became one of the group. He matched his gait with theirs and did what they did, which was nothing but walk around in the hot sun. Soon sweat streamed down his back and from his temples, wetting his hair. The helmet didn't allow even the smallest breeze to penetrate, and at this point, all he wanted was to pull it from his head and fling it aside. Just when he thought he might have selected the wrong group, the leader called an order and they shifted to a side lane and headed back in the direction of the temple.

The sun had begun to set at their backs when they once again neared the entrance of the shrine. Anyone who had once loitered around the front of the building was now gone.

Teck's heartbeat pounded in tempo to the footfalls of the soldiers, and the closer he got to the temple, the more anxious he became. He pushed aside his nerves and bolstered his courage. Maya needed him. With a deep breath, he mounted the stairs and followed the other men into the sanctum.

23

THE CAT WATCHED AS A maid carrying a tray made her way down the hall. Absently, he registered the smell of food. How long had it been since he last ate?

When she stopped directly in front of the door, his head rose and his ears pricked forward.

She shifted her load to lay it along one arm and, reaching into a pocket, produced a key. Quickly unlocking the door, she barely steadied the tray when it slid backward. With a sigh of thanks, she repositioned the tray, dropped the key in her pocket, and opened the door.

The cat was in the room before she took her first step.

* * * * *

SITTING ON THE BED, SYLVAN'S head lifted at the sound of a key in the lock. She'd tried to escape, even getting as far as the outer wall before being caught and led back to her room—her cell. A plush, beautiful room to be sure, but when you couldn't leave, it became a prison.

The maid, tray in hand, tripped into the room, but it wasn't she who held Sylvan's attention. A small glimmer of light preceded her. Dropping her head, the corners of her mouth turned up. Leave it to him to find her.

She'd never dreamed that Maya's maturing would break the spell she'd placed around the cabin—a spell that had kept them secure for sixteen years. She'd given up many things, gladly, to see to her child's safety. Her pedagogue only one of those things.

With a clatter, the maid placed the tray on a table. Performing a small curtsy, she turned and left the room. Sylvan heard the key turn in the lock and the girl's receding footsteps before she spoke.

"Hello, Nathaniel. I've missed you, old friend."

The shimmering intensified for a moment, and then the cat jumped onto the bed beside her. She gave a choked laugh, tears gathering in her eyes, as he bumped his head into her shoulder and ran his arched body down her side. As he circled her, she wrapped her arms around him and buried her face in his nape. His purr vibrated through her. The touch and sound of him filled spots she'd never realized were empty.

Curling together, they stayed unmoving for some moments. Finally, lifting her head, Sylvan gave the cat a kiss behind his ear. His luminous eyes opened slowly to regard her.

"I'm sorry, Nathaniel." Her eyes overflowed, and tears ran down her cheeks to her lips. "I know our separation has been hard on you, also."

Staring for a moment, the cat gave a slow blink. "Your child is amazing."

"Maya—you've seen her? Is she all right?" More questions crowded her thoughts, but before she could voice them, Nathaniel pulled out of her arms and leaped soundlessly to the floor.

"We need to leave this place."

"I've tried over and over again."

"Yes." He sat, his tail curling around his front legs. "But you didn't have me."

24

TIME HAD NO MEANING IN the pit. Maya may have fallen asleep, but in the total blackness, she didn't know if her eyes were open or shut. She was blind—without visual stimulation of any kind—and nearly deaf. If it weren't for the constant dripping of the water, she might have thought herself dead.

Once or twice, she thought she heard moans through the thick door but worried she might be hearing the echo of her own cries. And what did it matter if there were others in the dungeon with her? If they were here, they sat behind their own doors, living a half-life in their own hell. Not knowing if she, herself, would survive, she had no time to consider their hardships.

Once, she thought to call upon the plants. What aid they could be, she didn't know, but at least she wouldn't be alone. Laying her palms against the moist floor, she concentrated, but to no avail. She was too far down—there wasn't even a root for her to tap into. Finally, exhausted, she gave up. Sitting in the darkness, she allowed her mind to close.

WHEN A KEY TURNED IN the lock on her door, Maya thought her ears played tricks on her. Then the door swung open with a loud screech and light flooded her cell. Bowing her head and flinging an arm over her squinting eyes, Maya cringed. Footsteps entered the room and, slowly, she lowered her arm. Blinking rapidly, the light painful after so long in the dark, she looked toward the individual. Even blinded, she recognized the little man standing over her.

"Good morning, pet. How was your night?" When she didn't answer, he squatted in front of her, the sneering voice one she would recognize as his even if he didn't bring the torch for light. "Did you enjoy your accommodations?"

Unable to answer him, exhausted, throat parched, eyes watering, she stared at him. But he required no answer. He grabbed her arm, bruising the already-discolored skin. She tried to pull back from him, giving a soft cry of pain. He yanked her toward him, causing her to lose her balance and fall against his chest. She righted herself, having no wish to touch him. Giving her a slight shake, he dug his nails deeper into her skin.

"Come, pet. My master will see you now."

Outside the door, a soldier stood, this one different from the first, with a torch in his hand. Quickly, they again cuffed her hands behind her back and the man held her arm as they waited for the soldier to close and relock her cell. He took them up the long stairs. Weak from exhaustion, hunger, and the stress of the last twenty-four hours, Maya was barely able to keep her feet moving. For a moment, she was even thankful for the small man's assisting hand, though his grip remained painful.

Having reached the top of the staircase, the trio of them moved into the hallway. Pulling her with him, the little man left the soldiers behind and proceeded into the corridor.

Knowing this might be her best chance to get free, with no soldiers accompanying them, Maya planted her feet and threw her weight into resisting the man's pull. As weak as she was, her defiance had little effect, and with a laugh in her direction, he shoved her back into a wall. Before she could do much more than look at him, he'd slapped her across one side of her face. Tasting her own blood, Maya stood stunned with her head turned to the side, her expression covered by her hair. She'd had bumps and bruises growing up, running free in the wild, but *never* had she been hit. Still in shock, she was again grabbed as they continued through the building.

Another few turns, and the man led her to an oversized door covered in gilding. Where the sun broke through high windows and touched the door, it reflected and blinded her, causing her to squint. With spots in front of her eyes, she barely noticed when the little man opened the door and pulled her inside the new room with him.

"Master," she heard him say and felt him genuflect, pulling on her arm as his body bent.

Blinking rapidly to clear her vision, she looked through her hair to see a middle-aged man sitting on a dais. His chair much like a throne, she wondered if he was high-born. Perhaps a king from another land. She saw a mass of dark hair from his beard to the mane falling from his head.

The little man released her arm, and with a hand firmly on the small of her back, he thrust her forward. The momentum and her fatigue had her falling to her knees before the man. With her hands trapped behind her back, she barely stopped herself from landing on her face. Panting, head bowed, she struggled to catch her breath and keep some dignity, even prostrate before this man.

When she heard him stand and move down the stairs that separated them, she stayed still. Not knowing what to expect, she listened intently, prepared for anything. She inhaled as his booted feet stopped within view, and he crouched. With a sudden jerk, he grasped her hair and yanked her head back to stare into her face. His eyes flashed, and spittle flew as he growled, "With that devil's hair, you look just like your father."

* * * * *

THE GONG SOUNDED, AND TECK jerked awake. Disoriented, he sat and scanned the room from the pallet he'd collapsed on the night before.

The barracks. All around him men rose and began dressing in their uniforms—arm and leg guards, chest plates, and helmets. When he sat up, yawning and rubbing his eyes, Teck remembered the day before. The only thing that fit into his plan was getting into the temple. Before and after that had been keeping his head down and following orders. Now, to fit in and not draw undue attention, he followed suit and got ready. He couldn't believe he'd fallen asleep. His plan to find and rescue

Maya now delayed by hours, and any benefit he may have had using the cover of night, he'd now lost.

Fully dressed, he trailed behind, grabbing a long halberd and proceeding out of the building. In the courtyard, the soldiers moved into loose lines and waited. Teck waited with the army, looking around uncertainly.

The clump of boots drew everyone's attention to the main hallway. Three figures in full regalia moved through the door and stared at the soldiers, eyes glistening through slits in their golden helmets. Men straightened, fists gripping their weapons.

"Surveillance of Berth will halt until further notice," the middle soldier boomed. "On the direct orders of Master Cox, patrols will break up, and making full sweeps, will monitor the temple."

A hum of conversation moved through the men. He wondered if it had anything to do with Maya.

"Silence." Quiet fell. "This will continue until further notice." That said, the trio turned and exited the courtyard, their footfalls echoing as they moved farther away.

With their departure, the tension broke and the volume of voices rose. Confusion and speculation abounded, and men milled around. One man stepped forward and, with a gesture, drew the other men's attention.

"Line up!" he shouted. "Unit One—south corridors. Unit Three—north corridors. The rest of you will stay here and train. Prepare for a nightly patrol."

Men rushed to obey him. Deciding he'd learn more out than in, Teck slid into Unit One. He gripped his weapon, point in the air, and tried to blend in with the other soldiers. Following the man in the lead, they headed out of the barracks area and into a main corridor. As their boots left the courtyard and entered the hall, the sound reverberated down and back, masking how many men there truly were.

Other people in the hall—priests and young girls in gauzy garments—stepped hurriedly to the side, placing their backs to the wall. The first time this happened, Teck was surprised, but the wide eyes, quickly downcast, showed him that fear ruled these people.

Hallways opened every few feet, and the farther into the temple they marched, the more Teck felt a cloud weighing him down. How was he ever to locate Maya in a fortress this huge?

An hour later, when he was sure they must be nearing the final reaches of the temple, the men marched past a massive golden door. Carved and sculpted, it glinted from multiple overhead skylights. Stepping up and past the door, Teck started to feel a tingling sensation. He stopped in his tracks, concentrating on it. It was as if Maya were touching his mind, her unique scent filling his lungs.

"Maya," he whispered and swung his head toward the golden panel.

The company of men continued past the door and down the hall. He turned his head and watched them move away. With a scowl, he looked back to the door. He didn't know which way to turn. Moving toward the door, he laid his ear to it. It was cool against his cheek. Either it was too thick to allow sounds to transmit, or the room beyond was empty. Somehow, he knew this door led to Maya or to information about her.

He was preparing to chance it and push the door when it began to swing inward. His eyes bulged wide, and hustling backward, he stepped around a corner just as the door opened completely.

"Yes, my master," a small man said as he backed out of the room, pulling the door closed.

Teck stretched his neck but was unable to see anything but the barest sliver of the interior of the room. The small man turned from the door, straightened his shirt, and hurried down the corridor. Unsure what to do, Teck opted to follow the unit of soldiers again. Down the corridor and around the corner, he heard the unmistakable slap of boots on tile. When he hustled through a passageway, he caught the men and fell into line. No one even looked in his direction. Falling into step, he thought again of the room beyond the door and the intense sense of Maya. Tonight, he'd try to get back to that room.

25

IN THE CORNER, MAYA CROUCHED on her elbows and knees. Before the little man left, he cuffed her wrists to the front of a collar around her neck and then attached the cuffs to a chain that was bolted to the floor. Her tether to the floor was so short, she was unable to sit up, and her body ached. Throughout most of the day, she'd crouched and watched a progression of people move in and out of the room, each of them wanting something. They glanced quickly at her but just as quickly looked away as if afraid to draw her bad luck to them.

Midday, the man on the throne came down and again stood over her. While a fleet of servants loaded a large table with more food than he could possibly eat, he towered in silence above her. Once, she chanced to meet his gaze, but the hate in them had her turning away.

While he ate, he'd toss a scrap or two in her direction. Maya ignored them, but she worried if this continued, soon enough, she'd be begging for him to throw her more. With her stomach grumbling, only force of will kept her from grabbing at the food.

Soon, she was left alone in the room. She didn't know where everyone went or how much time she may have. Still leaning over the bolt in the floor, she worked the chains, attempting to get loose. But they were well made, and all she'd managed to do was cause her fingers and hands to bleed. Even the slickness of her blood didn't help her slide out of the cuffs.

When she heard footsteps approaching, she dropped back against the floor. She tucked her hands together under her chin and dropped her head, staring out through the veil of her hair.

The golden door burst open as the bearded man and the little man hustled in.

"Yes, my master," the small man finished. Maya didn't know what they were talking about, but she felt an almost overpowering revulsion for the deference paid to the man. Who was he? And what was his plan for her?

Grovel, grovel, little man.

The little man peeled off and approached Maya. For a moment, he stared down at her. She refused to meet his eyes, keeping hers cast to the ground. Ignoring him didn't work, however, and he reached for the chain attached to the bolt. Undoing it, he pulled, wrenching her arms until she stood. When he pulled the chain from her cuffs and dropped it to the floor, she readied herself, hoping he planned on moving her bindings to the back. Feigning fragility, she remained still until he'd unlatched one cuff from her wrist. With a thrust, she pushed him back. When he slipped and went down, she jumped over his prone body and raced across the room. Around the corner, headed for the door, she skidded to a halt when she came face to face with two uniformed men. They stepped in front of the gold portal and eyed her, their hands moving to the hilts of their short swords. Grabbed from behind, she was spun about to face the little man. His breath was coming out of him with a huff, and his face was red. A fist connected with her jaw, pain exploded, and blackness flooded her mind.

WHEN SHE WOKE, IT WAS to again face the total darkness of her cell. Her jaw ached, and she felt lightheaded. She knew where she was by the scent of moist dirt and rock and the sound of dripping water. A sigh exploded at the thought of the futility of her attempt at escape. There were simply too many of them, and she was too far within their stronghold.

With effort, she halted tears that threatened to spill from her eyes and returned her mind to her goal of finding her mother, and the plan to do that and how to escape this prison.

The image of the priest once again came to her. Where was he in this monstrosity of a temple?

Maya remembered sitting on the hill outside of Berth with Teck. At his gentle urging, she'd been able to somehow see the priest. She'd felt as if she'd been right there with him—and she could have sworn he knew she was there, watching him. Maybe she could do it again. Maybe she could see him and maybe even communicate with him. She had to do *something* to save herself.

Maya relaxed against the wall. She took deep breaths and closed her eyes. She concentrated on the image of the priest and thought of the look of his face and how he'd moved. Her lips quirked in a small smile when his image filled her mind. He came easier this time, maybe because she'd already made contact once or maybe because she had a face this time.

In her mind, the priest, Patrick, was sitting in a beautiful courtyard. Lush plants—trees, flowering shrubs, and grasses surrounded him. The only sounds to break the silence were the distant call of birds. He sat on an ornate bench, and on his lap was an open book. Her thoughts touched him and, immediately, his eyes lifted from the book to scan his immediate area.

"Hello?" he asked the open air. He felt her presence but seemed unaware of where the sensations came from.

Maya concentrated harder. Was she only able to observe, or could she communicate with the priest? His reaction indicated his awareness of her, but if she couldn't tell him of her needs, this connection wouldn't do her any good. She took another deep breath and relaxed, taking her mind away from the cell with its sounds and smells of dank water, and into the garden where the priest sat. The smell of fresh air perfumed with the heavy scent of flowers came to her, pulling her deeper into her mind. She sank to lie prone on the dirt floor of her prison, her mind flying toward the sunlight and birdsong.

26

WHEN THE SOLDIERS TURNED TOWARD the hallway leading to the barracks, Teck sidestepped into an empty hallway and, leaning around the corner, watched them continue. It was easy. Maybe too easy, he thought, but didn't take time to second-guess his decision. He needed to get into the room beyond the golden door.

For the past couple hours, he'd tried to memorize the direction they'd taken. Now, he moved back through the temple, only missing one or two turns and having to backtrack. Once, he had to hustle into a dark alcove to avoid being spotted by another complement of soldiers coming from the other direction. Pressed back into the shadows, he held his breath as they passed. The steady clumping of their boots covered the thumping of his heart. He didn't know what form his punishment would take if discovered, but it wouldn't be good.

Before too long, he again stood before the golden door. For a moment, its ornate beauty had him spellbound. He laid both palms against it. Its extremity, the very nature of something so opulent, was foreign to him. Though his parents were considered to be one of the leading families in Roadstead, he'd never known this level of extravagance existed. Wealth, to him, was being able to feed your family and stay warm through the winter months. This door and the temple that surrounded it were something beyond his imagining.

The figures carved into the entryway seemed to tell a tale but one he couldn't decipher. It remained just beyond his reckoning, though he strained to understand.

The sound of booted feet moving down the corridor behind him forced his mind to shake off the hypnotic effect of the gilded portal, and with a quick glance toward the sound, Teck cracked open the door and slid inside.

The room was dim, though not completely without light. High above the large, enclosed area, skylights permitted the remnants of the sun's rays to filter in. He stood with his back pressed to the door and listened for any sounds that might indicate he wasn't alone. For a moment, he worried the men who created the booted steps outside would enter, but without pause, they continued down the hall.

Teck sighed with relief and, for the moment, felt safe. With two steps, he cleared a wall that blocked the main room from his view. A raised platform filled most of one end of the assembly hall. Centered on the platform rested a chair very much like a throne. But a throne it couldn't be, as this land had no king.

He moved farther into the room and quietly stepped to the seat. Like the door, it was created with gold, but in addition to the gilding, it had gemstones inlaid. Walking around it, Teck ran his fingers lightly over the surface. A shiver ran from his fingertips to the small of his back. To whom did this chair belong? Who thought themselves so important as to use wealth in this fashion when people of the realm starved? In the pit of his stomach, a great anger began to grow. Before this was over, he would confront this person. He would have his answers. Pulling his thoughts together, he moved away from the chair to scan the rest of the room. He was truly alone here—at least for the time being.

Thinking to stay here, hidden in this room until nightfall, Teck moved along one wall, his shoulder to a corner. He'd remain vigilant, and if his luck held, he wouldn't be discovered. When the sun set, he'd head along the corridors in search of any signs of Maya.

AS THE SUN SANK INTO the mountains, Teck stepped from the wall. He'd remained silent and still for over an hour. With the rising of the moon, faint light shimmered softly from above.

Taking a final glance around the area, he shifted toward the exit when his eyes landed on something new. He angled across the room to the opposite wall and, with the toe of his boot, lightly kicked a bolt sticking out of the floor. Coiled next to and attached to the bolt laid a heavy chain. In the dim light, it looked like a snake ready to strike. Bending closer, Teck studied the floor near the chain where dark droplets marred the shiny surface. With the tip of his finger, he touched one to find it dry. He'd bet his sword hand the drops were blood. But whose?

Another finger of cold shot down his back at the certainty that he knew exactly who had been chained in this room—whose blood had dripped on the floor.

Undecided what to do and where to go, Teck rose and made his way toward the door. Thinking furiously, he walked with his head bent, his eyes tracking his steps. Nearing the door, another dark spot, more a smear, caught his eye. He crouched to study it and again came to the conclusion it was blood. What had happened here?

Pushing upright, he stepped forward and placed his ear to the portal, certain he wouldn't hear anything. There might be a whole battalion of soldiers on the other side and he'd hear nothing. He gave the door a slight push, amazed again by its balance as it swung easily and silently on its hinges. Beyond was the empty hallway, appearing bright after the dimness of the inner sanctum.

All was silent. He scanned the floor. Nothing. Slowly, stepping lightly, he utilized all his tracking skills in his search for additional signs. Partway up a hallway, he stopped, looking back the way he'd come, and then returned to the golden door. Two additional halls opened from there, and Teck set off down the far aisle. Moving slowly, he scanned left and right, eyes sharp on the lookout for dark stains on the shiny tile.

A few feet later, he found what he searched for. Dropping to his knees, he touched the circle. It too was dry, which told him it had dropped hours ago. From his vantage point near the floor, he scanned the tiles that stretched out before him. The shiny reflection made it easier to see the next sign.

Two drops.

Teck continued to move down the hall, following the trail of blood.

27

M AYA OPENED HER EYES. EXHAUSTION fell hard on her. She'd attempted time and again to communicate with the priest, but nothing seemed to come of it. He sensed her, even spoke to her, but she wasn't able to let him know who she was or where he could locate her. Fatigue made her lose her hold on him, and for the last few hours, she'd been trying to reconnect. Nothing. Each effort cost her more energy — already low due to her lack of food, rest, and her location. She needed to eat and drink, but to be rested and well fed wasn't going to happen anytime soon. Maya again closed her eyes and concentrated on the image of the priest.

* * * * *

PATRICK SAT STRAIGHT UP IN bed, the presence once again scratching his mind. In the shadowy darkness, he looked at the other beds filled with the men who shared his cell. The sounds of their soft, steady breathing reassured him he hadn't disturbed their slumber.

The cell he shared was one of many such accommodations within the temple. Each room had three to five priests in it, but little else. Their beds were plain but functional with thin, down mattresses and a scratchy wool blanket. In the corner sat a chamber pot, thankfully unused this night. Next to each bed, a pair of sandals from the various men took up a small space on the floor, and each of their robes hung on pegs on the wall near the door. A small window above allowed a sprinkling of starlight or moonlight. Tonight, Patrick felt more than saw the beds and men.

His bare legs hanging off the bed, he focused with his whole being to catch a hint of the spirit who visited him.

There it was. Closing his eyes, he concentrated and soon an image came to him. A cell—not totally unlike the cell he now shared—but colder and darker, with no furniture to rest upon. A prisoner waited within the cell for liberation. For him. Patrick examined his thoughts for a moment longer and then stood to pull his robe from the peg. He slid it on over his head and slid his feet into his sandals. He knew of the dungeons. He counted himself lucky to have never been in them personally, but now he had no choice.

Patrick froze as one of the other priests turned over and sighed in his sleep. He silently counted to ten, taking deep breaths to stay calm before moving again. When the door opened, a breeze from the hallway whipped into the stuffy room, threatening to wake the men. As quickly and silently as he could, Patrick pushed the door shut, closing the men in and the cold wind out. The same wind blew up his garment and he shivered. He needed to move quickly. Both to warm up and to avoid getting caught loitering in the hallway. It wasn't permitted to be out of one's cell after curfew. If he was caught, he might truly be visiting the dungeons.

The prisoner cells, he knew, were on the other side of the temple, near the inner courtyard. He would need to be stealthy to traverse the temple at night. The priests were not prisoners, but rules were strict and punishment swift for those who chose to disobey.

Moving silently away from his quarters, Patrick listened with all his being, but the corridor remained silent. Step by step he crossed the temple toward the prison cells. His thoughts jumped with questions about what he would do when he got there. Always, two guards watched the entry, their primary job to keep people out. How would he free the prisoner? And could this prisoner be the one he'd waited a lifetime for?

PATRICK LEANED AGAINST THE WALL where a hallway turned. Two guards stood at attention in front of a formidable wood door.

Okay. I'm here, now what.

Maybe there would be a changing of the guards and somehow, he might be able to sneak by them. He was pretty sure the door was locked. Closing his eyes, he took a deep, cleansing breath and tried to think of a solution, but when he relaxed, the image of the underground cell and the prisoner's distress filled his head. He had to do something—had to act.

Stepping around the corner, Patrick moved into the light of the corridor. Any relaxation in the bodies of the two guards disappeared as he neared. Their eyes locked on him, and even from a distance, he could see their grips tightening on their weapons.

28

TECK WATCHED THE ROBED MAN step from the opposite hallway. For some time now, he had watched the guards, the trail of blood leading straight to the door they secured.

The guards came to an instant alert and turned, watching the man advance on them. His sandals made small swooshing sounds against the tile, but other than that, the hall was silent.

"Halt," one of the guards said to the priest. "You have no business here. Leave before there is trouble."

"Um? Well now . . ." the robed man stuttered. He stopped in his tracks and his eyes widened as Teck stepped up behind the guards.

The first guard, the one who had addressed him, went down without a sound as Teck hit him alongside his head with the hilt of his sword. He fell so quickly, the second guard didn't seem to realize something was amiss at first. The impact of his comrade's head to the tile, however, caught his attention and he swung to face the intruder. He was too slow, and Teck's fist connected with his jaw, sending him into oblivion along with his friend.

"Oh, my," Patrick breathed.

"You," Teck said, pointing the tip of his sword at him. "Who are you?"

"Well, well . . . I'm . . . um . . . I'm Patrick." He stared in shock at the end of the sword. "I'm a priest of this temple."

At the word *priest*, Teck stopped.

"Priest? You're a priest here?"

Nodding his head vigorously, Patrick's eyes pleaded with the man not to hurt him.

"I'm looking for someone," Teck said. "I believe my friend is being held as a prisoner in this temple—in this dungeon."

"Yes, yes." Patrick's nodding became so forceful, Teck thought his head might come loose from his shoulders. "I, too, am searching for another. Mayhap we are looking for the same one?"

Tripping over his feet, the priest hurried to the first guard and squatted beside him to rummage through his clothing. Finding a large metal key, he turned a triumphant smile toward Teck. Dropping his eyes, his hands shaking, the priest moved away and approached the door. The key slid in soundlessly and the tumblers of the lock turned easily. With another glance over his shoulder at Teck, he pulled open the portal. Blackness welcomed them.

Glancing around, Teck moved a few feet down the hall and pulled a lantern from the wall. Back to the priest and the gaping doorway, he shifted to slip past him. The light from the lamp illuminated a small distance ahead of him, and at the edge of the light's glow, he saw the beginning of a descending stairway. Teck threw a look of uncertainty over his shoulder at the priest, then he faced the gloom again and started down.

Almost immediately, his ability to breathe became hampered. The air quality suffered in the enclosed passageway, and somehow it felt heavier—more difficult to pull into his lungs. The stairs were dangerous, wet with slime and dripping water.

The priest slid behind him, crashing into his back and threatening to send them both plummeting down the stairs. Teck glared over his shoulder, catching Patrick's eyes and scowling. Thrusting his hands into the air, palms out, the priest stepped back. Teck turned from him with a growl, continuing down the narrow passageway.

A few moments later, the stairway leveled onto a dirt floor. Raising his head and holding the lantern high, Teck saw locked doors down both sides of a corridor. The stench was overpowering, and it was only by sheer willpower and rapid swallowing that he held back a gag. The priest was not so controlled, however, as Teck heard him retching behind him.

"Maya," he called in a whisper, his voice loud in the heavy air. His only answer was the steady dripping of water. Glancing behind and up the stairs, Teck looked at the priest and then moved down the passage. Stepping up to the first door, he rose to his toes and held the light high to peer through a small window. As soon as he got close, he stumbled back, the bile from his stomach almost coming up with the stench wafting from the opening. Something was dead within the confines of that room, but not so long ago that it had passed the point of rot. It was dead before he and Maya came to Berth. Moving on, he made his way to the next door.

Tentatively, he moved toward the window. This one sat lower. When he slid the cover back, bars crisscrossed it. This time, while not pleasant, the air was breathable.

"Maya," he called. For a moment, there was nothing. He went to move on to the next door, when he heard a rustling. And then a cough.

"Maya?" Teck raised the lantern and squinted in the window. The stirring intensified and then something small knocked against the door. If he hadn't had his hand on the entry, he would never have felt it. Fingertips appeared over the lip of the window, nails broken and caked with dried mud and blood, the skin discolored. Teck remembered taking Maya's hand outside her mother's cabin the night before her Names Day.

"Maya!" he yelled, reaching through the bars with his own fingers to grasp hers. "I'm here. We're going to get you out."

* * * * *

PATRICK WATCHED THE MAN, HIS agitation plain. Looking up, he saw the small fingers within the man's grasp.

Faintly, he heard a voice from the cell. It crackled and then plainly he heard, "Teck. Thank the heavens." The priest looked back to the man. Teck. His name must be Teck.

With his hand still on the captive's, Teck turned back toward Patrick. "Do you have a means to open this door? Will the key work again?"

Stepping forward, Patrick held the key. He was still leery of the big man, even more so with his current intensity, and didn't meet his eyes. He tucked himself in, almost expecting a blow. Patrick's life didn't give him the experiences to be this close to someone this forceful. In the past, he'd always stayed to the back, unnoticed.

Teck's gaze felt hot enough to burn. Patrick slid the key into the lock and turned it. A sigh escaped his lips as a click sounded. He stepped back quickly as the man pushed him aside and wrenched open the door.

Patrick's breath caught in his chest. On the other side, barely standing upright, was a girl, frail and filthy. The big man swept by him to scoop up the girl. He clutched her to his chest.

"A girl," Patrick whispered. He hadn't even considered that the prisoner might be female.

"Come," Teck said as he turned from the cell, the girl still cradled in his arms, her face pressed into his neck. "We need to get her out of here."

"Yes, yes . . ." Patrick turned and, stooping, picked up the lantern from where the man dropped it when the door opened. "I know somewhere we can go. We'll be safe for a while, but we must make plans." Without another word, he headed back up the stairs, walking carefully on the slick surface. Partway up, he glanced back. The big man walked sideways, stepping up the stairs to accommodate the width of the girl's body. He had his eyes glued to the stairs and moved at a steady pace.

At the top of the steps, Patrick eased the door slightly and peered out. The two guards lay as they left them. Pushing the door open, he stepped into the hallway and allowed Teck and the girl to exit. When they were all again above ground, the priest turned to them. "Will you assist me in placing the guards beyond the door? It may give us extra time."

Nodding his agreement, Teck moved to the opposite wall. The priest heard him whisper something to the girl, who grasped him harder with her arms, burrowing deeper into his shoulder. The man rubbed her back and said something else. She nodded and loosened her hold. Gently, he allowed her to drop from his hold, her feet alighting the tile. Patrick couldn't see Teck's face, but his hand was soft as it rose to her cheek. A moment later, the man turned from the girl to grasp one of the guards by the feet. Showing no visible effort, he pulled the man within the landing beyond the doorway and then turned for the other guard.

When both men were behind the door, the priest turned the key in the bolt, locking them in. Pocketing the key, he turned from the door. The girl gazed at Teck, and a vibrant smile lit her visage. Patrick gasped. She so resembled her father. She was indeed who he was looking for. But he'd never imagined a female child. How would her sex change their plans? How did it fit within the coming of the Three? The man pulled her into his arms and then, sliding one arm under her legs, he lifted her against his chest. Turning back to the priest, he raised an eyebrow.

"Yes, of course. Please follow me," Patrick said and headed down the hallway. He knew they would need to hide right away. When the master of the temple found his prisoner gone, he would raze the town to locate her again. In doing so, it would be noted that Patrick had disappeared. His game would be finished, and he wouldn't be able to return to the temple. He needed to ensure he wasn't caught. The master of the temple was unforgiving when crossed.

Their luck held as they passed through an open courtyard. Approaching the main gate, Patrick saw a soldier he knew and dropped to a secluded spot, motioning for Teck to come near.

"I know this soldier. I'll call him away, and you and the girl slip through the gate. Continue down the street a block and I'll meet you." He stared at Teck a moment until the man nodded his understanding. Moving out into the main walkway, Patrick boldly approached the gate. When the soldier on duty called out a warning to him, the priest raised one hand and continued up to him. They were soon visiting and laughing, and Patrick moved the soldier away from the exit. Patrick kept the soldier's back to the courtyard and watched as Teck again picked up Maya and walked silently toward the gate. When they slipped through without incident, Patrick breathed a sigh of relief.

Making an excuse, he left the soldier to hurry back the way he'd come. Taking a circular route through the side of the temple, he hurried through an outer courtyard. In the distance, he heard the midnight prayer, the chanting of the priests floating through the air. Patrick looked back the way he'd come. No one followed him. A short time later, he exited by the public entrance, nodding at the armed guards. They didn't stop him, but he felt the burn of their gazes until he turned a corner and was out of their sight.

Patrick hurried along the street until he came to the back road behind the temple. He had his eyes open and aware, looking for any sign of the two he searched for.

When Patrick turned into an alley, he saw Teck with the girl behind him. They both deflated with relief when they saw it was him.

Moving toward them, he gestured with one arm. "Come, quickly. We must be away from here." When they stepped up to follow him, he stopped and extended a hand. "I'm Patrick."

The two of them looked at each other and then at the priest.

The man shook his hand. "Good to meet you, Patrick. I'm Teck. This is Maya."

"Patrick." The girl took his hand in both of hers. She looked at him for a moment, and then, dropping his hand, moved back to the man.

The priest stared at her, and then he turned and moved down the street, and the two followed close on his heels. Walking briskly, the trio moved through the city. Teck called out to the priest.

"We have belongings at an establishment near the city gates."

The priest stopped abruptly. "We can't go there. If they know anything about you, they'll know where you stayed."

Stepping forward, her hand on Teck's arm, Maya said, "But we must. There are belongings we can't leave behind." She looked at Teck, her eyes pleading. "And Rory. If we are quick, we can get in and out, possibly before they even know I am gone."

The priest looked at her with hesitation. This wasn't a smart move for them to make. They needed to use this time and get out of the city. And not just out of the city but away from here. Away to the catacombs.

Maya approached him. "Please. Even if we shouldn't, we must."

For a moment, he held her gaze and then, with a quick glance at Teck, he nodded. "All right, but we must be hasty. Where did you leave your belongings?"

After a quick discussion, the priest nodded. "Yes, I know that establishment." He turned and hustled down the next alley without looking back. Maya and Teck hurried to keep up.

A while later, the sound of the tavern reached their ears. Sliding along the wall, they continued toward the business. People milled around outside, their voices raucous. Even after everything that had happened to them, the tavern looked unchanged.

Peering back at the priest, Teck said, "You stay here with Maya. I'll go in and get our things."

"No," Patrick said. "Someone inside may recognize you. I'll go in. Just tell me which room your things are in."

Stepping forward, Maya held up a hand to them both. "You're both staying here. I'll go in." When they began to protest, she cut them off. "You're both wrong. Teck, you're much too big to remain unseen, and the staff will remember you. And you"—she turned to Patrick—"really? A priest in a tavern? You'll stand out like a sore thumb." Moving past them, she stepped out a bit into the street to peer down the road at the alehouse. "I'm little. No one will notice me. I'll slide in and out and we'll be gone."

Patrick could see the big man wanted to protest. He opened his mouth and then closed it without saying anything. Finally, he said, "You'll be careful." His words weren't a question. He stared at her with an almost terrifying intensity.

The girl moved toward him, taking his hand in both of hers. "I'll be careful." She nodded to emphasize her words. "I'm in, I'm out, and we're gone." He nodded in agreement. Reaching into a pocket below his tunic, Teck pulled out a key. Maya took the key and spun away to ease down the street, turning the corner at the tavern to enter through the back.

With Maya gone, the two men glanced at each other and then moved apart in the alleyway. Her presence joined them and with her gone, they were at a loss.

* * * * *

WHEN MAYA SLIPPED THROUGH THE back door of the tavern, she stepped into a busy kitchen. People stood over stoves that billowed smoke from the fires that heated them. Pots boiled, skewered meat dripped juices that caused small tendrils of steam, tubers were chopped, and plates clanked as they were roughly placed on a counter and filled with hearty foods. One man seemed to be in charge, spending his time glaring and yelling. The other people stayed well out of his way, heads down, working fast and hard. Sweat broke out across Maya's brow and down her back from the extreme heat of the room. How these people stood it, she didn't know. After just a few moments she felt like she was going to faint.

Keeping her head down, Maya slid past the counter and wove through the workers. She stayed well away from the yelling man, seeing no need to draw attention to herself. Successfully navigating the kitchen, she pushed through the door leading to the main barroom. The noise level erupted, causing her to wrinkle her brow and pull her head down between her shoulders. She thought the man in the kitchen loud, but he was nothing compared to a room of drunken revelers.

Dodging between inebriated patrons, avoiding groping hands and spilled drinks, she made her way to the base of the stairs. There she paused, looking up the stairs and then back around the room. The tavern was so full of patrons, she couldn't see more than a few feet. As she turned to proceed up the stairs, Maya felt someone take her hand. Looking down, she saw a small boy. He had a stock of bright yellow hair and the most beautiful gray eyes. He had a firm grasp of her, and instead of forcing her hand from his, she squatted next to him.

"What is it, little man?"

He didn't say a word and simply stared at her. A moment later, his head came up and, looking over his shoulder, he released her. When he looked back in her direction, she thought she heard a woman's voice call from across the room.

"Wyliam? Is that your name?" she asked and placed a gentle hand on his shoulder. He gave her a slight nod, turned, and disappeared into the crowd. She watched where he vanished for a moment more and then, refocusing her mind, turned to the stairway.

Quickly and steadily, she made her way up the stairs and down the hallway to the room she and Teck had briefly shared. A drunken man stepped out of a room with his arm flung over the shoulders of a scantily clad woman. Maya dropped her head and moved to the side along the wall, but they didn't seem to notice her, too caught up in each other to care about a lone person in the hall.

Maya extracted the key Teck gave her and unlocked the door. Repocketing the key, she took a deep breath, turned the knob, and slipped inside the room. The interior was dark and smelled musty and closed off.

"Rory," she whispered. Only silence answered.

With her hands in front of her, Maya moved into the room, feeling blindly for the bed with the small table next to it. She remembered a lantern sat on the table, and she definitely needed some light to gather their belongings.

Her shin hit the bed frame and she fell onto the mattress. Catching herself with her hands, she cursed. With a spin, she sat and rubbed her leg. The sharpness of the ache where she'd hit her bone abated with her touch, and dropping her foot to join the other on the floor, she scooted toward the head of the bed. When her knee encountered the edge of the table, she reached out gingerly to locate the lamp.

She felt for a small compartment in the lamp's base, retrieved a match, and scraped it against the side of the base. She squinted as the flame flared, and she quickly pulled off the shade to light the wick. Shaking out the match with one hand, she replaced the shade and scanned the room as the illumination spread.

Where is Rory? The last she saw the dog, they had left him in the room guarding their belongings. She looked around again as if she could have missed him. Sitting along the wall, just where they left them, were their packs and weapons. Putting the question of her companion away for now—she'd ask Teck— Maya hurried over to grasp her bow, running her other hand down the limb, feeling a renewed sense of wonder.

She snatched her quiver and strapped it over her back. Grasping the bags, she pulled them to the bed and placed the key on the bedside table. Looking at it for a moment, the feeling of anticipation she'd felt when first arriving at the inn filled her. So much had happened in such a short time.

Maya turned from the table and grasped first one bag and then the other, slinging them around her shoulders. At the door, she turned to survey the room and ensure all their belongings were with her. The room was once again empty except for the bed, table, and lamp. Turning the doorknob, she opened the door wide, closed it behind her, and walked down the hall.

The revelers were just as loud as when she entered, and she felt happy to leave the tavern. When she took the last step down to the floor of the bar, a hand caught her arm.

"Hey. There you are. Where's that handsome man?"

Maya turned and recognized the buxom barmaid from before. Maya stared at her for a moment and then turned away. This fiasco started with that woman, and she wasn't going to end it with her.

Out the door, through the people, and down the street, Maya hustled. When she neared the alley, she called out in a loud whisper, "Teck!"

Teck stepped from the alley and hurried to her. He took the bags and swung them onto his own frame. Together they turned to the back street to find the priest waiting at the entrance.

She placed a hand on Teck's forearm, stopping him. "Rory, where's Rory?"

Looking down at her, he hesitated.

"What?" Maya stepped up to him, noticing indecision in his eyes. "What's happened?"

"I'm sorry, Maya. I don't know where he is."

Teck told Maya of leaving Rory outside the temple. He quickly explained that he didn't have any choice. He couldn't take the dog with him and had nowhere to leave him.

"We need to find him. Where could he be?"

With a gentle touch, Teck took her arm and began to lead her down the alley in the direction the priest had gone. "Come on, Maya. Let's keep moving." He turned her back around, and although she looked over her shoulder, he kept an arm about her and moved her toward the city gates. Seeing them moving, the priest again turned to lead the way.

The priest led them back the way they'd come. At a main intersection, he turned, and Maya recognized the lane they'd traveled when entering the city. Silently, they moved through the buildings. This far from the business district, the town remained quiet with only the sounds of the night. Wind whistled overhead, night insects chirped to each other, and in the distance, she thought she heard an owl.

Leaning toward her, Teck explained more of the last time he'd seen Rory. "He's the only reason I found where you were being held. After you left the tavern, I couldn't track you through the city streets." Maya appreciated that he didn't bother to cast blame on what put her in the streets in the first place. "He scented you and led me right to the temple. I couldn't take him with me though when I pretended to be one of the guards. I had to leave him outside the temple. I'm sorry, Maya. I had hoped when we escaped, he'd show up."

With unshed tears in her eyes, she nodded her understanding. How could he ensure the dog's safety when he needed to rescue her? She'd been foolish to rush from the tavern in the first place. All emotion and no thought. Now Rory could be dead, and she may never know what became of him.

"He found you before. He will again." Teck sounded confident. He pulled her tighter to his side as they walked, Maya blind with the tears in her eyes. He was right. Rory may still turn up. She'd keep hoping.

EXITING THE CITY ENDED UP being easy. Even this time of night, the guards on duty were focused on people coming *into* the area, so they didn't spare a glance for them as they left.

Coming into Berth, the area had been full of people, carts,

and animals. Empty now, the large dirt road leading into the city seemed even larger with the area deserted of all activity. The scuffing of their footsteps echoed back at them in the cool night air.

Maya hurried, and catching Patrick, she walked beside him.

"Where are we going?" She stared sideways at him.

"Do you know anything of your family's history?"

"My family?" She glanced back at Teck. He shrugged and she looked back at the priest.

"We have a stop to make. There, that insight into your history will be made known to you."

"Wait." She grabbed his arm and stopped. "What do you mean? How do you know my family? Do you know what's become of my mother?"

The priest stared at her for a moment longer and then, turning, he continued down the path. Speaking over his shoulder, he told her, "We must hurry. They wait for you."

29

WHEN THE SUN BROKE OVER the horizon, Maya was asleep on her feet. They'd been walking for hours, and her body and mind felt numb. Even when questioned further, the priest refused to discuss it anymore, only saying they must hurry. Hurrying to where, or to whom, she didn't know.

The land became more forested, running water more frequent. The shelter of the trees and availability of drinking water was welcome and at first made the trip more agreeable. As the night progressed, and Maya's already tired and battered body waned, nothing would make their trek acceptable. She told herself to remember anything was better than the dungeons—the fresh air of the forest smelled wonderful and the plant life brought pleasure, but none of these thoughts worked. She needed rest and food.

"How much longer?" she called to the priest.

"Not too far now." His words would have made her happy if the exchange hadn't been the same for the last few hours.

"Not far now, not far now . . ." she mimicked with a shake of her head. She knew her actions were childish. She glanced at Teck to see a smile curving his lips. She couldn't withhold a laugh of her own. She was becoming rummy.

Once again she stepped up to the priest. "Who was the man in charge at the temple? He seemed to know my father."

Patrick studied her as they walked, but he didn't offer any explanations.

"Why did he want me? What did he want at all?" She stepped in front of him, but the priest just sidestepped her and kept going.

When she hurried to catch back up to him, she grasped his arm and swung him around. "Why won't you talk to me? All I want are some answers."

She began to feel nervous. Then, without giving her any answers, he turned and continued on. Over his shoulder he offered, "When we get to where we're going, all your questions will be answered."

30

THE SMALL MAN WATCHED RED droplets from his lip hit the floor. The wound throbbed. He knew enough not to look at the man who paced in front of him. The ranting had stopped, but that wasn't an improvement as the heavy silence, broken only by stiff footfalls, didn't bode well.

When the boots came to rest in front of him, filling the edge of his vision, he caught his breath. Salvation or death was now imminent—it all rested on the whims and judgment of the man before him. On the back of his neck, his nerves twitched, feeling like bugs on his skin.

His master squatted, his leather clothes squeaking with resistance. Waiting for a blow, the small man's breath quickened, and his body broke out in a cold sweat.

"Look at me."

Capturing his courage, the small man peered into his master's face.

"You will find her."

"Yes, Master," he rushed to agree.

When his master stood, a breath expelled from his lungs. The immediate threat had passed.

He needed to get the girl back.

31

PATRICK REACHED INTO A CREVICE of a tree and pulled out a wooden staff with what appeared to be mosses and cotton tied to the top of it. When he reached in again, he brought out a small metal box. Maya looked at Teck with a wrinkle in her brow. He gave her a small shrug.

"Patrick," she began, "what's going on?"

"We're here," he answered. Striking a match from the box, he lit the end of the torch. It flared immediately and then dimmed to a steady glow. Stooping, the priest replaced the box in the break of the tree.

"Come. We'll be able to rest soon." Turning from them, he continued up a small rise to a rocky wall. Beyond the wall, the ground continued to rise and the trees dropped away.

Maya opened her mouth to question his direction. But before she could utter a sound, the priest disappeared into the formation. Teck and she stopped so abruptly, they bumped into one another.

"Where did he go?" she whispered. Moving forward, Teck

took her hand and subtly shifted in front.

A second later, Patrick reappeared.

"Come, come. It won't hurt you. It's a hidden path, is all."

Moving forward to where the priest again disappeared, a hidden doorway became visible. Passing through, the departing silhouette of the priest could be seen moving down a tunnel. Picking up their pace, they caught up with him and followed, looking around as they walked. Staying close to Patrick, they took comfort in the torchlight.

The tunnel was dry, and the air smelled earthy. The only sounds were their footfalls and a slight sizzling coming from the fire on the torch. The tunnel's trajectory made a sudden shift downward. The temperature dropped.

A short time later, a light formed at the far end of the tunnel, and a filtered hum could be heard. They were closing in on a room within the mountain. The hum became louder and within it, Maya made out individual voices. Her eyes wide, she glanced back at Teck. Giving her a small smile, he reached out and ran a hand down her shoulder.

Patrick glanced back as if to ensure they were still with him before he moved through the entryway.

Taking a deep breath, Maya followed.

* * * * *

IN A COURTYARD, A FAIR distance from where Maya and Teck followed the priest, the cat stared up at the closed balcony doors. When he left Maya, the man, and the dog, he didn't bother to inform them of his decision to go. Finding his girl was his primary concern. Her trail was one he'd been on for almost two decades. Now, he'd tracked her to this spot, and it was imperative that he get inside the residence.

With a slow blink, his gaze shifted to watch a group of maids exit the building. Their chatter erupted into laughter only to be quickly stifled.

The cat's eyes tracked them as they entered a small outbuilding and soon, they reappeared, their arms full of baskets lined with an assortment of vegetables. Seeing his chance, the cat fell into step behind them.

All cats had a natural ability to camouflage, part of it coming from the cats' certainty they couldn't be seen. Over time, this confidence in their ability seemed to convince people they actually weren't there. This feline arrogance created an evolutionary development, and dirkcats could, over time, become almost invisible with the use of magic.

Nathaniel now used this ability to his best advantage.

The women slid into the building and the cat slipped between their legs to pad soundlessly down the hall and up a set of stone steps. The corridor led him further into the building. Within a step or two, his pelt shifted to blend with the muted browns and grays of the rock. Like a shift in the light, his fur shimmered for a moment, then the hall was empty.

Pausing at a door, he tilted his head, listening for sounds. A slight movement, perhaps the passage of a small body, came to him from within the room. Lying by the door, his body relaxed but his eyes remained alert, and his ears twitched as they caught every sound. He'd wait.

32

WHEN MAYA AND TECK STEPPED into the room at the end of the underground corridor, all talk ceased. Maya heard Teck's rapid breathing behind her and the pounding of her heart in her ears.

When Patrick dropped the burning brand into a vat of water, the silence broke. The sizzle and steam of the doused fire ignited the group like a starter before a race. Noise erupted, and men rushed forward.

A flood of bodies forced Maya backward and she felt Teck step up to brace her. His brawny arm came around her collarbone, and she reached up to grasp his forearm with both hands. His solid warmth reassured her, and she calmed enough to recognize the men's excitement—not aggression—in seeing Patrick.

"Brother." A man approached Patrick, a large smile on his face. They embraced and in the way of men, pounded each other on the back. Pulling away, Patrick glanced toward Maya and whispered something to the other man. What he heard lifted his eyebrows, and he leaned to look around the priest at the girl. She felt studied and perhaps judged when suddenly the man gestured to them, turned his back, and walked away through the crowd.

"Come," Patrick said to Teck and Maya with a cock of his head.

Moving through the mob of males, Maya was relieved Teck was with her. She was intimidated by the group—their noise, wildness, and masculinity.

When they passed through a doorway built into the rear of the room, the volume dropped noticeably, and she breathed a sigh of relief. The farther they walked, the more the hum of voices faded, and soon the only sound was the scuff of their steps. Maya slowed her pace until Teck moved beside her and, fumbling a bit, she found and grasped his hand.

At the touch of his skin, the memory of the night at her and her mother's cabin filled her mind. The smell of her mother's cooking and the budding attraction between her and Teck. Her present challenges seeming insurmountable, she wished to return to the innocence of that time. She longed to have her mother safe, to be snug in their home, wrapped in their quilt, dreaming of a special boy she had once hated.

With a squeeze of Teck's hand, she looked up at him. As if feeling her gaze, he glanced at her, grinned reassuringly, and then looked back at Patrick. She continued to watch his profile a moment longer, content to trust his guidance with the joining of their hands.

Sucking in a breath, she looked down and then forward. She

needed to fortify her resolve. Her dreams weren't to be, so it was best to prepare for what was.

On the heels of this thought, they reached the end of the tunnel. The man leading them pushed open an entry and waited for them to pass before shutting the door without entering. Maya stared for a moment at the closed door. Then she turned to take in the room they'd entered.

The space was sparsely, but pleasantly, furnished. Books lined one wall, and a small seating area was arranged on the other side. Across the room, in front of the bookshelves, a man stood with his back to them. His hair shone red in the light and reflected the brightness of several lanterns. Patrick cleared his throat and the man turned.

The man stepped forward and muttered, "Sylvan?"

Blood rushed from Maya's head, leaving her dizzy. Lights flashed across her vision, partially obscuring a man with a muted version of her own features. For a moment, she feared she might faint.

"What trickery is this?" Teck growled and stepped between the man and Maya.

The man continued forward, his body shifting to keep his eyes on the girl. "Sylvan, please . . ."

Maya placed a soothing and restraining hand on Teck's forearm. She stepped to his side and walked toward the older man. Patrick stood to the side, silent. Teck remained still, but his body remained tense.

"I'm Maya," she whispered. "Sylvan is my mother's name."

"By the gods," the man breathed. Grasping her shoulders,

he pulled her into a tight embrace.

* * * * *

TECK COULD BARELY KEEP HIMSELF still. He knew who this man was. Looking at him, he could only be one person—Maya's father. But, where had he been? How could he let her grow up without his name and protection? And now, he acted so happy to see her. Well, it was too late, he thought with narrowed eyes. Maya's safety and security were his responsibility. This man forfeited that right long ago.

When the man released Maya, he kept his hands on her shoulders. He gazed at her with unshed tears but spoke to the priest.

"Thank you, Patrick."

"Of course, Lord Bathsar."

Teck barely heard their exchange, his attention on the hands that still rested on Maya's shoulders.

Directing her toward the small seating area, the older man led Maya. Teck felt a hand on his arm and, with a shake, pulled himself from the image of Maya walking away from him.

"Come with me. I'll show you to a set of quarters."

Ignoring the priest, he turned his gaze back to Maya who now sat beside her father. He held her hand and she stared into his face. Teck knew he was all but forgotten in this new world of hers.

This was not happening. He'd just gotten her back—he wasn't going to lose her again.

When he took a step toward the pair, the priest tightened his hold on Teck's arm.

"Come on, boy. Leave them alone for a bit. She'll be safe." His voice was gentle as if he knew the thoughts passing through Teck's mind.

Teck stared at him, his thoughts awash with indecision. Taking advantage of his hesitance, Patrick directed him toward the door.

"Come on . . . give them a moment."

Teck was given a small chamber. He didn't like being shut out like this. He kept thinking about what could be happening, what her father could want now, after he'd never wanted anything from Maya before. His concerns grew as he formed more questions. Nothing was being explained to them, and he was again being separated from Maya.

Slowly, time passed—and Teck paced.

33

MAYA CRACKED OPEN THE DOOR and slipped in, her mind numb with the information she'd been given. Just the existence of her father had her in shock.

After talking for hours, Patrick had led her to a small room. When she inquired after Teck, she'd been told he was in a room just down the hall. It was into that room she'd just snuck.

Closing the door silently behind her, everything was eclipsed by the large man in the middle of the area. He looked haggard, she realized. When did they last sleep? Teck didn't say a word, just stood and stared with an intensity that had her breath stuck in her throat.

"Teck." She shuddered and took a step toward him.

He moved so fast, she'd swear she didn't see him shift— scooping her up in a hold so tight she feared he might break her. But she didn't care. She had what she wanted.

"Hold me. Please, hold me," she whispered, her lips touching his ear. His entire frame vibrated in response. He turned toward the bed and laid her down gently, stretching himself out beside her. Up on his elbows, one on each side of her shoulders, he still didn't say anything as his eyes burned into hers. Giving him a small smile, Maya touched his cheek.

"Make love to me," she intoned. "Make it so it's just you and me again."

He shifted to draw her under him, dropping his head to take her lips with his.

* * * * *

IN THE CALM OF MORN, Teck finished helping Maya button her vest on over her tunic when there was the sound of a commotion in the hall. A sharp knock sounded on the door. When it cracked open, Patrick leaned in. His hands still on Maya's shoulders, Teck almost growled.

Eyes open with shock, Patrick cleared his throat and then leaned back into the hallway.

"My lord Bathsar," he called.

Seconds later, the door was thrust open and Maya's father filled the space. He took in the intimate scene, his brows pulling down.

"Maya." He stepped into the room. "I didn't know where you were." He hesitated and then pushed on. "You weren't in the room you were given."

Maya turned, putting her small frame in front of Teck, her back against his body.

"No, Father. I'm not a child. I choose where I sleep." For all her brave words, her voice cracked at the end of her speech.

Both men at the door dropped their gazes, Patrick's skin reddening. Neither were well equipped to deal with a female. "Well." Her father cleared his throat and, looking her in the eye again, held out his hand. "Come, then. It's time to break our fast."

Reaching behind her to grasp Teck's hand, Maya stepped toward her father. She passed him, leading Teck without taking the offered hand. Patrick dropped out of the way as she advanced, moving down the hall. With a hard swallow, her father fell in beside her and Teck, leading them back to the main gathering hall.

When they entered the dining room, the men from the night before were absent. Her father led them to a vat surrounded by bowls, loaves of bread, and a large container of water. He opened the vat and ladled out a type of stew. Her stomach growled at the scent coming from it. At this point, she would eat just about anything. She couldn't remember the last time she'd eaten.

Turning, her father handed a full bowl first to her and then to Teck. She moved to get herself a tankard of water and a small loaf of bread. Putting her water aside, she placed a loaf in her bowl and put one in Teck's. They made their way to a long table.

A moment later, Maya's father sat directly across from Teck. Teck sat back and looked him in the eye.

"So, Teck, is it?"

Giving a curt nod, Teck volunteered nothing. It was obvious he didn't like this man, or really anything about this situation. Who was he to think he could step into Maya's life and begin making decisions? She'd done just fine without him until now.

When the man cleared his throat, Teck sat back, laid his spoon down, and stared back. The tension between the men was heavy, and Maya looked from one to the other, confusion coloring her face.

"Um . . ." she began in an attempt to defuse the pending explosion. Her gaze jumped again from her father to Teck and back again. "Teck's a friend from the village where mother and I lived. He came with me by his own choice. In protecting me, he's put his own life in danger, many times."

"Uh-huh . . ." Bathsar's vague response had her raising her eyebrows at him.

"Father." He continued to stare at Teck, so she leaned farther across the table. "Father." Her voice cracked with a sharp tone that finally drew his attention away from Teck.

His expression softened as he looked at her. "Yes, Maya?" When he said her name, it enfolded her in warmth.

"I wanted to tell Teck what you told me last night." She glanced at Teck to see now he looked at her too. "Can you tell me more?"

Nodding, Lord Bathsar recounted some of the tale of Maya's family history and the last time he'd seen Maya's mother.

"The Singh family have been the premier house in this land for generations—"

"Singh? I know that name." Teck sat forward and leaned his elbows on the table.

"Yes. I'd be surprised if you didn't." Lord Bathsar turned back to Maya. "The Singhs are Maya's family."

"What? But she and her mother live in a simple cabin . . . on the edge of town."

"Yes." Maya's father nodded. "But that's not the life she or Sylvan were born to. Her mother was trained to be an important landowner and statesman. The day of the tragedy changed all that."

"Tell us, Father. Tell us both what happened." Maya leaned across the table and placed her hand on her father's forearm, drawing his attention. "Explain to us what happened to my family."

"Before I tell you about that day, let me give you both some more background so you'll understand all the players." With a small nod, Maya asked him to continue.

"Your mother and I grew up together. Our parents' lands adjoined on one side. The Singhs were much wealthier than my family, but my father's granduncle was royalty in a small country, so it was always assumed the two families would join by marriage. The accumulative expanse of property would rival any other estate in the land. Sylvan was an only child, and the talk was she would marry my older brother." Bathsar stared down at the table, running his finger over a deep rut in the wood, seemingly lost in his memories.

"My brother was never a very pleasant man, even as a boy. It wasn't until years later that the level of his atrocities would become known, but as a young man, Sylvan and I only knew that when he was around, we didn't want to be anywhere near.

At first, our fear and dislike of my brother drew us together. Later, our friendship and then love grew.

"Sylvan pleaded with her father not to make her marry Mikel. Her father"—he smiled softly at Maya—"your grandfather, loved your mother very much. He wanted the families joined, but he also wanted his daughter happy. When he broached the question of perhaps her marrying *me*, Sylvan was overjoyed and the announcement was made. No one understood how my brother would react." Shaking his head, Lord Bathsar sighed deeply.

"What happened?" Maya grasped Teck's hand. Scooting closer, Teck took it in both of his.

"Your mother and I had a beautiful wedding. All the heads of state and landowners came. It was a gala event—the party of the season. Mikel was there and seemed resolved to his part. Everyone's lives moved on as normal.

"Afterward, Sylvan continued her training to learn everything she would need to know about running the Singh empire. I'd been in training too. Learning many things like statesmanship and finance, but as the heir, Sylvan would continue as the matriarch of the dynasty."

No longer able to sit and tell his story, Bathsar stood and paced the room.

"That day, about six months after our wedding, began as usual. Sylvan and I were just getting ready to rise and break our fast, when we heard the sounds of battle—the clash of metal and screams of terror." Lord Bathsar stopped his pacing, his eyes unfocused as his mind slipped back in time. "I didn't know what was happening, so even though she protested, not wanting to leave me or her family, I insisted she slip out through a hidden panel in the hall just down from our rooms." Focusing again to look at Maya, her father explained, "All the family quarters had escape routes built into the walls. They led to the river.

"I told her I would come for her when I knew what was happening, but until then, she would need to stay safe and hidden."

Standing to walk around the table, Maya stood next to her sire. She placed a hand on his arm, rubbing gently. "What happened, Father?"

Bathsar's eyes brimmed with tears. He placed his hand over hers.

"You're so like your mother. Not just beautiful, but kind. Strong." He touched her cheek, a small smile playing over his lips. Taking her hand, he led her back to the table where they sat. He cleared his throat.

"So how did you lose Sylvan?"

With a quick jerk, Bathsar's head spun to Teck. "I didn't *lose* her," he said, his voice gruff. Giving a final pat to Maya's hand, the lord sat forward and continued his tale. "After Sylvan left by the hidden tunnel, I went to confront the threat. I didn't know it when I sent her away, but it would be many years before I again left the estate."

Teck took Maya's hand as she moved back to his side of the table. "Were you attacked?"

Looking from the joining of their hands to Teck's face,
Bathsar answered his question in a soft voice. "My brother . . ."

34

MAYA'S EYES OPENED IN THE darkness of the room she shared with Teck. His deep and steady breathing — normally a comfort — did nothing to dispel the sense of foreboding that woke her. Her sleep had been troubled, her body tossing and turning, her mind restless. The story her father told, the answer to who instigated the attack on her family, who continued to pursue her, the master of the temple where she'd been held hostage, had her unable to relax.

Her own uncle. What quirk of fate or genetics could create such a monster? A man who would kill his own kin to see his desires fulfilled.

Now something else weighed on her. This was different, somehow changed from the disquiet she'd felt since her father told his tale.

Turning her thoughts inward, she tried to identify where the sensations came from. Her breath caught in her throat when she realized the heaviness, the waiting, emanated from an external source. It was as if her name were being called from afar. Like a scratching on her mind.

Maya swung her legs from the bed and stood. She couldn't lie still any longer. The air in the room was stuffy and warm with the heat of their bodies, and her shirt clung uncomfortably to her back. Pulling on her pants, she closed her eyes to concentrate on the voice that called to her. It beckoned, and she found she no longer had any desire to resist.

Slipping from the room, she quietly pulled the door shut and turned to walk down the hallway. This direction led to the main hall, but as she passed the large entrance doors to this room, she knew this was not the place. The emanation drew her onward.

The tunnel narrowed as she continued, and she wished for her boots as the temperature dropped. A chill moved its way up from her bare feet. Every few moments, a shiver racked her body, but she couldn't stop now. The farther she went, the louder the voice became in her head. No words were spoken, but still the call was incessant, pulling at her core.

As the hall darkened, Maya moved to the side wall and oriented herself by running a hand down the surface. Every so often, she came to the juncture of the wall and doorway. Sliding her hand over each door to where the wall again began, she continued.

Maya didn't know how long she'd walked before a change came over the voice calling in her mind. An excitement, an expectation—almost a frenzy—pierced her perception. In tune with this new excitement in the voice, her body flushed.

Ahead, the tunnel turned a corner and she saw a light. It

seemed to pulse, and as she neared, the beat of her heart synced with it. She swore she could hear the rhythm in her head.

She wanted to slow her progression, but the pull of the light was insistent, and soon it diluted her concern. Her body continued of its own accord, down the hall and around the corner. She was a piece of driftwood carried by floodwater.

She squinted at a door, closed but lit from the interior, light streaming from every crack and bursting through the keyhole. Maya shielded her gaze. The light, so bright, and the throb of its beat. She didn't know where it began and she ended. Her chest felt heavy and she heaved out her breaths. Surely, her heart would stop beating without the presence of this light.

Nearing the portal, Maya reached out a hand. When she touched the metal doorknob, a sharp sensation made her hiss and jerk her hand back. She scanned her palm only to realize it wasn't heat she'd felt but cold. The metal was freezing.

Grasping the tail of her shirt, she opened the door. A loud creak sounded, and only then did she realize how utterly silent it was—the intensity of the light had numbed her other senses.

Looking into the room, the illumination resided on a table against the far wall. Scanning left and right, the room appeared to be for storage. Crates and burlap packages waivered in the images cast in the brightness. Looking over her shoulder, Maya assured herself she was completely alone and then stepped into the room.

* * * * *

TECK SAT UP WITH A start, reaching out a hand for Maya. When all he felt was the cold blanket beside him, he clambered out of bed and lit a lamp. It only took a moment to see he was alone.

Pulling on his pants, his chest and feet bare, he grabbed the lantern and moved into the hallway.

"Maya," he called in a loud whisper but wasn't surprised when he got no response.

It was likely she'd gone to the great hall, perhaps to get a drink or something to eat, so he turned and headed that way. Passing a door, he halted as it squeaked and a face peered out.

"Has something happened?"

The priest, Patrick.

"Have you seen Maya, priest?" Patrick ducked his head between his shoulders at Teck's tone. Teck knew the smaller man was intimidated by him but couldn't worry about that now.

Stepping from his room, Patrick pulled the door shut and turned in the direction Teck had been going.

"Since you're out here, she's obviously not with you. I'll help you find her."

Appreciation filled Teck, but he didn't know how to express these feelings to the man. With a curt nod, he continued down the hall, taking for granted the priest would follow.

Just past the main gathering room, Teck noticed a shaft of light at the end of the hall.

"What's down there, priest? Do you see that light?"

Peering in the direction he'd indicated, Patrick craned his neck and lifted to his toes. With a small shake of his head, he muttered, "Nothing but storage . . . except . . ." Looking at Teck and then down the hallway, Patrick turned and scurried back the way they'd come.

"Priest!" Teck called, but Patrick kept moving. Teck turned and watched the priest, his brows drawn together.

Partway down the hall, Patrick stopped and banged on a door. The loud hammering reverberated up and down the path, drawing sleepy faces from multiple openings. Voices blended as confusion rose, and men stepped into the hall.

Lord Bathsar moved from the room Patrick had knocked on and, after a brief whispered conversation, he and the priest faced Teck.

Moving quickly to him, the duo stared down the hall at the illumination.

Grabbing Patrick by the arm, Maya's father hurried in that direction. Teck followed their rapid trail.

When they rounded the corner, the three men halted, hands thrown up in front of their squinted eyes.

"Maya," Lord Bathsar muttered. Looking closely at the door, Teck suddenly understood that Maya was in that room. He rushed forward, eluding the lord's grasp. Teck slowed his pace near the door, hearing the two men close in on him. Stepping through the threshold, he spotted a small silhouette against the far wall—the source of the light radiant behind her.

"Maya!"

As if in slow motion, Maya's gaze turned in his direction, her eyes bright with blue light, though she didn't seem to see him, and the muscles in her face were lax. No recognition registered and a moment later, she turned away.

Teck stepped forward, only to be halted by a firm hand on his arm.

"Wait."

Glancing at Maya's father, Teck flung off his grip. But when he pivoted back, it was too late. Her hands closed around a glowing orb on the table in front of her, and as she pulled it into her embrace, a force hit. The reverberation knocked them from their feet and threw them to the ground. Teck felt the floor beneath him quake as dirt and rock rained down from above.

35

THE LIGHT FADED SLOWLY, AND as Teck's sight realigned, sounds became evident—moans from the men next to him, voices from outside the room, and the tinkling of soil and rock sifting down from the ceiling.

Shaking his head to clear it, he peered to where he last saw Maya. A second figure stood with her. Teck rolled to his knees and pushed himself to his feet. He stumbled toward her.

Just steps from them, Teck stopped. The man stood in front of her. His gaze rested on her face—stoic, unmoving. She stared back at the man. Her eyes were wide but back to their normal green shade. Grasping her arm, Teck turned her toward him, but her head pivoted, and her gaze remained on the other man.

"Maya," he said and gave her a small shake.

The sound of a blade clearing its scabbard stopped Teck. He turned to face the threat, placing his large frame in front of Maya.

The stranger had skin of a darker shade than Teck had ever seen. The man was partially clad in trousers made of a fabric he couldn't identify. A reddish-brown, they shimmered in the defused light from the open doorway. Straps crisscrossed his chest, holding duo scabbards on his back. The hilt of one sword showed over his shoulder, and its twin rested in his hand. He no longer eyed Maya but now had his gaze fixed on Teck.

Taking a step back, Teck moved Maya with him. The room didn't afford much space, filled with crates and wrappings. With each step he retreated, the stranger paced forward.

"Bathsar!" he yelled blindly over his shoulder. "Get Maya out of here."

The sword whistled in the air as the man spun it, readying his stance to attack.

"Wait." Bathsar raised his voice and hands to step between the men. "Teck, you don't understand."

"Understand what?"

"He won't hurt her. There's no danger."

Teck risked a look at Maya's father, his eyes wide. "Are you insane? He has a weapon."

Lord Bathsar turned more fully to face Teck. "Because he thinks *you're* a threat—a threat to her."

"Wha—" Shifting his gaze quickly between the lord and the stranger, Teck paused.

"I'm telling you the truth. Step aside. He won't harm her— he's hers."

The words pierced Teck's heart, but he felt truth in them. Eyeing the warrior, Teck moved slowly to the side, allowing Maya to come into view. Her face still wore a spellbound expression, but at her appearance the warrior relaxed his stance, and the point of his weapon fell to the floor.

A light touch caught his attention as Maya laid a hand on his arm, stepping around him. She neared the warrior and Teck bristled, his muscles tensing.

A step from the stranger she stopped, her gaze running over his face. The warrior reached up, sheathed his weapon, and dropped to one knee all in one motion. Lifting his face, he gazed raptly at her.

"My lady," he uttered.

* * * * *

SITTING IN THE OTHERWISE EMPTY main hall, Teck, Maya, Lord Bathsar, and Patrick eyed the warrior who stood against the wall, his arms crossed over a powerful chest and his eyes never leaving Maya.

"So, you see, the firstborn of the Singh House receives their pedagogue on their sixteenth Names Day. It's been this way for generations upon generations. When you said she's been having dreams filled with light, I'd say the pedagogue has been trying to come to her."

Teck rubbed hard at his forehead. "What is this pedagogue? And where does it come from?"

Glancing from Teck to Maya, Lord Bathsar explained, "Long ago, eons ago, the eldest son of the then-Lord Singh chanced to save the life of a mountain sprite. She was loved by a powerful warlock. In return, the warlock granted Lord Singh a wish. He wished that his son, his only child at the time, be given the means to wisdom. Taking this wish, the warlock created the Pedagogue Seal."

"Pedagogue Seal, pff..." Teck muttered and rolled his eyes. Maya's father looked pointedly at him, his eyebrows raised. Teck pushed his seat back and stomped away from the table. Reaching the wall, he pivoted sharply and glared at Lord Bathsar. "A tale told to children. That's how you plan to help us?"

"Teck..." Maya began, confusion plain on her face, but he cut her off.

"No, Maya. This man disappears out of your life, leaves you and your mother to fend for yourselves, and now fills you with false tales about some wish granted by a warlock." He hurried to her and, dropping to a knee in front of where she sat, took her hand in his. "Let's leave this place. Just you and me."

"I know it sounds like a tale, but please, give him a chance. Listen to all of it." Her eyes implored him and his resolve wavered. "There's truth to the tale, if you'll just listen with an open mind. Where do you think the warrior came from? You saw the opening of the seal with your own eyes."

Teck released a deep sigh. Bringing her knuckles up, he kissed her hand. Setting it on her leg, he let his touch linger for a moment before standing. He sat and looked expectantly at Maya's father. "Well?"

Lord Bathsar stared for a moment, uncertainty and disapproval on every curve of his face.

"So, the pedagogue is a mentor. A trainer given to the firstborn of each generation in the Singh line. Each teacher is unique to the child and the life they'll lead. Each seal becomes active at the turning of the child's sixteenth year."

Maya heard Teck sigh. She wished he'd be more patient. This information he thought of as a tale, was the first viable clue they'd found. How else did he explain the man who stood against the far wall? Reaching out to him, she wrapped her hand around his. She caught his eye, and her lips turned up slightly in reassurance.

Turning from her, Teck interrupted whatever her father was about to say. "That," Teck said with a lift of his chin toward the warrior, "doesn't look like a teacher to me."

"I told you." Bathsar sighed. "The pedagogue comes in the form and with the knowledge the Singh heir requires. At this time, Maya needs a warrior."

"She has a warrior," Teck sneered.

Maya's soft voice cut through the tension in the room. "I'd like a moment alone with him."

"No."

"No."

Teck and Bathsar eyed each other, both suspect of any situation where they might agree.

"I wasn't asking permission." She stood and moved toward the warrior, saying over her shoulder, "Excuse us, please."

"My lady Maya." Maya turned to look at Patrick. "May I stay?"

Searching his face, she hesitated. Then with a curt nod, she turned back to the warrior. She waited until she heard the door close behind the two men. Raising her eyes to meet his gaze, she was momentarily taken aback by their intensity.

Clearing her throat, she asked, "Do you have a name?"

"Sentinel, my lady."

Maya took a step closer.

"Well, Sentinel, I for one don't understand this thing between us. Can you explain it to me?"

He squinted and peered at her. "I don't understand your question."

A cough sounded, drawing her attention.

"Um. Perhaps I might be able to shed some light on what's transpired."

With a final look, Maya turned from the warrior and faced the priest.

"Okay, priest. Speak."

"When the warlock created the spell granting knowledge to the first Singh heir, he either deliberately, or by accident, linked the two entities inexplicably together. We continue to see this fusion today."

"So, was this true for my mother?"

"Oh, yes. The link between your mother and her pedagogue was exceptionally strong." Patrick moved beside Maya. "If your father and he hadn't had such an adversarial relationship, perhaps they would have joined to locate your mother—I know your father has thought her dead all these years. I'm sure her pedagogue knew better, but when she disappeared, so did he. It was assumed his existence ended with her death."

Maya's eyebrows rose. "What do you mean, 'his existence ended'?"

"The pedagogue is breathed into life for the heir—to serve and teach them is their only purpose. Without the heir, the pedagogue has no function. No reason to continue."

"Are you insane?" She spun from the priest to the warrior, her eyes wide. She gestured to the warrior. "You're telling me his life is in my hands? I don't want that responsibility."

"I'm sorry, Maya. He is yours."

Turning away from the warrior, Maya paced the room, feeling the eyes of her teacher follow. She stood for a moment, hands on her hips, and then moved back to the men.

"Okay." She looked the warrior in the eye. "Tell me what I can learn from you."

As if but waiting for her to ask, the pedagogue's stance relaxed, and he began a litany of lessons and knowledge he would teach her—from statesmanship to swordplay. The world she was born into presented different challenges than any heir before her. No extended family, save her mother who was missing, and a newly discovered father. All inheritance and history—and the stability those things offered—taken from her before her birth. She would need to become more self-assured, more formidable, than all those before.

At his words, Maya felt a shiver move down her spine and up the nape of her neck. Could she be that person? Did she have it in her to vanquish the evil who had taken her family and legacy away?

Stepping back from the warrior, Maya looked from his stony gaze to the softer, understanding one of the priest.

Patrick laid a hand on her arm. "It'll be all right. We're all here to help you."

Shaking her head, she shrugged off his hand. "I don't think I can be that person you need." Turning toward the door, she cast over her shoulder, "I need to think."

When she opened the door, Bathsar leaned against the far wall, and Teck paced the hall. They both hurried toward her.

With this new information rattling around in her head, the two men behind her, and now two in front, she felt like a caged animal. Her only thought was to escape.

Before Teck could reach her, she sidled past her father's outstretched hand and headed toward the exit of the encampment.

"Maya," she heard Teck call behind her. Not wanting company, she broke into a sprint and cleared the hidden door. She heard footsteps behind her for a few feet, but with no obstacles, she soon outdistanced Teck.

Her speed was her ally as she ran into the forest. The flash of her passage through the trees caused disruption—grazing deer raised their heads, small ground animals scampered, and birds took flight.

Sometime later, panting, sucking in great gulps of air, and unable to run any farther, Maya skidded to a halt before a stream. Bending at the waist, with her hands on her thighs, she concentrated on delivering oxygen to her starved lungs.

As her breathing slowed, the sound of the stream drew her attention. The soft gurgling of water over stones calmed her mind a little. She glanced up and was momentarily blinded by sunlight bouncing off the water's surface. The damp, mossy smell of the stream reminded her of the stream near home.

Undone by the memory, Maya collapsed beside the water on the grass.

* * * * *

WATCHING MAYA DISAPPEAR INTO THE forest, Teck slowed and stopped, knowing he'd never catch her. She'd always been fast. All he could do was wait at the entrance of the cave for her to calm and return. What insight she'd gained during her time in the room with the priest and the newcomer, he didn't know. He would need to trust that she would tell him when she was ready.

36

CASSANDRA STOOD ON THE HILLSIDE; the wilds of the forest spread out before her. She loved to observe the world like this. Fruitful. Vibrant.

Her tongue flicked out to run along her dry red lips. Her skin flushed a rosy hue, and her eyes shone with desire.

Spreading slowly around the spot where she stood, a black stain encroached on the land. The grasses, once tall and green, were now blackened, burned. When the rot spread far enough to reach a sapling, the poison colored its trunk with death, crawling up the soft bark into the leaves.

Cassandra, humming to herself, took a step across the hillside, walking slowly. She moved from one spot to another and left behind footprints of dead, burned grass. As she continued her morning stroll, her cheeks became flushed, her lips even redder, the life of the land siphoning straight into her.

When she stopped, turning to survey the banquet before her, Cassandra's laughter pealed across the valley, startling deer and birds. The birds that flew too close fell from the sky.

Hitting the land, their bodies impacted as piles of ash, their life force adding to her meal.

Soon, she thought. Soon she would gorge on this world.

37

THE SMALL MAN SAT ON his mount on the ridge and watched Maya disappear into the forest. When the big man halted in his pursuit of her, a smile touched the lips of the observer. With a whispered order, the troop of men moved forward. Soon, a small detachment of them moved in the direction Maya had disappeared, while the bulk of men headed toward the hidden encampment.

* * * * *

WHEN TECK MOVED BACK INTO the tunnel, three impatient faces waited for him. He stepped to the side and walked to his quarters.

"Where is she?" Lord Bathsar inquired.

Without turning, Teck answered, "She needed some time alone."

The lord grabbed him by the arm and spun him around. Teck wrenched his limb out of Bathsar's grip as his face became a hard mask.

"Do you really think alone and in the forest is the safest place for her to be? You can't be that dense." The two men stood toe to toe, neither willing to give an inch. Teck knew Maya wasn't safe in the forest, but his pride wouldn't allow him to admit he'd lost her. The more the older man pushed, the harder Teck pushed back.

Patrick stepped up beside the men and, with gentle hands and words, got them to step back from each other.

"My lord. We'll go out and find her. Perhaps we could give her a moment to clear her head. The information she's been given is a lot for her to take in, I'm sure." Patrick spoke to Lord Bathsar in such a way as to turn him from Teck and the look that still colored his face. The last thing any of them needed was for the relationship between the two men to erupt into violence. With an inner sigh, he thought of them as two bulls in a field—neither willing to give the other any space.

Lord Bathsar nodded in agreement when he looked up. Spinning, looking left and right, he stopped and yelled, "Where is he? Where is the warrior?"

The three men whipped around, only to realize Sentinel had disappeared.

* * * * *

MAYA STARTLED AT THE SOUND of footsteps coming through the brush behind her. She'd been so lost in memories, she'd only just noticed the presence.

Spinning on her knees, her hand already pulling her hunting knife from the sheath at her waist, she stopped. The warrior advanced, looking down without expression.

"Leaving the shelter of the encampment is not wise."

Turning back toward the stream to again plop fully down, Maya did her best to ignore him. Silence stretched out and still neither of them spoke.

When birds took flight in a noisy explosion of wings and calls, Maya looked up and saw the warrior was at attention. Rising to her feet, she once again gripped the handle of her blade.

"Come," the warrior said and, without waiting, stepped into the trees and brush, leading her in a circular path back to the encampment.

Sentinel grabbed her arm and pulled her down among the briars and grasses. Just as she was about to ask him what he was doing, she heard the unmistakable sound of horses and the creaking of saddles.

Crouching even lower, eyes wide, she watched as a troop of men passed closely by their hiding spot. She recognized their red-and-black uniforms as those of the soldiers in the city. The ones protecting the temple. She realized how foolhardy it had been to leave the hidden settlement, and how lucky she was that Sentinel had come after her.

After the group of horsemen passed them, she and Sentinel rose to their feet. They checked behind them every few moments as they made their way back to the camp.

Watching where she placed each step, Maya followed

Sentinel until they approached a hilltop overlooking the hidden doorway. Dropping to their bellies, the two crawled to the edge of the drop-off. Below them, swarms of mounted men milled around. Amid them was the small man from the city. He was speaking with another man, gesturing with his arms and pointing to the forest, but they were too far away for the conversation to be heard. Once, the small man stopped his yelling and pacing and stared at their hill. Maya's breath caught, and though she knew he couldn't see her at this distance, she still felt as if he stared right at her.

At a shouted command, the men dismounted as one and moved up the hill toward the door to the encampment, pulling their swords from the housing on their hips. The collective sound echoed up the hill, and Maya hunched her shoulders as if to avoid its cut.

"We must help them," she whispered to the warrior.

Saying nothing, Sentinel watched the army swarm the entry, his frame as still as if he were carved from stone.

Maya heaved an aggravated sigh and she ground her teeth, slapping her hands into the dirt. "If you won't help, *I will*." She moved to stand. Fast as a snake strike, the warrior grasped her arm and pulled her back beside him.

"Stay where you are, or they'll have you too," he hissed.

"We can't just sit here and let them be captured or killed."

He watched the activity below them. With a stoic expression, he looked up to the horizon and then at her.

"Please, Sentinel. We have to at least try. Teck is in there. My father. And Patrick. We can't just leave them. I won't just leave them."

Giving a curt nod, he said, "Come," and snake crawled backward down the hill.

When they reached the slope of the hill where they were concealed from the army, they stood and trotted the rest of the way. Reaching even ground, Sentinel turned and faced her.

"You wait here, and I'll find your family."

"No. Absolutely not. I'm going with you."

Sentinel's eyebrows drew together and the corners of his mouth pulled down. "It is unwise for you to follow this path."

"I'm going."

Staring at her for another moment, the warrior gave a curt nod and turned to jog through the forest. Maya stayed on his tail, almost running into him when he abruptly stopped. So intent was she on not being left behind, she didn't notice they'd reached the clearing by the hidden door. Now closer, she saw the evidence of the number of horses and riders. Grass that once stood tall, now crushed by hooves. The scent of broken greenery permeated the air to such an extent, breathing became difficult, and she thought she might sneeze.

The men guarding the entrance both fell with soft thuds when short blades hit them mid-chest. The warrior retrieved his blades and wiped them on the fallen men's cloaks to clean the blood. Sliding the blades back into hoops on his belt, he stepped over them and cautiously approached the door.

Maya followed him, stepping gingerly over the bodies, her eyes fixed on them. Her top lip curled. Getting used to dead men would take some time. Already, the crisp, coppery scent of blood assailed her nose and she caught her breath, holding it as she moved past them.

Coming up to Sentinel's back, she placed a hand on his bare shoulder and waited while he cracked the door. They stood together, silent, listening intently.

Sounds of fighting—swords clanging and men's groans of pain—came to them, but at a distance. The warrior looked her in the eye and then turned from her, pulling the door open so they could slip through.

Deeper into the tunnel, torches lit the walls. Sentinel and Maya crept toward the fighting. Maya's head swung back and forth, her eyes constantly on the lookout for Teck and her father. As they neared the first turn of the tunnel, the sounds increased in volume. Sentinel stopped and regarded Maya. She knew what he was thinking, but she wasn't going anywhere.

"Let's go," she whispered to him, and after a moment more, he moved around the corner.

The sounds and smells impacted her senses and almost overpowered her. Men lay dead or dying, coating the floor, their low moans coloring the air with despair. Blood flowed freely, and arms, legs, and still bodies blocked their way. After a moment of shock, Maya blocked out the carnage and began scanning for her men, breathing a deep sigh when she failed to see Teck, her father, or Patrick among the dead and wounded.

Continuing along the corridor, the warrior and Maya slid to one side or the other to stay well away from the fighting. Stepping over the debris of bodies and fallen weapons, they searched. As they sidled past a pile of bodies—a place where

men from the caverns had huddled up but still died—Maya
bent to retrieve a short sword. She felt better with the steel in
her hand—more capable and competent—although her ability
to use it was limited. The fighting men didn't seem to notice the
man and girl moving through the hallways, their attention on
the battles before them.

Past the dining hall, Maya dared to move into the main
room, but no living being resided there. Bodies littered the floor,
and after determining none were who she sought, she shook her
head at Sentinel and they moved on. Exiting the doorway, two
men coming down the tunnel confronted the warrior. Shifting
Maya behind him, he again pulled his long knives and engaged
the invaders. They were overmatched, even two to one, and
soon Maya and the warrior were stepping over those bodies.

Maya finally located Teck in their shared room. Five men
were backing him against a wall, their backs to the door.

Maya saw recognition on his face as he disappeared under
the marauders. She jumped forward to assist him, but Sentinel
thrust her behind him then stepped into the fray. The sound of
his blades clearing their scabbards cut sharply through the
room, drawing two of the men's attention. Leaving the assault
on Teck, they raised their weapons. His blades became a blur,
their whir a song, and he didn't slow his assault.

Maya's mouth gaped in awe as she watched the beauty of
his fighting skill. He was fluid motion, liquid death. Before the
two fell, two more rose to take their place, the third pulling Teck
up with a blade at his throat. Sentinel never paused as he
continued to play his instruments, the song they sang haunting

and devastating as the sharp cry split skin and drew final screams of pain. Soon, just the four of them remained alive in the room.

"Stay back," the lone enemy shouted. "Stay back or I'll slit his throat."

Wiggling and throwing himself backward, Teck couldn't dislodge the man and only managed to have blood running down his throat.

"I swear, I'll—"

The twang of metal cut off all other sounds. Teck looked over his shoulder at the man, now impaled on a sword that ran through him and into the stone wall. Confusion froze the man's face.

"Are you insane?" Teck yelled, advancing on Sentinel. "You could have killed me."

Passing Teck, the warrior gripped the hilt of his sword and yanked it from the man and wall with a hard grunt. The body slid down the wall, leaving a red smear behind. Turning, Sentinel walked past Teck again to take Maya's arm.

"We must leave this place."

"My father. We must find my father."

Pulling her toward the door, Sentinel muttered, "He'll find his own way. It's time to leave."

Looking over her shoulder, Maya caught Teck's eye and he hurried to catch them. Within a few moments, the three of them left the tunnels behind.

38

ONCE AGAIN, CASSANDRA PACED THE ramparts of the castle. The girl was on the move and Sentinel was free. Neither of these things mattered, because she still had one secret advantage, one asset that not even Caleb knew of.

It had been a long time coming but was soon to be free.

A bracing wind blew over the walls of the castle, chilling her skin. Cassandra turned her face into it and reveled in the sharp slap of it against her.

She would win. She would win because her brother and his champions were weak. She could never be defeated. This world, and all the others, belonged to her.

With the coming of Sentinel, she was sure Caleb's confidence was overflowing. But let them come. The Three and Three would come to be, but they would never become One. They would never unite because one of the players was hers. Just one bad fruit and the whole barrel was rotten. Without this one, they would never be strong enough to triumph over her.

The cat. Sentinel. Two of the pedagogues were released. But just a little longer and her plan would come to fruition. All the long plotting would pay off and she'd see her brother crushed.

39

MOVING SWIFTLY THROUGH THE FOREST, the trio didn't think too hard about where they were going. It had been many hours since they'd fled the tunnels, and the only truth each of them knew was they were alive.

Maya forced her feet to keep moving and kept her eyes on Sentinel's back. She couldn't think anymore, the needs of her body a raging presence in her otherwise-numb existence. She pushed on, a force of will the only thing keeping her on her feet. Where they were going, she didn't know, and at this point she didn't have the energy to care. Later, when she'd fed her body and rested, she would wail at the injustice of losing the father she'd just found. But for now, she concentrated on placing one foot in front of the other.

Teck moved around and ahead of her. Jogging slightly, he stepped up to Sentinel and grabbed his arm, swinging him around.

"We need to stop. We need to find food and water. We need rest."

Pulling his arm away, the warrior turned and continued.

"Hey!" Teck yelled, but he got no reaction. Maya walked around Teck and followed Sentinel.

Teck stopped her with a hand on her arm. "Maya, we need to stop. We need water and food."

Maya looked at him through eyes glazed with exhaustion. In the back of her mind, a buzzing had begun. She couldn't hear herself think. If she stopped, she might not get started again.

"We have to keep going, Teck. We have to follow Sentinel," she mumbled and turned.

With a clench of his jaw, Teck followed them up the hill.

Not long after, Maya's head jerked up. Water. She could smell water. Glancing at Sentinel, she watched his path change. He smelled it too. Within another few hundred feet, the group cleared a tree line and found a quickly running stream.

Maya walked past Sentinel, down the bank, and right into the stream. When she got to the middle, she squatted and drank water scooped into her hands. The cool, fresh liquid filling her mouth and running down her parched throat was one of the best things she'd ever experienced. Her body opened to take in the liquid, energy returning to her worn muscles, lungs, and brain.

"We can't risk a fire tonight, but I will search for food."

Maya watched Sentinel rise from where he'd been drinking to move into the forest. Catching Teck's eye, they stared at each other, exhausted.

Finally, Maya sloshed her way back to the bank. Plopping down beside Teck, she rested her head on his shoulder.

Questions about the little man from town ran through her head. How did he find them? Where were they to go now?

After a time, the sound of footsteps came from behind them. She and Teck turned with what energy they could muster as Sentinel moved out of the forest. In his arms, he carried a variety of the wild's bounty—nuts, roots, and berries. It wasn't much, but it would have to do for tonight.

Sitting at the edge of the trees, the warrior beckoned Maya to join him. When she moved to him and sat, Teck followed and they consumed all he had found. Teck soon fell asleep against a tree and Maya laid her head on his lap. The warrior sat and watched the night descend.

The next day they would begin weapons training.

40

TWO MONTHS LATER, THE TRIO wandered into a small forested community. Life on the run, moving constantly, living off the land, seeing other people few and far between, and continuously training—sword, knife, and hand-to-hand—had altered who they were or could be. For weeks they'd traveled, constantly moving to avoid detection.

During this time, Teck made another bow and a number of arrows for hunting game, but nothing so fine as the one lost in the tunnels. He thought to try to create another for Maya but each day, watching her train with the warrior, his heart hardened. Each day she became better and better with the twin blades until their song called to her, too.

Maya now practiced with two swords of her own. Weeks ago, while passing through another small community, they stayed the night. Sentinel had the blades forged for her. The look on her face when presented with them had Teck catching his breath and remembering an evening at the cabin. She had traced a soft finger over the bow he'd created for her, her eyes alight as they were at the sight of the swords. The gifting of the blades, he knew, was the beginning of the end for them—for the life he had hoped to have with her.

Now, as the people in this small town either stepped out of different storefronts to watch them or, in some cases, scurried to hide as they passed, Teck realized how they would appear. Their path moved almost as a circle that would bring them back to the city that they had fled so long ago. Battle-hardened and dusty from travel. Their eyes were suspicious and wary.

It was unusual for them to venture into a community, but their stock of provisions had become dangerously low, and game was scarce. If they could do some bartering in this town, they would be able to set off again with full bags.

When Sentinel paused and turned to enter a shop, Maya and Teck fell in line behind him. He wasn't their leader, but they had made a habit of moving as one. A bell above the door jingled as they entered, but inside, silence reigned. The only break in the hush was the scuff of their shoes on the hard plank flooring.

"Ah . . . help you folks?"

Teck and Sentinel stopped their exploration of the shop to look at the speaker. With a smile on her face, Maya approached the man behind the counter.

"Good morning."

He smiled at the girl and her pleasant greeting while still keeping an eye on the two men. "Good morning, miss. There something in particular you might be lookin' for?"

"Yes, sir. We'll need provisions. Interested in some

bartering if possible." She engaged him, drawing his attention from the men. She'd found, in the past few months, that people were more trusting of her than of her companions. She needed this man relaxed and willing to trade.

"Well and sure, barterin's a way of life in these here parts. Question is, what you got to trade?" When he continued to look her in the eye and not peruse her body as some men would have, she decided to take his question at its face value. They might be able to make a short stop in this town.

"If you need any heavy lifting done, my two companions and I are able to put in a good day's work. I'm a fine hand in a kitchen, too, if you'd be interested. Bake a mean pie." She smiled at him and, willing to be friendly, he smiled back.

"I might have something for you," he said, nodding. As he walked to the side of the counter and toward the rear of his shop, the man gestured. "Why don't you three come here and I'll show you. We'll talk terms."

MAYA DROPPED A LOAD OF lumber at the rear of the building and turned, wiping sweat from her forehead and neck. Looking back the way she'd come, Teck and Sentinel tore down the final wall to an old shed on the side of the store property. The owner needed the building gone — said something about expanding — but wanted the cut wood saved. He told them that if they could get the work done today and have the spot cleared, he'd get them supplied with flour, jerky, some stored vegetables from last harvest, and even a piece of fruit or two.

As they traveled, Maya had been searching for the right

plants to get fruit from, but this land was populated with trees and plants that didn't produce anything but nuts.

Just as she started back to grab another load of lumber, the back door of the shop opened, and a group of men stepped out. Among them was the owner of the store. He fidgeted but led the group to Teck and Sentinel.

Subtly, almost without notice, Teck moved to position himself within easy reach of his sword. Sentinel, never without his, crossed his arms over his bare chest and eyed the men. Maya stopped behind them to observe and placed her hand on the long knife in her belt.

The group of men cautiously approached the area, and without speaking, stood and gaped at Teck and Sentinel. For a long moment, no one said anything.

Finally, deciding someone needed to take the initiative, Maya walked up from the rear of the group. "Hello, gentlemen, can we help you with something?"

Almost as one, the group of townsmen turned and looked her up and down, only to turn back to her companions. Maya's back stiffened, and her jaw thrust forward at the obvious insult. Just as she was going to say something, Teck stepped up.

"What can we help you with? We have work to do here." His tone didn't brook any nonsense. All the men but one responded by dropping their eyes. Within their ranks, a tall man dressed finer than the others stepped forward. Maya shrugged and turned to find a close place to sit in the shade and listen.

With a quiver in his voice, tone deferential, he spoke directly to Teck. "Yes, sir. I'm Jonathan, the mayor of

Wealdhaven. We understand from Marcus that you and your companions are looking for work in exchange for traveling provisions."

"That might be true," Teck said, moving up to the group. "What do you propose?"

"Well now, sir. We have a slight problem we thought you might be able to help with."

The village men spent the next half hour filling them in on a band of cutthroats and thieves that habitually came to this small hamlet. While in town, they robbed, raped, and wrecked as much as they could. If lucky, the townspeople disappeared while they were there. It seemed the founding fathers had taken all they were willing to take.

It had been a while since the band had been to the village, but everyone knew it would be just a matter of days, if not hours, before they again crossed their borders.

"What does this have to do with us?" Teck asked as he turned from the men to seat himself on a pile of wood.

"Well, sir . . ." The mayor stopped and looked at his companions. He swallowed hard. When he turned from them, his mind seemed made up and he stepped to Teck. "We would like to hire you and this other fellow to rid us of this problem."

Teck looked from the man to Sentinel and then, leaning forward, elbow on his knee, he glanced at Maya with raised eyebrows.

"Gentlemen." Having drawn their attention, Maya stood and walked toward them. She stopped ahead of where Teck sat, now with him on one side of her and Sentinel on the other.

"What exactly are you proposing?"

Seeming to realize who was in charge, the men had the decency to look abashed but gave her their full attention.

"Um . . . well miss." Perhaps now playing to his audience, the mayor said, "Our women are sure scared with these men about. They're wantin' to leave and make a home somewhere else, but we've all"—he turned to include the entire group of men—"got time and blood in this town. It's ours, earned by us."

Nodding, she looked to her feet and then back at the men, catching each of their eyes. "As I said, what *exactly* are you proposing?"

When the mayor faltered, Marcus, the owner of the store, stepped forward. "We'd like those men dead, ma'am. Dead and gone. Out of our lives forever."

Maya waited to see if he or any of the other men would have anything to add to his proclamation. When they remained silent, she again nodded. "Let me speak with my companions." She turned from the men.

Teck was standing by the time she reached him and, with Sentinel, they moved off to the tree line.

"What do you think?" Teck asked.

Maya looked from one man to the other, her decision already made. "I think, I hate injustice and the evil taking advantage of the weak . . . and we need provisions."

TWO DAYS LATER, WHEN MAYA, Teck, and Sentinel pulled out of Wealdhaven, they each carried a new pack loaded with provisions. The service they'd paid, just one more day in their new existence.

* * * * *

ORSON AND A UNIT OF soldiers rode into the small forest community. It was prosperous and lively. People moved about, going from shop to shop or visiting with each other, and children ran through the streets playing.

In front of a store, men loaded a wagon with merchandise. Dismounting his horse, Orson heard banging and, following the sound, saw new construction going up right next door. The smell of newly cut timber filled his nostrils.

A man who seemed to be in charge noticed him. He wandered up to him.

"Howdy, stranger. I'm Marcus and I own the store right next door. Can I help you with anything?"

The man had an open, friendly face. Orson disliked friendly people. They always seemed to be hiding something behind those smiles. He thought it was too bad they were in a hurry, as he'd like to carve that friendly face from the man's skull.

Plastering on a smile of his own, the small man pulled out a sketched rendition of Maya. "I'm looking for this girl. She will be traveling with a man—a large man with black hair."

The shop owner took the drawing and looked it over before handing it back to Orson. With a shake of his head, he said, "No, sir. I've never seen that girl."

"And you see everyone who passes through this town?"

"Yes, sir. Seems that everyone stops at the store. Everyone

needs something," he said with another grin.

Orson turned from him to regard the town and his soldiers. Taking a cloth from his jacket, he wiped the sweat from his brow and the back of his neck. He nodded. "Thank you for your time." Then he walked back to his unit.

"Remount!" he yelled.

The man, Marcus, stood for a bit watching the soldiers ride out of town. Even after they were out of sight, he continued to stare the way they'd left. Then, with a mental shake, he turned back to direct the men building the expansion to his store.

41

THE SUN'S DESCENT COLORED THE world in yellows and reds as Teck skinned a rabbit and tended the fire.

A woman, he thought. *I've become a woman.*

Too much had happened during their time in the woods. Too many changes. He'd changed—and not for the good. And during that time, Maya had changed. Not only physically— becoming leaner and stronger—but mentally. She rarely confided in him anymore. They were no longer a couple. She and Sentinel were as one, and he found himself alone in their group.

The clang and rasp as sword met sword drew his attention. Looking up from the spit where a rabbit sizzled, he watched her fluid movements. His breath caught and he had to turn away lest he do something rash. He missed her. He missed their time together.

Unable to keep his gaze from her, he again turned to watch. Mesmerized by her ability, his heart ached. How beautiful she was. More than ever before—a force to be reckoned with. He had every faith she would find her mother, take back her heritage, and free this land. He just didn't think he'd be there to see it. He didn't think he could.

Lost in his thoughts, Teck didn't at first realize the sparring session had ended and that the fighters now approached him. The sound of their voices, low and jovial, broke his reverie. They squatted by the fire, drinking water and cleaning their blades. Neither of them spoke to him or thought to include him in their comradery. They tore into the rabbit without thought of thanks. Not that it mattered, as thanks was not something he would accept, his new position in their group a thing of shame.

When Teck rose and moved into the night, neither noticed nor tried to stop him, their minds full of the mastery of their art form.

TECK WATCHED THE SUN DESCEND, his thoughts on their camp and whether he would be returning to it for the night. When a twig snapped behind him, he turned to see Maya walking through the brush. It surprised him she had sought him out— that she'd even known he was gone.

"Teck, there you are."

He turned away from her. To see her, to remember her, caused him pain. "What can I do for you, Maya?" His voice was low and brisk.

Maya sat beside him. He felt her watching him, then she laid her hand on his leg.

"I didn't know where you'd gone. And then you didn't return."

With a quick glance in her direction, he mumbled, "I'm surprised you care."

"What's that supposed to mean? Of course I care." Taking his hand, she shifted fully to face him. "Teck. Tell me what's going on with you lately."

Teck looked at her, not sure what he could even say that wouldn't sound like he was whining or that would matter at this point. When the last of the daylight struck her hair, it caught his eye—maybe for the last time. His heart constricted. He missed how it used to be between them. Leaning in, Teck placed his lips upon hers. His pulse leaped when he felt her ready response to his kiss. He placed a hand next to her hip and the other around her small waist. Pulling her toward him, he lifted her and moved her forward. She straddled his lap and wrapped her arms around him, leaning into their kiss. As he rolled her to lie under him, his worry and angst for the future faded in his rising passion.

* * * * *

ROLLING FROM HER BLANKET THE next morning, Maya shivered. The fire was out and the morning frosty. Winter would soon be upon them. The camp was quiet, both the men already up, their blankets empty.

Reaching for her waterskin, she swished her mouth and took a long drink. Looking around the campsite, she wondered why Teck hadn't started a meal to break their fast. She recognized Sentinel's footsteps long before seeing him.

Glancing over her shoulder, her words caught in her throat. His eyes were intense, his mouth tight.

"What? What is it?"

Stopping to look down at her squatting form, the warrior said, "He's gone."

Maya scrambled to her feet. "Who? What do you mean, 'he's gone'?"

"Your man. He's left."

Spinning in a circle, Maya shook her head. He must be mistaken. Teck wouldn't leave her. He couldn't.

Hurrying to his blanket, she pulled it up to realize only a small extra blanket lay in his spot. She threw it aside and searched for his pack and bow—both were missing. Catching the vague sight of footprints in the grass, which were quickly disappearing as the sun rose, she raced into the forest, following the trail. She heard Sentinel behind her but continued to track Teck. In her head questions reverberated. She knew he wasn't happy, but why would he leave her?

She'd traveled about a mile, no longer following any trail, just walking blindly. When she stumbled, tears running down her cheeks, Sentinel stopped her with a hand on her arm.

"We need to go back."

"I can't," she cried, turning on him. "Don't you see? I can't just let him go."

Taking a step back from her, the warrior wore a blank expression.

"You go back and get our things," she said. "I'll track him. We should find him by nightfall." She glanced away from him, her mind already heading down the trail after Teck.

"I won't leave you, and we're not going to find him. He doesn't want to be found."

"Don't say that! He's not far. We'll find him soon."

"No, Maya." Placing an arm around her shoulders, the warrior turned her in the direction they'd come. With little force, he caused her to take first one step and then another away from the direction Teck went.

Looking over her shoulder, Maya resisted once more. Sentinel continued back toward camp, his restraining hand on her. Laying her head on his shoulder, Maya wept while Sentinel led them.

With no more words, they gathered their belongings. Packs loaded, bedrolls contained, weapons sheathed, they headed out. Their path led them away from the course Teck took. Maya couldn't help thinking she was moving farther from one destiny and closer to another.

42

THE FORCE OF STEEL MEETING steel reverberated up Maya's arm, causing numbness in her shoulder. By the time she'd parried and spun, she no longer registered the sensation. Kicking out, she tried to sweep Sentinel's legs out from under him, but he leaped over her and planted a foot between her shoulder blades, pushing her to the ground. Hitting face first, Maya rolled and, with a sword in each hand, bowed her body to spring to her feet. She was just in time to catch the arch of his weapon on hers. With a sideways twist, metal slid across metal, throwing sparks. She backhanded with the hilt of her weapon, catching Sentinel on the temple and driving him to the ground. Teeth bared in a feral grimace, she leaped on his chest and laid her sword along his throat.

Stillness reigned as they faced one another, inches apart, each panting for breath. This was the first time she'd bested her trainer, and the knowledge was only now slipping into her consciousness. Slowly, she came out of her battle haze.

Maya sat up on Sentinel's chest. Pulling her sword from the

proximity of his throat, she reached over her shoulders and sheathed each weapon. Standing, she stepped from him and then offered a hand.

Sentinel's gaze moved from her eyes to the extended hand. He grasped her wrist and, with her assistance, rose from the ground.

Later, Maya and the warrior ate their meal in silence. She gazed into their fire, lost in thought, but he watched her.

She was ready.

* * * * *

THE LITTLE MAN LOOKED AT his mount with a grimace. The girl continued to elude him, and without her, he was unable to return to the city of Berth and all its comforts. He and his men had been on the road tracking her for months, and if he had to get on this horse for many more days, he just might take a sword to it.

Twice, he thought he had her and twice she'd managed to slip through his grasp. His scouts came back with enough information to continue on her trail, but he'd long ago given up hope of a quick acquisition.

The time on the road plagued him. He dreamed of home and his soft bed and softer women. Time spent in his special rooms and how they had run red with the blood of his victims. Daily his gut churned with the hard, cold fare of travel. He wished for the time he had the girl in cuffs and wondered why he didn't work harder to keep her that way.

If he didn't find success soon, he feared his master would send another to take his place. When that happened, he would never be going home again.

He *must* find the girl.

43

MAYA'S ARMS FELT LEADEN, AND she could barely lift her swords to defend herself against the thrusts coming from Sentinel. The passion of before, the day she'd bested him, had eked out of her slowly, leaving this devastation. All her anger, all she'd come to feel from Teck leaving, had now turned to sorrow.

Why did he leave me? What could I have done differently?

The world seemed so faded and unimportant. She wasn't eating as she should, and when the warrior asked her opinion as to which direction they should head, or where to spend the night, she would shrug and look away from him. She knew he was getting tired of her apathy. She heard his sighs and perceived the looks directed her way, but she didn't have the energy to care.

Another day of travel was behind them, and now she sat on a log half watching Sentinel skin a hare for their meal. The evening was turning chilly, but even the meager heat of the fire held no appeal for her.

* * * * *

WATCHING FROM THE OPPOSITE SIDE of the flames, Sentinel wished Teck were here so he could run him through with his sword. When Maya's emotions were blunted, Sentinel's were at their most intense. This was unacceptable. He needed to find a way to break Maya's despondency. They needed to be training. Just because she'd beat him once didn't mean she didn't need to practice anymore. How could he get through this barrier she'd erected?

Moving the rabbit from the center of the heat, Sentinel stood.

"Come." He pulled his swords and walked away from her to a small clearing.

May looked up from the fire, watching him until he turned to face her. She glanced into the fast-approaching dusk. Insects began to swarm, and a breeze picked up.

The swoosh of metal through air caught her attention, and her gaze shifted back to the warrior. He stood and stared at her, daring her to come and play.

With a deep sigh, Maya pushed to her feet. Slowly, she wandered to her bedroll and belongings and, stooping down, grasped the hilts of her swords. She'd been taking them off as soon as they made camp—a new habit on her part. Standing, she again faced Sentinel. Her arms felt like lead weights, and the last thing she wanted to do was raise the weapons. She glanced longingly at her bedroll.

Moving within range, she ducked and stepped back when he swung at her. Her eyes felt tired and heavy, her limbs laden. Swinging again, the warrior's sword came within inches of her face. She jumped back from it, her heart thudding. Again and again, he swung, and she stepped back until he threatened to drive her into the surrounding forest. A final thrust had her tripping over a tree root. Her instincts kicked in. She caught her weight on one crouching knee and stopped the plunge of his sword with the blunt edge of hers. Twisting her wrist, she forced his blade away and pushed to stand. When he again swung, she caught the force with hers and began to drive him backward. Her emotions dissipated as her brain took over. She could see their battle as if from afar and, in a nanosecond, was able to compute his next move. Thrusting and parrying, she continued to drive the warrior back across the clearing. Sentinel watched her face and body, and a small smile lifted the edges of his mouth.

Maya felt the flow of the battle, and a warmth filled her that had been missing for days. The clang of steel on steel and the dance of battle forced out the despondency left by Teck's absence. Her mind and heart turned to this new warmth and embraced it.

When she stepped forward to parry with one sword, she brought the other around to catch him. Sentinel moved with her, his weapons catching hers as they flowed like a river across the clearing. Unable to find an opening in his defense, Maya's frustration grew, and her senses constricted to a pinpoint and then opened wide.

The burn of her magic ignited and flowed through her blood. She could see and feel everything. It was as if she were a part of every tree that encircled the glade, looking up from each blade of grass they moved on and around. She felt the sun and breeze on a hundred different surfaces and heard the call of birds and the sounds of their battle from the perception of a hundred different individuals. Her breathing calmed, and her heartbeat slowed. She began to move faster, her motion fluid, her strikes fierce.

* * * * *

SENTINEL MOVED BACK AND THRUST as Maya worked her weapons on him. He knew she was growing frustrated with her inability to breach his defenses. Soon he would have her. Patience was his ally. She was still young and inexperienced. Losing today would be a good lesson in keeping one's head.

When Maya's breath altered imperceptibly, his hands tightened on his swords and his eyes narrowed. For a moment he watched, waiting to see what might happen, and then the girl began to move faster. A burst of light had him squinting and drew his attention from monitoring the motion of her body mass and swings. Only instinct kept him in the fight when her eyes shone a bright blue.

Faster and faster her swords flew until they were just a blur. Almost running backward, defending where he could, Sentinel shouted, "Maya," and louder, "*Maya!*" when she didn't respond to the first.

When she skidded to a halt, Sentinel kept moving until only a dozen feet separated them. Grasses and vines shot out and wrapped around his legs. He wavered as he caught his balance, unable to move his feet. Only then did he realize the clearing was smaller. The trees had pulled toward them, blocking out a rim of the evening sky. It seemed as if the air were being sucked into a vortex, and they were in the middle.

"Maya," he said gently. When the girl blinked rapidly and shook her head, Sentinel's breathing eased.

"Wha—What happened?" She touched her forehead with a shaking hand. Raising her gaze, she looked at her mentor.

When her eyes returned to their normal color and brightness, he heaved a loud sigh. The brambles and vines fell from his lower limbs and he was able to approach the girl.

Maya rubbed her eyes. "What just happened?"

With a shake of his head, Sentinel touched her arm. "I don't know, but we need to figure it out. It will make a powerful weapon in the war."

44

MAYA WOKE TO THE CALL of a rooster. She blinked. The noise confused her as it seemed unusual in the city, but here it was and here she was. The city of Berth.

Light snuck under the tattered curtain covering the lone window in the room she shared with her mentor. Last night, they'd made their way into the city. When they'd first walked the streets, people stopped to stare, and Maya quickly realized it was the warrior drawing their attention. His look was exotic, unusual, and many of the citizens had never seen one such as him. With no desire to be discovered, Maya led them down an alley. She took two cloaks for cover from a line.

But their precaution came too late.

Circling down a street, Maya and Sentinel were hemmed in by several men. Maya couldn't tell if they were friend or foe. The men watched them closely, their actions jumpy, but their faces gave away little or no emotion.

Stepping toward the wall of the alley, Maya and Sentinel threw off their cloaks, the swirl of cloth through the air a harsh sound. They pulled their swords and covered each other's back. Maya caught the glint of the late afternoon sun off the edge of one of her weapons, and an eagerness filled her. With a twist of her wrist, she spun the hilt, causing the blade to cut through the heavy air, calling its song of death and destruction.

"Wait." A man stepped forward with a placating motion. He moved closer, holding his hands up, palms forward. "My name is Manuel. We're here to help you."

Maya kept her stance, weapons at the ready, knees bent. She felt the heat of Sentinel at her back and heard his steady breath.

"Who sent you?" she spoke in a loud, growling voice.

"My lady, your father is in the city. We have been watching for you for months."

In the past year, Maya had grown distrustful of many things, and now, she was not willing to give these men the benefit of the doubt though for a moment her heart jumped with the promise that her father was alive. Even though it was some time ago, her experience in the prison was fresh in her mind, and she had no intention of repeating it.

"How do I know I can trust you? That you come from my father?" Her eyes shifted from face to face.

"Your sire, he said to tell you, 'We search for Sylvan.'" The tension in the small space felt thick. She caught Sentinel's eye. He waited also, allowing the decision to be hers.

After a moment, Maya dropped the tips of her weapons, signaling for the warrior to do the same. It was time for them to trust someone. They couldn't wander the city with no direction. Sheathing their swords, Sentinel and Maya stepped forward into the group of men.

NOW THEY WERE AT AN inn and she had yet to see her father. The only information given to her was that he had gone out into the surrounding communities to talk with the leaders.

Waking in her room alone, she lay still, contemplating what would be expected of her. With no answers forthcoming, her mind slipped easily to thoughts of Teck.

She couldn't get her heart or head around the fact that he'd left her—and done so without a word of good-bye. All she could do, the only way to survive, was to push the feelings far down into the bottom of her being and concentrate on the search for her mother. And the destruction of her uncle.

Climbing from the bed, she peered out the window for a moment, watching the bustle on the street in front of the inn. This was a busy place. They would have to be extra careful not to be seen by the wrong people.

The soft swish of the door opening behind her had her looking over her shoulder, her hunting blade already leaving its housing. She reseated the knife as a smile lit her face.

"Hello, priest."

"My lady," he breathed and moved into the room, his shoulders slumping in relief. "It is so good to see you. We didn't know where you'd gone."

Nodding, she stepped toward him. "You've been with my father?"

"Yes. We had to flee the caverns, but your father wouldn't leave without you." He shook his head and looked down before again meeting her gaze. "I'm sorry, my lady Maya, but I finally convinced him to leave even though we didn't know where you were."

Maya stared at the priest and he was again unable to meet her gaze.

"Think nothing more of it, Patrick. We're all here and quite well." Turning from him, she grasped her primary weapons and slung them across her back then headed for the door. "Will I see my father today?"

"Yes, he and the council will meet by noon and then they wish to speak with you." He hurried after her as she left the room. "Is Teck with you? I didn't see him this morning."

Her stride caught for just a moment, then she hurried down the stairs. Her words carried back to him. "No. Teck is gone."

WHEN MAYA LED THE PRIEST into the hallway, noise from the common room filtered up the stairs and hit her like an invisible force. Though almost undefinable, she knew the sound was of many people. People eating, talking, and even at this early hour, drinking. It was a common enough sound, familiar to all inns and taverns. It took her back to the first evening in this city. When she and Teck left their room to find dinner. The volume increased for a moment, and the pain in her heart swelled with it before dissipating. *He left me*, she reminded herself. He was the one without the courage to see this through. Tightening her jaw and straightening her shoulders, she waited for Patrick and then walked with him into the crowd.

Maya's eyes swept the group. All men, she observed, except

for a few serving girls. They hustled among the males, agilely sidestepping when necessary to avoid the off-hand pinch or rub.

The sound of a door opening caught her attention. Swinging around, Maya saw her father enter with four unknown men. He hurried forward and laid gloved hands on her shoulders, gazing into her face.

"Maya, my dear," he whispered before kissing her cheek. When he pulled back, she swore there was a tear in his eye.

"Father." She nodded at him and then scanned his face, her lips turning up in a smile. "It is good to see you again. I'm glad you are well."

Keeping a hand on one shoulder, Lord Bathsar turned to the men he had entered with. "Gentlemen, may I present my daughter, the Lady Maya."

The men all dipped their heads in respect, but they threw furtive glances at the hilts of the swords peeking over her shoulders. While her father talked of their escape and trip to the city, she blatantly eyed the men of the council. Their gaze shifted from her weapons and fell to their feet. No warriors, she noted. Politicians. Spokesmen. What good would they be in the battle to come?

"I have something for you, my dear," her father said, his words drawing her attention.

"You do?" She couldn't imagine what her father might have for her. His hand rose and, with a nod, Patrick went back up the stairs. She scowled at him and then turned back to her father. "What do you have for me?"

"You'll see. It'll be just a moment."

Her attention was caught by the conversation between some of the council members after a while, so she didn't notice Patrick until her father spoke to him.

"Thank you, Patrick."

She turned to her father and the priest, a small smile playing around her mouth. When she saw what her father held, the blood drained from her cheeks, and despair drew a knot in her throat.

"I found it in the tunnels. I knew I would see you again. I would never have given up until I found you."

Maya took the bow from her father. Her fingers tingled when she touched it. She couldn't believe he had it. That he'd found it and kept it safe.

"Father . . ." She stumbled over the words of thanks. She'd thought it lost and had hardened her heart against the pain of not only losing Teck, but his gift. Now here it was. Her heart thumped, swelling within the housing of her chest, and a flush colored her cheeks.

"I know how much this bow means to you. And Teck. Won't he be pleased to see you have it again?"

Maya didn't answer. All the hurt and anger at Teck's leaving surged back into her. Her father said something else, but the roar in her ears drowned out everything.

"Maya," her father said, touching her arm. Giving herself a mental shake, she again gave him her attention and raised an eyebrow.

"I asked where Teck is."

She turned from him. "Teck is gone."

"Gone?"

The front door opened, admitting a burst of sunlight, fresh air, and her warrior. All talk in the room ceased except for a few startled gasps from the circle of councilmen. She ignored them and intercepted Sentinel's path to her.

He pulled back the hood of his cloak. As he leaned into her, his gaze ran over the bow.

"There are no whispers of your mother." Pausing, he scanned the room, causing more than one set of eyes to drop. "But the people are oppressed. They all fear the temple and what it contains."

"My uncle."

* * * * *

THE SMALL MAN LOOKED AT the body of the soldier at his feet. Slowly, he leaned to wipe the blade of his knife on the dead messenger's cloak.

Straightening, he breathed in and held it for a moment. Releasing the air, he turned to the waiting men.

"Mount up," he ordered, and they scurried to obey him.

Finally, he thought, they'd head back to the city. According to the messenger, the girl headed that way. He preferred to enter the city with her bound and in his custody, but maybe, he could catch her before her presence was known. Then it could be he who gave her to his master.

Mounting his despised horse, his lips turned up in a smile. No matter what, soon he'd be back in his house. A long bath, good meal, soft woman, and fresh bed were all in order.

45

MAYA AND SENTINEL MOVED LIKE wraiths down the darkened streets toward the temple.

An hour ago, a message had come in. Amid a battalion of guards, a prisoner had been delivered to the temple. Somehow, Maya knew it was her mother.

While her father and the council quarreled about what to do with this information, she and the warrior slipped out of the tavern. They'd head to the temple and see what could be discovered.

Moving street to street, sometimes taking alleys when the thoroughfares became occupied, they slipped silently toward the center of town. Cloaked and hooded, they more closely resembled shadows than people.

Almost within sight of the temple walls, a commotion reverberated down a lane. Many people talking. And another sound—low and guttural.

Maya stopped in her tracks, her head cocked. Something. There was something in the sound. It made her heart pound.

Sentinel stood a few paces beyond her and looked back. She angled down the lane and followed the sounds of revelry, Sentinel on her heels.

Stopping in front of a large paneled door, she listened to the sounds within. Laying her hand on the wooden portal, she leaned forward then swung the door open, and the volume intensified. Sentinel followed her inside.

A sudden cheer arose. Catching Sentinel's eye, Maya headed forward. The hall she entered was dark with a glow at the far end. When she cleared the doorway, Maya looked down into a room. A fighting pit was at its center. A horde of men surrounded it—drinking, placing bets, or arguing in loud voices.

Her eyes and ears took in everything, every nuance. Somewhere must be a hint as to why she was drawn to this location.

The crowd quieted as a man stepped into the middle of the ring.

"Betting is closed. White box. Black box. All bets are closed." And then he walked to the side where other men assisted him out of the pit.

With swirls of sound and motion, curtains were pulled from boxes on opposite sides of the arena. Maya's breath caught in anticipation, but the pit remained empty. Nothing rushed from the boxes.

Behind and around the crates, men took long staffs and jammed them into the boxes. Whatever was housed within did not want to come out.

With a growl and snap, a huge, dirty white dog leaped from the box to the right. It turned and snarled at the men who jeered and brandished their sticks. The crowd roared in appreciation.

With her heart in her throat, Maya's eyes pivoted to the other box, somehow knowing what she would see. Her breathing was loud in her ears as all other sounds muted. Time seemed to slow as first a snout and then the whole gray dog stepped from the box.

"Rory," she breathed, her shoulders collapsing with the expulsion of air.

He was much worse for wear, the last year showing on his frame and in his eyes. Thin to the point of emaciation, his hip bones protruded, and his shoulder blades were prominent in his movements. But his eyes. In his eyes was the glow of kill or be killed.

The white dog snarled and leaped forward. The gray pivoted, and they circled each other. Each dog snapped and snarled, trying time and again for the other.

The roar of the crowd waxed and waned with the movement of the dogs.

Then, there was a blur of motion—too fast for the eye to follow—and the white dog lay with blood streaming from its throat at the gray's feet. The crowd fell silent and then burst into cheers and boos. Some had won and some had lost.

What had he become? Maya wondered. What had they done to him?

Without a thought, she stepped forward and dropped to the floor of the arena, dust rising around her. The big, gray dog swung his head in her direction and all conversation stopped. Loud in the room was a low rumbling coming from the throat of the brute.

Slowly, deliberately, he turned in her direction and began to stalk her—head down, his growl gaining volume.

"Rory," she said, and dropping to one knee, she held out a hand.

The dog didn't give any indication of hearing her or acknowledging she might be something other than another adversary.

Maya's brain spun. How could she get through to him? Why didn't he recognize her? Then it came to her. She was still cloaked and hooded. What scents she carried were many.

Carefully, she reached to untie the lacings of the cloak at her throat. Sliding back the hood, she pulled the garment from her frame. The dog had begun to circle her, and she shifted slightly to keep a wary eye on him. Her pulse hammered when the dog issued a low keen.

"Rory!"

* * * * *

THE BEAST, WHICH WAS ONCE Rory, watched the being in the arena. He could still taste the blood of victory on his tongue and knew he would soon kill again. She spoke, but he didn't know the language, didn't understand the words—he was drowning in the call of his need. *Kill*, it said. *Kill and fight another day.*

Moving to the side and rear of the person, he watched as

she pushed back a hood and pulled off a cloak. That was good. So much easier to get to the throat.

"Rory," she said, and the stalking paused, the growl halting in his chest. His eyes remained on the girl as the flesh at his nostrils twitched. Something, some memory, pressed at the back of his mind.

"That's it. That's a good boy. That's my Rory."

At the words *good boy*, the memory exploded in the dog's mind. The girl. *His* girl. Like sunshine leaking into a room, the memories pushed out the darkness of his existence. His whine, almost a moan, came low in his throat. Stretching his neck, he sniffed again in her direction.

* * * * *

MAYA'S MOUTH TURNED DOWN SADLY as the whine hit her ears. *By the gods*, she thought. *What have they done to my Rory?*

"That's it. That's a good boy." Stretching her arm farther, she called to him. "That's my Rory."

The dog's tail lifted to a more natural position, and his head came up from the attack posture he'd maintained as he advanced on her. Sniffing again, he walked toward her hand and gave the fingers a tentative lick.

Maya smiled, and a tear fell as she ran her hand along Rory's snout and head. Burying her fingers in his mane, she showed her trust by bringing her face up next to his and hugging him.

He was thinner than she thought. She needed to get him out

of here. The whispers about a new prisoner to the temple would have to wait. Rory needed her now.

Just as she pulled back to look him in the eyes, his gaze shifted to latch onto something behind her. Slowly, looking over her shoulder and then pivoting on her knees, Maya looked at the men entering the arena.

The announcer was in front, men with thick sticks stalking behind him.

"Who are you?" the first man shouted.

Standing, Maya placed herself between the men and the dog.

"He's mine. I'm taking him with me."

The man chuckled and glanced from his compatriots to her.

"The dog is mine, girl. He stays here, and you will leave, or we'll find a way to make coin from you, too." At his words, the men laughed and jostled each other in agreement.

Reaching over her shoulder, the sound of the blade clearing its housing was loud in the room. "I don't think so," she said. "Either step back or join the dead on the floor."

The men stopped laughing and looked at each other, waiting to see what their spokesman would do. When he moved forward, Maya's knees bent into a crouch, ready for battle. Something about the look in her eyes must have given him pause, because he didn't move again. Looking at the spectators and then back to Maya, he again chuckled and shrugged.

"Take the dog, girl. There are plenty more where he came from."

Maya waited another moment, her eyes glued to his face.

When his gaze fell, she returned her weapon to its housing on her back. Laying a hand on the dog's head, she glanced to her side and only then noticed Sentinel standing at the edge of the pit. He gave her a nod, and with a final look at the men, she walked toward him, Rory sticking to her side. When she reached the wall of the pit, she crouched to wrap her arms around the dog. Once, she never could have hoped to lift him, but this animal was far changed. He weighed almost nothing compared to what he once did—and she was far stronger than she once was. She faced the wall and the waiting warrior. Sentinel grasped the dog and pulled him onto the platform. After Maya retrieved her cloak, she accepted the hand he extended to assist her up. Within moments they were together above the fighting arena. Sentinel turned to head back the way they'd come. After giving the men and the fighting area one last cursory glance, she followed him, the dog staying close to her side.

46

PATRICK CRIED OUT AS ONCE again the pain erupted. It began each time in his center, near his heart, and spread throughout his body until it reached the tips of his toes and fingers. A moving entity slithered through his veins and nerves to branch out into every fiber of his skin. His entire frame felt as though it were being roasted over a fiery pit.

"Remember," the small man said, his eyes on Patrick. "You belong to my master. You will do as he says, or the punishment you receive will be far worse."

Patrick nodded vehemently, sweat flying in all directions. "Yes. Yes, I understand." Chancing a glance upward, Patrick watched the small man pace in front of him. With a burst of courage, his gaze flicked to the dais where Mikel Bathsar sat watching the torture. His face was blank, as if he were somewhere else.

"My lord. My lord, please," Patrick began and tried to crawl toward the landing. His scream echoed off the walls of the golden room, and he rolled into a quivering ball as the pain once again shot through him. But he had managed to gain Mikel's attention.

After a moment, Mikel said, "Speak."

"My lord. I am just a humble priest. I know nothing of the resistance, or of your brother."

A heavy sigh erupted from Mikel and he pushed himself to his feet to tower over the cringing priest. When he kneeled, Patrick shrunk back, trying to make himself small.

"If that is true, priest, and if you value your life, you'd better find some information."

Rising from his crouched position, Mikel Bathsar stood for a long moment over the prone man. Turning on his heel, he strode out the back entrance of the throne room and Patrick thought for a moment, a blessed moment, that it was over. He realized this was not to be when the pain began to again spread through his body. Before his scream filled the room, he heard a low chuckle of amusement.

47

MAYA WALKED BETWEEN HER FATHER and Sentinel as they moved toward the temple. Rory kept pace with her, his shoulder often rubbing her leg. Behind them filed uncountable men and women—the resistance.

The news of the new prisoner had traveled fast through the city and into the ranks of the rebellion. Even through all the gossip, little true information was known. And now the word was out that her uncle, Mikel, had a new queen. Some said she was deadlier than him, if that were possible.

The council's consensus was the resistance should hit hard and hit fast. Mikel and his new wife should be taken prisoner if possible, and if not, they would be killed.

As the group moved through the streets, playing children were scooped up by mothers and people ran inside to close and bar their doors and windows. Dogs barked or ran to hide and stare at the mass with tails tucked and heads down. The sounds of so many booted feet bounced off the stone walls to reverberate down the streets.

When the temple came into view, looming above the skyline of the other buildings, a murmur moved through the ranks. This place had a reputation that did much to undermine the confidence of the people who'd come to fight for their freedom. Too large a group to gather and speak with, the council, which included her father, simply looked at each other and continued.

When they rounded the final corner and the entry of the temple stood before them, it was to come face to face with a battalion of temple guards. Well trained and unremorseful, they were a different breed from the farmers and shop owners who faced them.

With a ringing battle cry, the temple guards rushed the mass of civilians. The resistance split in the middle as many ran in terror. But many stood their ground, the clang of steel against steel a testimony to their bravery.

Maya pulled her swords as she watched the first group of soldiers move toward them. She firmly planted her feet, shifting back and forth slightly to better ground her boots in the dusty road. With a battle cry of her own, she engaged the enemy and repelled them. On one side fought her father and on the other Sentinel as they made a secure area and covered each other's backs.

Stepping over the fallen, she chanced a glance about and saw Rory take down a man who tried to come at them from the side. No quarter was given as his time in the killing rings showed. Moving forward, cutting a swath through the men, Maya and those around her neared the temple stairs. Her blades ran bloody as she thrust and hacked to clear enough space to move forward. Just as she thought they might be successful in their bid for entry, a fresh battalion came at them from the alleys on each side of the temple stairs.

With a thrust in the belly of the soldier she battled, she pulled her sword free and sidestepped nearer to her father.

"We're being cut down!" she shouted at him.

With a quick glance in her direction, he acknowledged her words with a nod and began shifting toward a side alley.

"Maya!" he hollered and pointed with his chin toward the escape while taking down a soldier.

She caught Sentinel's eye and pointed to the alley. He nodded in response but continued to fight three soldiers who backed him toward the street. Maya jumped a body that was bleeding out and cut down one of the soldiers. Sentinel took off a head of one man and left the other screaming in the dirt holding a stump that sprayed blood where his forearm used to be. With their backs together, Maya and Sentinel began to move toward the alley. Maya caught sight of Rory amid the fighting and, giving a shrill whistle, had him running to join her.

She and Sentinel fought to reach her father who was battling a man at the mouth of the alley. They pushed and hacked their way out of the main fighting area in the street then paused within the alley to assess what direction to take.

"They knew we were coming," Lord Bathsar said aloud.

Sentinel nodded. "Yes."

"Come, let's make our way back to the council headquarters. If we weren't given up by someone who knew its location, it may still be secure. We need to get the council together and reformulate a plan." Maya's father turned away from the sights and sounds of battle and began making his way through the alley. Maya watched the fighting for a moment more, and then with a gesture at Rory, headed after her father, Sentinel close behind.

It was many blocks before the sounds of the battle faded. Maya and Sentinel continually turned to watch behind them. With their retreat covered by her and Sentinel, Lord Bathsar hurried to reach the inn.

The streets were mostly deserted as they neared the location where, for days, the council hid. It was as if the entire city were at the temple, hiding, or dead in the streets.

Pushing open the door, the only question on their minds was, what had happened?

THREE MORNINGS LATER, MAYA WOKE to the sound of deep breaths coming from the floor beside her bed. For a moment, she thought she was back at the cabin in the clearing. Safe from all the evils in the world. Then the light from the rising sun hit her face and she remembered where she was and what had happened. The room's sparse furnishings, smoldering fire, and locked door confirmed it. Turning over in her bed, she leaned over the edge to view the sleeping canine. He slumbered soundly. After a couple days of proper feeding and fresh water, and a good brushing to loosen the layer of filth on his coat, he was beginning to resemble the dog she'd raised.

That first night, he'd lain by the fire in the common room

for a time while she conversed with her father and the other men about plans for the next few days. Soon, she tired, and when she stood to head to her room, he was right with her. She knew she would never leave him again. No matter where she went, he would go.

Now, days later, leaning over the edge of the bed to watch the dog sleep, she was overcome by a bout of nausea so intense she had to jump from the bed and collapse beside the nearby chamber pot.

When she quit gagging, she wiped her mouth on the sleeve of her gown. A small whine caught her attention.

Rory's large brown eyes were curious and pleading.

"It's okay, boy. I'm okay. Just ate something off one of these last couple nights. I don't think the kitchen here is cleaned very well." Patting his head, with a small groan she rose to get a drink from the water pitcher then spit it into the pot. Picking up the chamber pot, she set it outside the door. She grabbed her clothes and dressed quickly. After purging her system, she felt normal.

"Let's get you outside and then get us something to break our fast." Rory seemed to agree as his tail wagged hard enough to move his lower body.

48

THE DAY OF THE BATTLE, the three survivors had entered the inn with hopes of finding the council intact. This was not to be. When it was obvious the tide had turned, the council had fled the field to regroup inside the walls of this tavern. Looking around at the bloody faces, the dawning realization came that over half of them were gone.

Some sat, a glazed look in their eyes. Some ranted as they moved about the main room, their blood still hot and vengeance in their hearts.

Lord Bathsar sent sentries out to watch for soldiers and runners to ascertain if the inn was safe. When the news came back in the affirmative, he set to righting the men surrounding him.

"Yes, my brothers. We have taken a mighty hit. But we must calm ourselves and formulate a plan."

"A plan?" one man yelled, his voice cracking with emotion. "What kind of plan can we make? You saw the army. How can we even begin to hope to stand against that?"

The other men roared in agreement, their fear a palpable entity that colored the room with a scent of rust.

Rising before the men, Lord Bathsar held up his hands. They would need to calm down so each could help devise a way to beat their common foe.

"Men," Lord Bathsar yelled. "Men, please. If you would only calm yourselves and quiet, we could begin to figure out a way to continue on our quest."

"What can we do?" An older man with a portly belly stood and gestured at him. "You talk and talk of planning, but when we do confront Mikel Bathsar, we realize we can't stand against him. He and his soldiers are too strong—too many." A rumble of agreement drowned out the protest Lord Bathsar would have made. "I for one," the man continued, "will be taking my family and fleeing from the tyranny and oppression of this city."

"And how far do you think you'll get?" he shouted to be heard over the commotion of the gathering. At his words, some of the men looked his way. "How far do you think you'll have to go to free yourself from Mikel's grip?" With no answer to his questions, the crowd of men looked at each other and then back at him. "It is here and now that we must make our stand. If we run now, we'll be running for the rest of our lives—and the rest of our children's lives."

"And what of his new queen?"

Lord Bathsar looked around at the faces, not sure who'd asked the question.

"She needs to die alongside him." His voice was quiet in the large room. Men stepped forward as if to hear him better. "The worst thing would be for us to allow her to live, only to find there will be an heir to Mikel's madness."

One man, an elder among his people, stood. "You speak casually of the slaughter of your family." He glanced at the men. "Not only your brother, but perhaps a child of his. Your own blood."

Lord Bathsar stepped toward the man. "I loved my family. A beloved mother and father. My in-laws. All of whom were slaughtered by a crazed brother. I know now, he can never be saved. His cruelty and insanity are bone-deep." Again, he scanned the room. "I don't say it lightly, gentlemen. Mikel and all his madness must end. We must end it."

The buzz of conversation rose again, but not to such uncontrolled heights. The men tossed ideas between themselves, tasting and rejecting concept after concept. Lord Bathsar moved among them, listening and contributing to each idea. He calmed one group and invigorated another. Maya watched her father from the back of the room, realizing what a natural leader he was.

When he walked up to Maya and Sentinel, he placed a hand on her shoulder.

"What thoughts have you, my daughter?"

Maya squinted and looked out into the sea of men, listening to them quarrel and discuss the situation they now found themselves in.

"I think my uncle is too powerful for a frontal attack. We need to consider another type of warfare."

"What are you thinking, Maya?"

"Perhaps a small party might be able to sneak into the temple. If we were able to kill Mikel and his new queen, everything would be in turmoil. With them gone, there will be a void. A void for the council to fill. The war would end before it even began."

Her father looked out into the main room without speaking for so long, Maya thought he might not have heard her. As she was about to restate her idea, he moved to look down at her.

"And do you know who you'd want to accompany you on this raid?"

The fact that he rightly assumed she'd be going filled her with pride. She'd become a force to be reckoned with. She could hold her own in the worst of battles and under the lowest of conditions. If he hadn't wanted her to go, she would have fought for the right.

"Let me give it some more thought. I need to come up with a real plan and not just the beginnings of an idea." Turning to Sentinel, she gestured to the rear of the room. He followed her without comment.

THE MEETING BROKE UP SOME hours later. Men filtered out of the inn, wary of being watched. The night was quiet, the noise and death of the battle long past. Sentries still prowled the area, on rooftops and down alleys. The men needed to stay vigilant for Mikel's retribution.

Inside the inn all was quiet. And Maya had a plan.

Once again, her thoughts turned to Teck. This would have been so much easier if he were with her. He had knowledge of the temple and talented fighting skills. Would she ever get over missing him?

MAYA WOKE EXCITED TO SPEAK with her father. In the act of dressing, she became ill again and purged the contents of her stomach. Her body felt weak and sweaty. Sitting on the edge of the bed, she slowly caressed Rory's head, her excitement abated. His fur and warm breath helped to calm her nerves.

Maya slowly made her way to the basin and splashed water on her face. She took up a cloth to dry herself. Rory stood and faced the door. When she opened it, Sentinel waited.

She spun back into the room, tossed the towel to the bed, and leaned over to grab her swords from the floor. The steel made a low scream as she set them into their housings on her back. Grabbing her long knife from beside the bed, she slid it into its sheath at her belt then spun to Sentinel and followed him out the door and down the hall.

The great room teemed with men, all vying for her father's time. Maya decided it would be best to catch him later when he became free. She clicked to Rory and headed outside to give him some time there. The dog sniffed around the building and down one of the alleys, lured by the scents of garbage and dead things. When she headed back toward the inn, he turned and trotted to follow her back.

On their way into the inn, after Maya swung by the kitchen to gather some meat scraps for the dog, she walked toward the main dining area, laughing at something one of the men in the kitchen had said. Sitting at a table across from Sentinel, she reached for a mug of water when the old woman whose husband owned the establishment set a steaming bowl of mashed oats in front of her. Placing an aged hand upon her shoulder, she whispered in her ear.

Tendrils of vapor rose from the bowl along with an earthy, appetizing smell. Though she stared at the meal, Maya's thoughts turned inward.

What could the old woman mean? That couldn't be right.

Her expression blank, Maya raised her head, wondering if Sentinel heard the woman.

Slowly, routinely, Maya grasped her spoon and began to eat the mash. The scent didn't lie, as the flavor was appealing and soothed a stomach she didn't know still ached. She consumed the meal, her thoughts in turmoil.

Thinking back, she counted the days, the weeks, since Teck left. It just couldn't be. This would change everything.

49

MIKEL STARED AT THE CROWD of men. As his eyes passed over them, they lowered theirs.

Good, he thought. *They are wise to cower. How could this rebellion have happened? And how is it they were unable to find the leaders?*

He looked at his queen. Finally, this beauty was his. And she was worth the wait. She had become so much more than he ever imagined. So much stronger. With her at his side, he would accomplish everything.

"My master."

Mikel Bathsar tore his gaze from the woman seated beside him. Of course, it would be him. The one man in the land who would dare approach him at this time. Orson.

"My master, I have a report from the outer edges of the city."

Mikel contemplated a time when Orson would become a problem. For all his loyalty and abilities, he may be becoming too bold. Shifting, he crossed his legs and reached toward his queen. He ran a finger over her pale hand where it rested on the arm of her chair.

"Speak, Orson. Tell me a tale that will satisfy my anger." He leaned forward. Orson looked into his burning eyes a moment longer and then dropped his gaze.

"The lookouts at the outer posts send word that none have passed from the city. The rebels must still be within the walls." Orson kept his gaze on the first step of the dais, his voice low and submissive.

"Good. That is very good." Mikel stood and began pacing in front of the thrones. His hands clasped behind his back, he watched the floor disappear in front of him, and when he turned, he continued on the same path again.

Stopping, he faced the crowd of men.

"General," he yelled. One man, in a shiny uniform with a long sword strapped to his hip, stepped forward. He was grizzled with sun and wind-worn skin but had the upright bearing of a lifelong soldier.

"Yes, my lord." Genuflecting, he stayed in a subservient position, waiting for Mikel to give him his orders.

Mikel waited for the men to stir in the silence—to think they could whisper among themselves. When one shifted from one foot to the other, he glared at him, and the man froze. Giving it a moment more, Mikel spoke to his general.

"Take a battalion, go house to house, building to building. Find the rebels."

"Yes, my lord." The general dropped to one knee.

When Mikel moved down one step, the general's head fell

even farther between his shoulders. In a cower, he waited.

"I want them brought back to the temple alive." Stepping down beside the general, Mikel leaned forward until his breath was against the man's ear.

"Do you hear me, General? I want them *alive*. I will have the pleasure of questioning them and granting their punishment."

"Yes, my lord. It shall be as you command."

Mikel stood straight and turned from him to stand before his queen. "Good, General. Good." He caressed the cold, pale cheek of the woman who sat before him. When she tipped her head, eyes locked on his, the blackness of her orbs made desire run through his frame. "You are dismissed. All of you."

The commotion behind him was quiet, but he knew the men rushed to clear the room. No one wished to gain his attention. All wanted to avoid his eye. As it should be. They would do his bidding, or they would pay. Perhaps he would give one of them to his bride. He so enjoyed to watch her at play.

50

RORY STRETCHED HIS NECK TO rest his nose against the girl's foot. She wasn't acting right, he could tell. Something was wrong with her, but he wasn't sure what it was.

When the old woman approached, he lifted his head to observe her but didn't otherwise move. The old woman said something to his girl and when she moved away, the leg he leaned against twitched. He issued a low whine and inched forward to resume his place with his nose upon her booted foot. Every time the noise level increased in the great room, his eyebrows shifted, and his sight moved toward the disturbance. He didn't know for what, but he was on guard. Taking his cue from his girl, he prepared to defend.

* * * * *

WHEN MAYA FINISHED HER MEAL, she took a deep breath, enjoying her calm stomach. She couldn't think about what the old woman had said. She would put it from her thoughts. She needed to finish her quest to find her mother and free the land of her uncle.

With this foremost in mind, she turned to locate her father. He sat across the room, visiting with some of the council. The priest, Patrick, sat with them. He leaned forward, his eyes rapt on the speakers.

With a lift of her leg, she turned on the bench and lifted her chin, standing to move to another empty table in the room. Lord Bathsar excused himself from the men he sat with and moved to join her. Patrick followed. Seating themselves at a table, Maya turned and gestured to Sentinel to join them.

When her mentor seated himself next to her, she paused to look the three men over. Almost absently, she touched Rory's head when he leaned out from under the table. Rubbing her thumb along the hard bone of his skull between his eyes, she felt the warmth of his breath and was thankful for his presence.

"I have a plan. I know how we can kill Mikel Bathsar, but we'll need the council's help."

Lord Bathsar nodded. "Yes. I will be able to rally them. Their egos took a hit with the defeat at the temple, but they must realize we need them to succeed."

Maya gave her father a small sample of what she would need from the council and their men. As she began to lay out the grander plan for him, the plan to get to Mikel, he stopped her.

He looked first one way and then the other to scope out the room. "We require privacy, more privacy than this, for this discussion." He gestured about the room, including the men who were part of the council. "Leave now and meet me in my quarters this time tomorrow. We'll discuss this in full and see if your plan has validity. I'll speak to the council."

Nodding in agreement, Maya stood, Rory moving quickly to escape from under the table where he rested. Sentinel shifted around to her other side, fingering the handle of his knife.

"Yes, Father. That's a good idea. I need you to tell me if there are errors in my thinking. To fail this time, I know, will mean death for us all." Her gaze flickered, and her hand lay on her belly for a brief moment.

Patrick leaned forward, his eyes moving from one to the other. When his glance chanced upon the dog, his gaze stopped. The dog was staring at him. Keeping his eyes on the man, a low growl issued from the dog, and Rory's upper lip quivered. Even from across the table, Patrick saw the hair rise on the dog's neck and back. A snarl vibrated in the dog's throat, and a chill moved up the priest's spine.

Patrick sat back, keeping his eyes locked on the canine.

Maya glanced at the dog, her eyes widening. "Rory," she admonished him. "Be a good boy. That's just Patrick. You know Patrick."

The dog calmed, but his gaze didn't shift from the priest. As Lord Bathsar and Patrick moved out of the room, the priest glanced over his shoulder at the dog.

Hurrying, he caught Lord Bathsar just as he rounded a corner. The streets were full of people selling wares and buying wares, with children running between them. It was as if the day at the temple had never happened. But Patrick knew better. It was his fault so many men and women lay in the street in front of the temple. So may corpses no one could claim for fear of being killed themselves. When the stench finally drove worshipers away, the soldiers came and gathered the bodies to burn. This left all the families without closure over the deaths of their loved ones. How was he to live with the guilt? And it wasn't over. Would it ever be over?

When Lord Bathsar entered another building, Patrick held the door for a moment, looking around them before slipping inside and pulling the door closed.

"Lock it."

Squinting in the low light, Patrick looked from Lord Bathsar to the men behind him. With a slight nod, he turned to throw the bolt and lock the door. He shouldn't be here. He didn't want to hear the plans these men made. When Mikel came for him again—and he would—he knew he wouldn't be able to withstand the pain. He'd talk. He was weak.

* * * * *

LORD BATHSAR LOOKED AT THE men who filled the room. The members of the council were present along with other leaders in the community. Leaders who had survived the bloody morning at the temple. He needed to enlist their help. But how to get their assistance without disclosing the entire plan? He didn't know all of Maya's ideas yet, but a distraction would be necessary. And these men would make a wonderful distraction.

"Men," he began, drawing all attention to him. "As you know, we suffered a defeat the other morning at the temple. But we are not finished."

A low murmur rippled in the room at his words. One man spoke up, stammering. "Lord Bathsar, you can't mean to say that we will be going back into battle."

"That is exactly what I am saying."

The murmur turned into a roar. Holding his hands up in a calming gesture, he shushed the men. Slowly they quieted but didn't calm.

"I tell you we can do this. And we *must* do this."

The noise level rose again at his declaration, but when he opened his mouth to again speak, the men quieted on their own.

"Mikel Bathsar *must* be defeated. The people and even the land on which they live will not exist much longer with him having free rein." Some of the men were nodding and looking to their compatriots, seeing if they also agreed.

"Obviously, a full-frontal attack is not the way to go." Lord Bathsar stepped from the raised platform on which he stood. He moved through the room of men, speaking loud enough for all to hear but making the conversation a thing between friends.

"I propose we prod at the beast of Mikel's army from the side. We will cause a disturbance within sight of the temple, but when soldiers come to confront us, we will lead them away. We will lead them into a larger force that will neutralize their threat. We will continue this with small groups until they change tactics—then we will change our tactics."

"To what end?" one man yelled out.

"Well, now, I'm not exactly at liberty to say. We'll be planning and plotting as we go, based on what the army does. We'll have to be thinking on our feet. Our plans *must* stay between us." Saying this, he looked each man in the eyes. He held their gaze for a moment before moving on to the next. "Our previous plan was leaked. Mikel knew of our coming. To triumph, we must keep this plan a secret."

51

MAYA NEEDED SOME TIME ALONE. She had so much on her mind that it felt as if her thoughts were going to explode and run out of her ears. She needed to think about her plan for her uncle, to think about her mother and where she might be, to think about Teck—why he'd left her and where he might be. And to think about her future.

Telling Sentinel she would be back in a moment, and telling Rory to stay, she walked away from them, concentrating on not hurrying—on making it appear as if everything were okay. As soon as she rounded the corner of the building, she broke into a run. People moved out of her way but turned to watch as she sped by them. She didn't know how far she'd run when her chest began to hurt, and the sound of her breathing was harsh in her ears. She pushed past the pain and continued to flee her ghosts.

When she pulled up alongside a building, she had to lean against it, bent over with her hands on her thighs to catch her breath.

Once she could again breathe normally, she looked left and right, scoping the area to determine where she was. With a deep sigh, she admitted that she was lost.

She looked up at the building she'd leaned against. It was taller than those around it—almost four stories. Down the street she spied a doorway into the building. Without stopping to think about it, she moved to the opening. The door wouldn't open. She threw her weight into it, and it gave with a screech of metal on metal. The inside was dark, but she didn't hesitate as she stepped over the threshold and pulled the door closed behind her.

She leaned her back against the door to give her eyes a moment to adjust to the darkness. Soon, she could make out large bundles, and by the smell, she guessed them to be baled wool. A storehouse then.

She moved carefully into the room. When the clouds outside cleared, a beam of light filtered in through cracks in the walls. Dust motes filled the light as if a universe of stars were playing in the small rays. Across the room, through the cubes of shorn wool, Maya saw a set of stairs leading up. She moved between and around the bales toward the flight.

When she reached the stairs, she stopped for a moment to survey the room. Above, she heard the sounds of doves cooing, and the burst of wings, but on the floor where she stood, it was as if she were the last person on the planet. She sighed, reveling in the feeling of finally being alone, of not having anyone watching her, monitoring her actions and reactions.

She slowly mounted the stairs, and when she reached the

second floor, she paused to scan it. More storage. Grain, it appeared. With her hand on the rail and her head up, she climbed the wooden steps. They gave subtly under her feet, but other than an occasional moan, they remained a silent witness to her passage.

When Maya reached the top floor, one that was completely empty but for a few balls of dust, she moved away from the staircase to wander the room. Across from her the sun broke through the splintered planks of a window shutter. The light spilled onto the floor and bounced to light the entire area.

Making her way toward the window, Maya pushed the shutters open. The vista of the city opened before her, making her catch her breath. Always within her was a yearning for the cool green of her valley, but here in this urban sprawl, she admitted it had a beauty all its own. The city stretched for miles, the rooftops a myriad of colors and shapes. Smoke rose from chimneys, making its way slowly to disperse in the sky. The tendrils of vapor belied the hints of a breeze by rising as straight as the chimneys from which they emerged.

The sun, just beginning its daily descent, shot rays to reflect upon surfaces of the city so they sparkled like jewels. Birds, feeding on the leavings of the human population, now took wing readying for their roosts.

Maya felt a calmness come over her senses as she peered out over the makeup of the city. Sitting, she leaned against the wall, her arm crooked on the windowsill. Exhaustion hit her as she laid her chin on her arm and enjoyed the fading sights and sounds of the district. Her eyes became heavy, her breathing deep and regular, until she dropped into sleep.

SOMEHOW, SHE KNEW IT WAS a dream, but still the fear of the unknown moved through her.

She moved like smoke, drifting through rooms floored with tile. In her dream it was completely silent. No footfalls announced her entrance into another room. No sounds of other people. Her breath caught, and her heart constricted. She knew this room, though her sight was indistinct as though she peered through a fog. A golden chair sat upon a dais and next to it another, like it but smaller. As she neared, a man rose from the larger chair. When he moved toward her, she tried to pull back, fear moving through her, but the mind controlling this body felt no fear.

His smile was evil, and her stomach clenched. When he held out a hand, as if to assist her, her own reached out. She stared down at the appendage, unable to control it, and gasped at the pale gray hue of her skin, the dark tints of her nails— overgrown and broken in places.

The man said something, his lips moving, but no sound invaded her dream. Raising the hand he held, he laid a kiss upon the back of it, looking at her with adoring eyes that held the stark gleam of madness.

Turning toward the chairs, he preceded her to the smaller one, her hand still held in his. When she turned and sat, he looked down on her for a moment before spinning to face the room.

Many men faced the dais. The man appeared to be

addressing them, his arms gesturing and his back moving as he took deep breaths—still she heard no sound. The men parted and a single man was pushed forward. He was terrified. He dropped to his knees, pleading.

The only reaction from the man facing them was to turn toward her and smile. When he reached a hand to her again, she read the word, "Come," on his lips and willingly reached to him with her gray, crooked claw. Her perspective changed as she stood and, looking out, saw the room was massed with bodies of men. All of them attentive to the front of the room.

Being led to the kneeling man, he was offered for her perusal. When she released the guiding hand of the man in charge and stepped down with the prisoner, all the men fell back from the two of them.

Reaching for his upturned face, she gently wiped tears from his cheeks. When hope began to filter into his eyes, she straightened and moved back. Her hands held out, she felt her throat vibrate as she spoke.

Fear saturated the kneeling man as a mist, black as night, seeped from her skin. It grew and surrounded the man whose mouth gaped in a silent scream. Faster and faster it swirled. It constricted until blood began to run from his nose, eyes, and ears. With a final move, she clenched her fists and the mist crushed the man.

Dissipating quickly, the mist left nothing but a broken remnant of what was once a living being. Blood stained the marble floor. As it moved and spread, men stepped back.

Maya turned her eyes from the sight to look at the man on

the dais. His face was split by a wide grin. Hopping down the step, he again took her hand. At his touch, Maya's dream self shuddered.

WAKING WITH A START, FOR a moment Maya didn't know where she was. The room was dark and her position on the wooden floor leaning against an open window made her body stiff. The full moon had risen above, and its light shone over the town, giving it the appearance of somewhere magical and mysterious.

Realization came seconds before she heard the door close on the ground floor. She tensed to stand, and the unmistakable click of dog toenails sounded on the stairs. With a stretch, she came upright, and seconds later Rory skidded into the room, making his way to her. He was followed closely by Sentinel. She should have known they would find her—this wasn't the first time Rory had tracked her.

"Sentinel," she said with a nod of her head.

"Maya," he replied. "You've been gone too long." When he walked across the room to her, she turned, and together they looked out over the city. The full moon shone on the rooftops, illuminating the buildings. When a shadow crossed the moon, Maya noticed a large owl swooping down to disappear into the street.

"We need to be getting back," the man intoned.

"Yes, I know. It was just a welcome feeling to be away from everyone. I miss the cool and quiet of the woods."

"I know. Soon we will make our way home."

She turned fully to look at him. His profile was dark in the room with some speckled moonlight shining in his eyes. "Do you really believe that?"

He was still for a moment and then turned to look at her. "Your destiny will take you much farther than this city. You need to believe this for it will happen."

After a moment more, she turned from him, and with a pat on her thigh to call the dog, she moved to the stairwell.

52

ORSON WATCHED THE WITCH, HIS master's obsession. Admitting his own failings was always difficult, but in this instance, it would be ridiculous not to admit his fear—at least to himself. Her power was something he'd never witnessed before. And coupled with her evilness, she was a being to be feared.

His mind moved to ways she could be used. The man with control over her would be a powerful man indeed.

His eyes shifted to Mikel Bathsar, confusion filling his mind. He'd been loyal to his master for years. Their goals aligned. Now, ambition for himself and avarice for the witch moved forward above all things. With her came not only power, but the ear to their mistress. The true power of this world. Cassandra.

His gaze moved between them as Mikel offered the witch his hand, prompting her to stand and move toward the men who filled the room. When her power erupted like a mist from her small frame to surround a man kneeling before her, his spike of desire made him stagger. As the condemned man imploded, body parts falling, blood splashing, he wet his lips, mind atwitter with ideas.

Foremost of them, was the knowledge that Mikel Bathsar must die.

53

T HE NEXT MORNING, MAYA AND Sentinel, with Rory between them, stood outside the doorway of her father's quarters.

When the door opened, she stared for a moment at her sire. She'd never realized, until this moment, how much she resembled him—other than their red hair. She'd always been told how much she looked like her mother and had been able to see the evidence of that for herself. It had been obvious from his first reaction to her—after all, he had thought she was Sylvan—but now, she saw the likeness. Their eyes were the same shape and so was the curve of their jaws. Her heart swelled.

What would it have been like to have been raised by both parents? How would her life have differed? Who would she be?

Her attention caught when her father stepped back to allow them into the room. He muttered, "Good morning," as they walked past him.

At the center of the room, Maya turned and faced him. She heard Sentinel continue to the rear of the room and knew he would be backed to the wall, his stance alert for any threats even in this seemingly benign space.

"So, Father, were you able to meet with the council? What did they say?"

He gestured as he approached her. "Please, have a seat and let us discuss what our plans should be."

She inclined her head and, turning from him, walked to one in a set of chairs in front of a cold hearth. She seated herself on the edge of the chair, the crossed swords on her back stopping her from fully relaxing back. Her father took the other chair to face her.

"Can I get you anything?"

"No. We're fine. Please, can we get this plan decided?"

With a nod, he stood again and looked at her and those with her. Sentinel stood behind her, the dog at her side. With a deep breath, he told her of his conversation with the council.

"They are afraid," he said.

"I'm not surprised. After the rousting we received at the temple, they would have to be idiots not to be afraid. But can we trust them to obey your orders and do what is necessary to distract the soldiers?"

Her father placed a hand on her shoulder. "Yes. They will do what is necessary." Giving her a gentle pat, he turned and sat across from her again. "Now tell me, Maya. What is your plan to kill my brother?"

54

THE CORRIDORS OF THE GREAT temple were silent. Moving along the aisle, aware of every nuance and sound, Maya couldn't believe their luck. Her plan was going off without a hitch.

Accompanying her, on what some would define as a fool's errand, were Sentinel and Rory. Her father and four additional men whom he trusted above all others followed them.

Their plan had begun early that morning with small groups of men causing disruptions at different locations in the city. As they'd hoped, units of soldiers were dispatched to stop them, and when the soldiers came into sight, the townsmen engaged the militants. This contest was happening all over the city, and the temple was soon emptied of most of its guards.

She and her small group watched the temple, and after seeing what they considered to be one of the last available units leaving, they slipped in—right through the front door.

Now, they moved down the hallway in search of the room with the golden door. In the back of her mind, she again wished

Teck were with her. Not only for his strong sword arm and bright mind, but because, like her, he'd been to the room and would most likely remember the way. Her experience in the room was foggy and how she got to it even foggier. Trial and error were all they had and, already, they'd been searching for longer than she'd like. The longer they spent wandering the temple, the greater the chance of running into trouble. With her swords held at the ready, she flowed down the halls in front of the small band.

When a low growl issued from Rory, she froze. Listening hard, she heard the soft tread of boots and the whisper of a voice. She flattened against the wall and the men were quick to follow. When a dozen soldiers came around the corner, for a moment they all stood like a tableau and gaped at each other. Then the stillness was broken as the soldiers engaged them.

A young man fell, and she stepped on him to pull her sword out of his belly. Not looking at his face, Maya blanked her mind to the minimal years her opponent had lived. They each had their fate and hers was to live through this day. Many would fall, some from her swords and some from others'. There was little she could do except ensure she wasn't one of the fallen.

The force recoiling up her arm, Maya blocked a strike from another soldier. With a quick spin, she stooped and slashed his thigh with her other sword. When he stumbled back, she crossed her twin weapons at his neck and took his head with a decisive cross pull. Blood splashed her chest and neck, but she never noticed. Moving forward into the fray, she engaged another combatant.

This man was older than the rest. Watching for his first move, she could see he had more experience. Waiting for his chance, he engaged her when another drew her attention. The clang and rasp of weapons rang harsh in her ears, and the force of his strike was so strong that her hands and arms numbed. The effort to hold her swords proved too much, and with dismay, she felt her fingers open and her weapons fall to the floor.

Leaping back once then twice, she barely managed to avoid being gutted by his wild swings. When he whirled again, she rolled into him, at the same time pulling the long knife from her belt. Coming to her feet, inches from his body, she voided his advantage of reach and strength. Just as he arched his neck to render a head butt, she thrust her blade under his chin.

The man's gasp filled her ears. His weapon fell, his eyes wide and questioning. A small pool of blood gathered and ran from his mouth. Grasping the handle of her blade firmly, she pulled it free. The soldier toppled backward like a felled tree.

Bumped from behind, she swung to defend, only to pull up short when she saw it was Sentinel who now stood back to back with her. Hurriedly, she searched for her father and Rory. Sheathing her knife, she took her swords from the floor and surveyed the carnage. All around them lay the bodies of soldiers and half of the men who had come with her.

Rory trotted over to her, his muzzle red and dripping. He had once again proved his worth in battle.

Maya, her father, Sentinel, Rory, and the two remaining men from the city moved away from the fight. It wouldn't be long before the evidence of the melee was discovered. If their time was short before, now they were out of it.

The small company moved stealthily through the halls. When Maya saw a bright reflection coming from around the corner, she slowed and once again flattened herself against the wall. Mimicking her, the men pressed back. After she glanced at them to ensure all were prepared for anything, she peeked around the corner. Reflecting the sun from a window in the ceiling was the golden door.

Maya turned to her companions with a triumphant and relieved smile. With a gesture, she led them around the corner and to the door.

She leaned in to listen for activity on the other side. After a moment, she directed a negative shake of her head to her father.

"What do you think?"

"We have no choice but to enter," her father said.

She gave him a long look and then turned to the others with them. Steeling herself, she faced the door and pushed it open.

55

ORSON STOOD TO THE SIDE of the dais. He kept his eyes on the witch and Mikel, waiting and watching for a chance to change his fortunes.

For a moment, the dais was full of people. Servants crisscrossed the area, filling wine goblets and serving food. Shifting, he moved back and forth in an effort to keep Mikel in his sights.

When the main door pushed open and the girl stepped through, he wasn't surprised. It was as if fate sat on his shoulders. This was it. This was the moment he'd waited for. The moment that would change his life.

"Well . . ." Standing to walk to the front of the dais, Mikel Bathsar didn't seem surprised either. "It's taken you long enough."

* * * * *

MAYA STEPPED INTO THE ROOM. Through the ringing in her ears

and the loud thump of her heart, she barely heard Mikel's words. Then, she understood.

We've been betrayed. Again.

When Rory leaned against her, she absently noted the weight of his body as the rumble of his growl moved through her. Vaguely, she saw the forms of many people on the dais, but she couldn't rip her eyes from her uncle.

"Come, come. Don't be shy," he said and stepped forward. With a lofty lift of his hand, he waved for her to come nearer.

Pushed from behind, soldiers ripped her weapons from her hands. She stumbled, almost falling as her leaden feet and legs moved closer to him, her mind full of memories of her last time in this room.

"Oh yes, sweet niece. You and your band thought you were so smart. But I had the advantage. My little mouse in the wall— so don't feel too bad."

When he gestured again—this time beside him—the soldiers pushed a man forward. Not even trying to catch himself, the priest, Patrick, landed on his knees before Mikel, his head bent to his chest in defeat.

"Patrick?" Her father stepped to her side, his head shaking. The broken man didn't give any indication he'd heard him.

"Ah, yes." Mikel inhaled a deep breath and blew it out. "I always knew it would end like this. Those you trust, your friends and loved ones, they all betray you."

"Mikel." Maya's father took another step forward. Scanning around him, taking in both Patrick and Maya, he again faced his brother. "Let them go. Brother, let them go and take me. It doesn't have to be this way."

"But it *does!*" Mikel screamed. "The only way it could ever be was with me *winning* and you *losing*." Mikel stepped to the edge of the dais. "Don't you see, brother? I *hate* you." Spittle flew from his moist lips. "I have always hated you. Since the moment you were presented to me cradled in my mother's arms, you have taken from me."

His vehement emotions moved him as he stepped down the stairs from his platform. "Everything I've ever wanted, you got." Stepping back up the stairs, Mikel backed across the dais, servants fleeing in his wake. "Even the woman I love."

With a whip of his arm, he stepped to the side, indicating the figure in the smaller chair.

Her father choked, "Sylvan?" A gasp exploded from Maya's lungs when she directed her attention to Mikel's queen. Her mother. Or at least, a form of her.

Garbed in an opulent gown of red and gold, her figure was resplendent. It was her eyes, however, that drew Maya's attention. They were black, and a light fog seemed to hover around her frame.

"Mother." Maya tried to rush to her, but her father caught her by the arm.

"Wait, Maya. This isn't right."

Turning back to his brother, her father stalked toward him. "What have you done to her? Free her from your influence this instant."

With a laugh, Mikel threw back his head. "Oh, brother. How little you know. She's under no influence of mine. This power is all her." Mikel stared at the woman for a moment and then, with a sad shake of his head, he muttered, "You never did understand her potential. It always resided in her. She is magnificent. Only now has she become all she can be."

Maya pushed past her father, heading toward the woman on the platform.

"Mother!" she yelled just as her father again caught her arm. Spinning her, he grabbed both of her upper arms, forcing her to face him.

"Maya!" he shouted, but her attention was locked over her shoulder, trained on her mother. He shook her. "Don't rush off. All is not as it should be."

"But, my mother. What's happened to her?" She again pulled from him and started forward.

"Maya—" Sidestepping him, she slipped by.

Maya stopped just short of the steps. When Sylvan's head pivoted toward her, Maya sank to her knees. Her eyes. The orbs were black as pitch, but still they somehow swirled. Her hair, once a warm chestnut, was dull and lanky with streaks of gray. The pallor of her skin was that of a person who hadn't felt the warmth of the sun in weeks. And she'd lost weight. Always small of frame, now the bones of her face and body were sharp and seemed almost to pierce her skin.

Maya's face fell into her hands, a sob shaking her frame.

"Now I have the power—and the woman. You, brother, are nothing."

Maya gave a start when she realized her uncle stood beside her. She pulled back when he grabbed a lock of her hair, but he held it, pulling until it hurt.

"This illicit spawn of yours is nothing." He flicked the hair away from him. "Now, finally, I have it all." Mikel spun, gesturing to the room at large.

"*No.*" Leaping to her feet, Maya took a half step to the solider next to her. Twisting, she drove her elbow into his jaw and drew his sword with her other hand, the rasp of it loud as she pulled it from the scabbard. She was already turning before his body hit the ground.

She swung toward Mikel, her arms cocked, elbows pulled back, sword straight out from her body. With a lunge, she thrust the weapon forward, through his chest and out his back.

Mikel's breath expelled from his lungs. He bent in a slight crouch. His eyes wide, he gaped down at the hilt protruding from his chest, blood beginning to stain his tunic.

Maya staggered back into her father's arms, surprise evident on her face. The room fell into stunned silence except for the sound of Mikel's low cough and a sudden splash of blood on the tile. When he tumbled backward, he lay half on his back, half on his side, resting on the sword tip.

With an animalistic growl, Sylvan surged to her feet, causing all eyes to swing toward her. The light mist that hung over her darkened and swirled. She strode forward, arms raised.

Soldiers scattered at her approach until only the small band of rebels stood in her sights.

"Mother!" Maya yelled and took a step toward her. She knew the woman who'd raised her, the woman she loved, was in there somewhere.

She skidded to a halt as Sylvan's gaze fell upon her.

"Child!" she screeched and thrust her hands forward, the mist following her demand.

"Sylvan. *No!*" Maya's father yelled. He rushed forward, shoving Maya out of the way.

Landing hard on her knees, Maya looked over her shoulder. Caught by the mist, her father was almost invisible within its swirling mass. A chill swept through her body at the image of her mother, who stood on the dais, arms raised, eyes swirling like the mist that held her father. A maniacal smile split Sylvan's face, and blood dripped from her lip where she'd bitten herself.

Maya surged to her feet. Strong arms encircled her from behind, trapping her arms against her body. She fought the grip but couldn't break their hold. With a twist of her head, she caught sight of her jailer—Sentinel.

"Let me go!" she wailed. "I must do something. I have to save him."

He hauled her toward the golden door. "No, Maya. Be still. We must leave this place."

She shook her head at him and continued to fight, a guttural howl beginning in her throat. Her vision blurred as her eyes turned a bright blue. The floor shook as if strained from below, and they tripped and almost went down. A roar erupted in the room as the floor was ripped apart from beneath. Vines and roots surged through the gap. A loud crash sounded as more vegetation broke through the large skylight to the back of the dais. Slithering greenery was soon everywhere, almost obscuring Maya's already hampered view of her parents.

A screech erupted in the room, and her eyes were drawn back to the faint image of her father within the gray cocoon. With a surge, it gave a violent start and shattered his body.

She screamed, her vision flashing with images of body parts, blood, and torn clothing. From the carnage, Maya's eyes darted to Sylvan. Just as Sentinel pulled her out the door, the ceiling of the room gave a mighty crack. Broken pieces rained down. Maya's last image of her mother was of her being crushed under its weight.

Once free of the room, Sentinel released his grip on her body but retained one on her arm. Turning, he began to move back through the temple, pulling her weeping body with him. Glancing behind them, he moved quicker when the golden doors groaned then flew off their hinges, forced outward by a sea of green, whipping vegetation.

Down winding hallways, Sentinel pulled her. Maya ran alongside him, but she continued to trip and almost fall to her knees. Only his aid kept her upright and moving. At one point, Maya realized Rory ran beside them, and Sentinel hurried to get the three of them free of the temple.

When they pushed their way to the outside, the light of morning was just breaking.

They were dirty, exhausted, and heartbroken.

The city streets were deserted. It appeared as if all the citizens had fled. A cool morning breeze blew from where the vendors' shops were located, ruffling scarves and drapes.

Sentinel released Maya's arm and she slid down to the top

step of the temple. With her head in her hands, her fingers clutching her hair, she took deep, ragged breaths, straining to control the sobs that shook her.

After walking partway down the street, Sentinel turned in a circle, looking for threats. Seeing nothing, he moved back to her and extended his hand. "We must be away from here."

Not raising her head, she muttered, "What does it matter? Everything is gone."

"Not everything."

Slowly she lifted her face. As the morning sun hit him, it came to her that he was correct. He stood before her proud and fierce. A shaft of sunlight glinted off the strap of his empty weapons harness, causing her to squint.

"You are right, Sentinel." She wiped tears from her cheeks. Reaching up, she took his hand and allowed him to help her to stand. Laying a palm against his cheek and the other on Rory's head, she managed, "All is not lost."

"And more, Maya," he said, laying his hand on her midsection.

Taking her trembling hand from his face, she placed it upon his. She glanced down and then back to his eyes with a nod. "Yes. Now there is more."

The girl, the dog, and the mentor returned to the top floor of the storage building. Nothing had changed since they had been here a few nights ago.

With a quick glance around, Maya could see no other footprints than their own. No one had been here. No one had disturbed their things.

She hurried to the corner of the room and stared down at their belongings. Packs for each of them, bladders full of water, and her bow.

She was right to make this plan. This last plan. Never again would she be ill-prepared.

Her father was dead, her mother was dead, and Teck was gone. She would take all that remained, all that still mattered, and leave this place.

SOME DAYS LATER, WHEN MAYA and her companions neared the port of a small town, she was assailed with the scents of fish and saltwater. Birdcalls echoed in her ears. It felt like a lifetime since she was last at the water's edge.

She and Sentinel had come to a decision to leave this land. They would go afar and begin anew. She would raise her babe and try to forget all the loss and pain.

Strapped to her back were two newly forged swords, her bow in her hand. Other than the weapons and Sentinel, she looked like the girl who had begun this quest. But inside she was changed. The grief of loss burned through her to temper her thoughts, emotions, and power.

With a sad smile but a hopeful heart, she turned to Sentinel, and together they boarded a ship leaving for a distant port.

56

TECK STARED AT THE RECEDING shoreline and felt his first stirrings of anticipation. The first time in a long time. For months he'd traveled the lands, fighting with himself on whether to return to Maya or continue on his own. Nothing had felt right. Even the thought of returning to the town of his birth filled him with discontent.

Then, one day not so long ago, while in a small port town, he'd spoken with a group of sailors and his fortune had changed. The ship they sailed on was heading to foreign lands. There they hoped to begin a new venture, to return one day as wealthy men. It seemed like the answer to all his hopes and dreams. A new beginning.

He watched his homeland retreat from the bow of the ship. Choppy water separated him from what was, and with a final sigh, Teck turned his attention to what would be. Leaving the stern, he took a flight of stairs to stand beside the captain at the helm.

"Teck, your new adventure begins, my boy." Captain

Albarso clasped a hand on Teck's shoulder and then turned to again face forward.

"Yes," Teck answered. In the auburn light of the fading day, he couldn't help but be reminded of a young girl's flaming locks. Her smile and shining green eyes called from the watery depths. This would be a good move for him. Somehow, he would forget her, his plans for them, and his heart would heal.

With a lift of his chin, Teck faced the future.

57

CALEB STARED OUT AT THE sea, his mind focused on what he'd seen.

The Three and the Three. He knew who they were, who they would be. They would need to come together at the right time, right place, and with the right motivation. To become the One. The challenge was still there. He could still lose this contest, but confidence filled him.

His belief in the goodness of all mankind filled his heart. Trials lay ahead for the Three. Hard times and mighty challenges, but he was confident they would triumph.

* * * * *

This ends part one of *The Pedagogue Chronicles, Book I: Maya's Song.*
Continue the story with *The Pedagogue Chronicles, Book II: Sylvan's Guise.*

ACKNOWLEDGMENTS

Driven Digital Services

Kingsman Editing Services

Did you enjoy this book? Visit your favorite retailer
and leave a review to help other readers discover the magic
of *The Pedagogue Chronicles*.

* * * * *

vickibwilliamson.com

Facebook.com/FindingPoppies

Made in the USA
Monee, IL
20 July 2021